VETERANS' AFFAIRS

JOSEPH HIRSCH

BLACK ROSE writing™

ISBN: 978-1-61296-666-3

PUBLISHED BY BLACK ROSE WRITING

www.blackrosewriting.com

Printed in the United States of America

Suggested retail price $16.95

Veterans' Affairs is printed in Palatino Linotype

For Norman Hirsch

PRAISE FOR VETERANS' AFFAIRS

"If you can imagine George Saunders reinvisioning *Going after Cacciato* after repeatedly watching *Jacob's Ladder*, then you have some idea of the phantasmagoric ride you're in for while reading *Veterans' Affairs*. You'd need to have Tim O'Brien ghosting around still, and maybe you'd want to build a catbird seat for Kurt Vonnegut and Kenzaburo Oe as well. Only then can Tom Robbins show up to dose everyone. Now you're ready. From its Voltairean narrator, Joseph Sullivan, to its realistically drawn (and wounded and querulous and sympathetic) hospitalized veterans, Thigpen and Jones, Joseph Hirsch's novel embraces the obscene facts of the human body, both at love and at war, let loose through the horrors of life—and the afterlife. Among the many emotionally demanding, prize-winning novels and story collections now emerging from our recent wars, *Veterans' Affairs* will occupy a singular, necessary place." – **John Joseph Ryan, author of** *A Bullet Apiece*

"In prose carved with a knife, Hirsch has written the novel all of us fear: the truth of war, whether it's pretty or not, whether we like it or not. In *Veterans' Affairs*, faced with ghosts and his own inadequacy in the face of the horrors of war, Joey Sullivan must struggle through the traumas of others before he can face his own. We owe it to ourselves to read his story." – **Rusty Barnes, author of** *Reckoning*

"*Veterans' Affairs* creates an authentic-feeling struggle of a damaged veteran trying to come back to life, and then takes that familiar type of story into a wondrously uncanny new dimension. It solidly grounds the reader, but also thrusts them into the unknown. Gratifying to read even when unpleasant, it gets a grip and hangs on ruthlessly." – **David S. Atkinson, author of** *Not Quite so Stories, The Garden of Good and Evil Pancakes*, **and** *Bones Buried in the Dirt*

"I'm not sure what happened to Joey Hirsch to make his writing so bizarre, but I suspect the US Government had something to do with it. Regardless, it's to the reader's benefit: his new book *Veterans' Affairs* is as funny as it is strange: it's like *G.I Joe* meets *Casper the Friendly Ghost*, only if Casper was no longer so friendly, due to war-related PTSD." – **Fiona Helmsley, author of** *My Body Would be the Kindest of Strangers*

"A captivating and poignant story of an anguished soldier and the gossamer thread that anchors human sanity." – **L.E. Fraser, author of** *Skully, Perdition Games*

VETERANS' AFFAIRS

"Death must be so beautiful. To lie in the soft brown earth, with the grasses waving above one's head, and listen to silence. To have no yesterday, and no tomorrow. To forget time, to forgive life, to be at peace."
— Oscar Wilde, *The Canterville Ghost*

"They came round about me daily like water; they compassed me about together. Lover and friend hast thou put far from me, and mine acquaintance into darkness."
Psalm 88, Verses 17-18, New Testament, *King James Bible*

CHAPTER ONE: THE MADCAP'S NIGHTCAP

It was a Wednesday night, and, like on any other night, I had a decision to make. I could either commit suicide and sleep forever, or I could take my meds and conk out for the remainder of the night. I was starting a new job in the morning, so I decided not to kill myself.

The last time I'd attempted suicide, I'd called my brother (an ex-heroin addict) and asked him if he could get me enough dope to overdose. I'd heard that an overdose was actually the most pleasant experience in the world, that being revived and intubated was actually the painful part.

My brother refused to euthanize me, though. Instead, he drove me to the VA hospital, where I spent a week on an inpatient basis. I was going to start to work in the morning, and I needed to get some sleep.

I walked over to the windowsill, which faced Ludlow Avenue. My pill bottles were lined up in front of the window, glowing in the light reflected from the gaslight globes scattered throughout the neighborhood.

I poured myself a full shot of Nyquil, and uncapped several other bottles. I dropped an Ambien, two Clonazepam, and a Percocet in the sweet solution. I wasn't sure how good the cocktail was for my organs, but it helped me sleep.

I walked out of the living room, and into the bedroom. I got in bed and nestled under the covers. My dog, Tiffany, came bounding into the room and wormed her way beneath the blankets. The coarse, gray wires of her terrier coat felt good against my naked skin.

"Good night, Tiff."

I closed my eyes, and I was back in Iraq. We were doing a twelve-man foot patrol inside the city the combat engineers had cordoned off with massive bulldozed berms of earth. Now there was only us, some insurgents, and anyone unlucky enough to find themselves trapped inside of the city when the engineers sealed the town. I felt bad for the Iraqis and for myself.

"My friends," Matthias said, "We are about to find out once and for all who is the *awat* up in this bitch."

Matthias was directly in front of me, the pattern of his ACU Camelbak dusty from constant use. He held his M4 at the port arms position and walked ahead of me as we reached the traffic cloverleaf.

Sergeant Omero's voice came from behind me. "Sully, tell Token to open up his stride. We're bunched the fuck up like a centipede."

"Mathias," I said.

He half-turned, and I saw his ballistic glasses were fogged as hell. I wondered how he could see anything. "What?"

"Walk faster."

"Yassah boss. I's powerful sorry." He sped up his pace, walking faster toward the local police cantonment marking the beginning of the downtown district. Mathias had picked up the nickname "Token" because he was the only black soldier in our twelve-man team. I didn't feel sorry for him. They called me "Porno Tits," on account of how I could never get pectoral definition, no matter how much working out I did. My man-breasts poked through the moisture-wicking BDU shirts we wore. I would frankly rather have porno tits than to be prematurely balding and with shriveled testicles, like our resident king of anabolic steroid abuse, Sergeant Carter.

"I don't mind being *awat*," Dondy said, from somewhere to my six. I didn't turn to look, because the collar attachment of my vest gave me Indian burns and chafed whenever I moved my head to the left or right. "*Awat* is good shit."

Awat meant "soft cake," and it was what the insurgents called us. I had to agree. We were pussies, at least compared to the unit we had replaced. They came storming through here with twenty-ton Bradleys and Bushmasters blazing. The fighting vehicles were small enough to chase insurgents down the narrow alleys of the *souks*, too. They knocked over baskets of figs and dates in the open-air markets, as they bodied fleeing terrorists and made new stucco patterns on the walls of the alleys.

"Fuck!" I heard Dunfy whine, from somewhere behind me. He ran to catch up with me, weighed down with SAW ammo and a spare barrel. He walked until he was standing alongside of me. Sergeant Omero didn't bitch about us being bunched up, though. He must not have cared whether or not me and Dunfy got knocked off by a sniper or an RPG on our way to the IED kill zone. "My shin splints."

"Man up, douchebag!" Sergeant Carter shouted.

"I don't get shin splints." Matthias said. "Thank God for the slave genetics."

I looked up, toward the empty blue sky. One of those blimps was floating directly overhead. It was watching and recording the movements down below, and broadcasting them back to one of the larger forward operating bases. Sergeant Carter once showed me security footage from one of the blimps, wherein a local Iraqi farmer in checkered *kaffiyeh* and white dishdasha sodomized a camel.

I tried to avoid Sergeant Carter whenever possible. Sometimes it couldn't be helped, like right now. He ran, the slosh of water from his Camelbak and the clank of metal from his weapons and ammo accompanying him as he booked until he was alongside me and Dunfy.

"I've got a little theory."

"Please, Sergeant," I said. He outranked me, but that didn't mean I had to put up with everything he did, or said. Smoke curled upward from a stack of tires that never stopped burning up ahead of us. It reminded me of the perpetually burning tire fire on *The Simpsons*. I'd actually bought a bootleg DVD with ten seasons of *The Simpsons* on it, from one of the Hajji bazaars. I was looking forward to bringing it home and showing my brother my find, if and when I got out of Iraq. The Hajji who sold me the DVD said *The Simpsons* was haram, because Homer drank beer and no one in the family respected the father.

Sergeant Carter brought me out of my thoughts. He spoke, as we walked closer to the city. "If you pat someone on the ass after a play in football, as long as you say 'Good game,' it's not gay. Right?"

Sewage from clogged mains flooded the path at our feet, made a wet sloshing sound and darkened the suede of our desert boots. Something thicker and redder, either blood or radiator fluid, floated inside of the stream. Decrepit electric power generators chugged in front of us and spouted brown smoke.

"I guess," I said.

"Well, if I suck a guy's dick, it's not gay right, as long as I say 'Good game,' afterwards?"

"Sounds legit," Mathias said. Then, "Oh shit."

I unslung my M4, Dunfy hoisted his SAW, and even Sergeant Carter got serious. The last time Mathias said "Oh shit" like that was when he found a charred arm dangling from a power line. This time, though, he laughed after he said it. We all relaxed.

"Bush!" Mathias said. He started laughing. I had yet to meet a single black soldier who liked George W. Bush (most of the white guys didn't even like him at this point). Mathias got quite a kick out of the mule walking into our midst, on whose side someone had written "Bush" in blood. Hopefully the blood belonged to a sheep, but maybe it belonged to a man.

Sergeant Carter slapped the beast on its rump and it walked on past us. "Don't fucking touch it!" Sergeant Omero said. "You don't know what kind of diseases it has."

"I have gloves on," Sergeant Carter said.

"At ease!" Sergeant Omero was a Staff Sergeant, and outranked Carter, but there was always tension between those two. The steroids probably had something to do with it, since both of them juiced.

"Stay alert, stay alive," Sergeant Omero said.

"Bullshit," Dunfy muttered to me. "You think being alert is going to stop a fucking RPG round?" He shook his head and gazed up at the sun, white as a light bulb left turned on for days.

A rusted Chevy Caprice was on our left. The remnants of a Datsun pickup truck were slammed into its back bumper, as if the cars were mating with each other. Our platoon entered the city, spreading out. Dunfy and I remained asshole to elbow, though. It was just like in the chow line at basic training, where we would queue up and the drill sergeant would say, "Get as close to the man in front of you as you can. Make your buddy smile!"

"I don't understand," Dunfy said, and nodded toward the building at our left. His Kevlar was a bit too big for his head, and it rattled around. He needed to adjust the Velcro pads inside his helmet, I thought.

"I know," I said. Almost all of the buildings in town had been looted and stripped. Even bricks were taken away in wheelbarrows and put to use for god knows what. This first building was left untouched. Even the hedges were still trimmed, spelling out something in Arabic that I couldn't understand, since I couldn't read the language. I'd managed to pick up some German using Rosetta Stone, before our unit deployed, but Arabic was too much of a challenge for me.

"It's Ba'ath Party Headquarters," Mathias said, as he halted, and got down on one knee. "These *awat*-ass niggas are still all scary and shook, even though that Joseph Stalin-looking statue in Firdos Square done been pulled down for a long, hot minute."

"He's the real *bou-bou*," Dondy said, halting by the Caprice. He leaned against its hood, which probably wasn't the smartest idea. There could be an unexploded shell inside for all he knew. It could be nestled under the radiator and waiting for the slightest touch. If it was hooked to infrared, then something as small as a wave of his hand could get the IED to go off.

"What's *bou-bou*?" Mathias said.

"It means boogeyman," Dondy said, and motioned with his head toward the *souk*. There was no one on the street, no vendors at the stalls. The crates where tobacco, rugs, knives, fruits and vegetables once sat were now empty, except for a thick layer of dust. "It's what the Iraqis call us. The moms scare their kids by saying the *bou-bou* man will get them."

Mathias stood up, grinning. "Bou-bous. I like that."

"I got one more rule," Sergeant Carter said. He spoke to me or Dunfy, whichever one of us would listen.

I tried to ignore him, stared down the street toward the mosque a few blocks away. It was a bright spot of color in the otherwise gray and brown world that was Iraq, just like the building with the hedges and hibiscuses. The outside of the building was covered in blue terrazzo tiles that made me think of ancient Roman atriums, and the roof was topped by a beaten gold Cordoba dome that always made me think of that wailing call-to-prayer. I loved a lot of things about Iraq and the Iraqis, but I was careful to keep that to myself. The whole country was composed of nothing but camel fuckers like the one caught on that security blimp, as far as Sergeant Carter and all the others who set the tone of the unit were concerned. Even the Iraqis who helped us, at the risk of their own lives and the lives of their families, didn't get much credit in the eyes of the average American soldier.

Take Matthew, for instance, the one 'terp (interpreter) who showed us a house, in which there was a basement where a laptop sat by itself on a table. Some of the open windows on the computer featured hardcore pornography, Bang Bros. videos of girls getting sodomized by the pool or catching cum shots in the backseats of sports cars. Other windows featured schematics, blueprints, and diagrams for various kinds of explosives, remote detonation devices, and triggers.

Matthew had made us clear out of the room. He said that he once saw a trap like this, where a bomb was planted inside the computer that was triggered when someone clicked the mouse.

Sergeant Omero called in EOD and we waited outside the building with Matthew. "Hey," Dondy had said, "I thought you Muslims weren't allowed to look at porn and shit. Doesn't the Koran say so?"

Matthew had flipped the front brim of his chocolate-chip boonie hat up and said, "Your Bible tells you not to do things that you as Christians still do, yeah?"

"Touché."

Sergeant Carter brought me out of my thoughts. "If I say 'no homo,' after I say something else, the first thing I said gets cancelled out." He squared himself to me. "You feel me?"

A heavy wind picked up, and I instinctively scanned around. Strong winds were good, because if there were cardboard boxes around and they weren't moving in a stiff wind, it meant there was a good chance that an IED might be planted inside.

I didn't see any boxes, though. I only saw a few pages from the fundamentalist fish wrap *Hawza*, al-Sadr's newspaper that Coalition forces had shut down awhile back. Something black moved on the path up ahead of us, and I ignored Carter and the stiff wind. Dunfy, Mathias, and I watched a funeral procession carrying a pine coffin up the marble steps of the beautiful little mosque. The dome was radiant in the sun, so hot I imagined I could hear it humming through the case of tinnitus I'd picked up after being in so many explosions and firefights.

There was never time to say, "Wait a minute, let me put my earplugs in," before a battle. I couldn't just walk around with earplugs in all the time, or else I might miss something.

Carter kept talking and I looked back at him. The wind tousled what little bit of hair on his head the steroids hadn't already caused to fall out. I wondered how small his balls were at this point. "Like if I say, 'I'd really like to suck Brad Pitt's dick while George Clooney fucks me in the ass, uh…no homo,' then I'm in the clear. I'm not gay. See how that works?"

"This nigga's crazy," Mathias said, laughing.

Dondy, Sergeant Omero, and the rest of the platoon had made their way to the city square. The mule had done a circuit around the platoon, and was now in our midst. "Looks like we got a mascot," Ski said, and patted Bush's rump.

"That's a no-go," Sergeant Omero said. "Frago from higher says no mascots."

"Why's that?"

"Cuz of diseases. You don't know what that fucking mule's got. That's why I told this dipshit not to touch it." Sergeant Omero pointed at Sergeant Carter, who was busy extracting a can of Skoal wintergreen from his shoulder pouch. He looked at Mathias. "Why you calling me 'nigger?'"

"I didn't." Mathias leaned forward, taking the pressure from his sappy plates off his back. "I said 'nigga.' There's a difference, but a country-ass, sister-fucking hillbilly like you can't make the distinction."

They went back and forth like this constantly. Sergeant Carter had been detailed to get dinner for the whole platoon from the DEFAC before we saddled up for this mission, and he had singled out Mathias while taking orders. "Let me guess. Fried chicken, fried in extra Crisco lard, Texas Pete hot sauce…"

I ignored them, and shifted my weight from my left to right foot. I watched the funeral procession disappear inside the mosque. Sometimes when driving on the roads in Iraq, I would see coffins strapped to the tops of the vehicles. One time I saw a wooden coffin no larger than a beer cooler, which I was sure contained an infant corpse.

"'Nigga'," Mathias said, "not 'nigger.'"

Carter didn't understand that Mathias used the word "nigga" just to mean person. He was from the Bronx. Once I mentioned there were some Jewish relatives on my father's side of the family who still lived in Brighton. He had nodded and said, "There's still mad Jewish niggas in Brooklyn." He didn't mean that there were angry, black Jews in Brooklyn; he meant there were many Jewish people there.

"Hey," Dunfy said, and then the mule looked at me. Bush spoke. "Your buddy Dunfy is going to step on a hidden pressure plate that's on top of an oil barrel that contains a three-hundred pound, one-hundred and fifty-five millimeter shell, in about two minutes."

"Mules," I said, "don't talk."

"This is a dream," Bush said.

"I know," I said. "But this all really happened."

Bush with the bloody rump snorted, and said, "Both can be true. Something can really happen and also be a dream."

"I'll take your word for it." I uncoiled the snaking, black PVC line of my Camelbak and flipped the cap off. I bit and sucked cool water like a baby suckling at his mother's breast.

"Look up," the mule said.

I looked up. The blimp was now a giant, pink flying pig, like the one that Roger Waters used in his concerts. There were amplifiers nestled beneath the shortened wings of the pink dirigible. Psi-ops messages broadcast over the *souks* of the city, and my mother's voice said, "I said you should have joined the Navy."

I fell on my knees, my kneepads absorbing the trauma. Everyone in the platoon joked that Sergeant Omero never forgot his kneepads on a convoy, the implication being that he was good at kissing ass/sucking dick of the higher-ups in the chain-of-command; he was trying to make Sergeant First Class pretty hard.

"I'm sorry, Mom," I said to the underbelly of the pink pig.

"You're selfish," Bush said. "Her brother went to Vietnam and put her through hell for a year when she was a sixteen year-old girl. Now that she's in her fifties and she should be thinking about retirement, you went to Iraq. That was a war that didn't have to be fought, and you made her worry about you."

"I know. I put a bunch of miles on her heart," I said. "But I think my brother's heroin addiction also hurt her. I'm not the only one."

There was an explosion. I lost my vision in the white, blinding cloud. Bush kept speaking. "This is how you get your mild traumatic brain injury."

"No shit," I said. I was no longer in Iraq. I was floating in space, floating in bed with my Terrier-Chihuahua mix coiled between my legs. The thing I didn't understand about my TBI was how I got it in the first place.

When you watch old World War II movies, you may have noticed soldiers leave their helmets unfastened, with the straps dangling. The reason they did this (at least according to the drill sergeants in basic training) was because, when there was an explosion, one's brains could get rattled to soup if their helmet was attached to their head.

The drill sergeants called leaving your helmet unstrapped "John Wayning (sic)" it. The temptation to John Wayne it was always great with those old-fashioned helmets, since they were hot and uncomfortable. The new helmets were padded with soft cushions that made keeping them fastened a much easier task. These newer helmets were supposed to absorb all of the force of the blow from an explosion.

If that is the case though, then I have a question to pose. I'll pose it to the mules and the pink pigs and to my mother for that matter. Why does my head still hurt, and why is Dunfy's body lying in a plot in Arlington cemetery?

CHAPTER TWO: MY NEW JOB

Third shift hours at the VA were from midnight to 8 a.m. My boss, Joe Hasford, wanted me to meet him at the emergency triage station around 11:30 p.m. I set my alarm clock to wake me at ten.

I woke up, set three eggs to boil in a pot on the stovetop, and then showered and brushed my teeth. I fed Tiff a package of Caesar wet dog food, and took her for a walk around the block.

It was still dark, and the gaslights glowed up and down the streets. The bulbs on the marquee down at the Esquire Theatre flashed, and the neon from the pubs splashed out onto the sidewalks. I walked with my right hand in my pocket, clutching a plastic dog poop bag. I kept the leash in my left hand.

A couple came toward me as I walked up the street. I sidestepped them, getting a strong whiff of perfume and shampooed hair as the female half of the pair passed me close enough to brush my shoulder.

I sighed. I hadn't had sex in years. I'd had erectile dysfunction since coming back from Iraq. My hair was shot through with gray, and my hands constantly shook. I would frankly rather pop a handful of Percocet than make love to a beautiful woman at that point, even if I had the ability.

The neighborhood where I lived didn't help my depression, either. There was nothing wrong with Clifton. It was a charming little gaslight district with all kinds of amenities, ranging from an ice cream parlor to a floral shop and art deco theatre. It was also the neighborhood where I grew up, though. It made sense for me to live here, since I went to school at the University of Cincinnati and I was now starting to work at the VA within ten minutes' walking distance. But this was the neighborhood where I lived when my parents broke up. They got divorced after being married for twenty-five years, and the fallout was ugly. This was the neighborhood where I'd met my first girlfriend and got my heart broken. The Catholic school I attended as a young man was only a few blocks away. I remembered its statuary and icons that made me feel guilt when I went home and masturbated, or snuck a joint in the gym bathroom across from the Church of the Annunciation.

The neighborhood was haunted with too many ghosts for me. I felt like a ghost myself walking around there, cut off from the flow of life. I'd felt out of place in college, since I spent my twenties working odd jobs and in the Army, which made me a full decade older than most of the undergrads. I'd dealt with the awkwardness and got my degree as a registered nurse, though. And now it was time to go to work.

I walked Tiffany to the edge of Burnett Woods. She crapped. I picked it up in the plastic mitt, and then dropped that in the trash can. I crossed the street and ran back into my apartment, which was above an Afrocentric notions shop called Third Eye Boutique. I had my breakfast upstairs. Then I washed my hands and kissed the dog goodbye, and headed back outside.

The VA was a ten minute walk uphill and I trudged in the dark. I headed toward the moon pinned to the horizon, buttressed by floating clouds. I was nervous about my new job and several other things. I hadn't worked a real job in years. I'd been surviving on the Montgomery G.I. Bill's Basic Allowance for Housing, along with my VA disability money and Social Security. I was sure I was going to lose the latter once I started working. I didn't care. I would rather work than sit around the apartment all day, with my thoughts and medications.

The hospital was eight stories of red brick, surrounded by an annex of trailers and a multi-level concrete parking garage. Encroaching condos, upscale eateries, and other hints of gentrification loomed around the VA. The university's buildings- everything from the microbiology center to the high-rise dormitories- kept spreading farther and farther, threatening to draw all of uptown into its orbit.

I looked up into the windows of the nearest college dorm building. I stared at a room with a light on, glowing in the lonely night. I invented a life for the student who lived there. I imagined an Indian engineering undergrad, contemplating slitting his wrists as his father chastised him on a Skype call for getting a 3.8 GPA this semester.

Parking was usually a bitch at the VA, which was why I was grateful to be walking and working nights. The lot was mostly empty now, and the incessant sound of construction that rattled my brains during the day was silent. I walked toward the Mylar-skinned shelter where vets and nursing assistants shared cigarettes from time to time. I headed for the emergency entrance, a set of automatic double-doors beneath a fluorescent light fixture, when I heard someone whisper.

"Sullivan! That you?"

"Yeah." I walked toward the voice, and the glowing coal of the cigarette. It was the senior RN, Joe Hasford. I'd met him earlier when interviewing for the job. I was frankly surprised that I landed the gig, since I'd been treated on an inpatient basis at the hospital for suicidal ideation. I also came here to get treated for my traumatic brain injury, which was mild according to the Gloucester Coma Score system. Then again, everything at the VA worked on a points system. If you were a vet, you got a certain number of points; if you'd been injured in wartime, you got a certain number of points for that, too. It was an odd hiring system with a strange set of criteria. The more fucked up you were, the better chance you stood of getting the job, apparently.

"Here," Hasford said. He held out a lanyard from which dangled my new Common Access Card. I took the lanyard and hung it around my neck. I glanced at the photo on the laminated card. I didn't like the way I looked; I'd gained a ton of weight since getting out of the Army, thanks to the General Tso's chicken and pain pill diet I was on.

Hasford's neck squeaked as he turned his head from left to right. He wore a white cervical collar, comprised of plastic and metal. It stretched his neck and caught several strands from the gray ponytail he wore. He'd explained to me the first time we met that he had four herniated discs in his neck. He'd also had bone grafts and a titanium plate surgically attached to his vertebrae to hold everything in place. I wasn't sure if he should be working, but it wasn't my business.

"You ready for the shit?" he asked.

I nodded.

"I mean maybe literally." He held out his pack of Winstons to me. I shook my head. "You got to keep an eye on Thigpen's colostomy bag. His nephew punctured it with a fork the last time he was up there."

Hasford took another puff on his smoke, and I noticed a faded India ink tat on his left arm. I glanced at it. It was a rifle of some kind, bayonet jammed downward and helmet lain over the buttstock and draped with dog tags, funeral-style.

He caught me looking, winked, and smoked. "You like that?"

I didn't say anything. "You know what it is?" I shook my head. I had an M4 and M16 in Iraq. Whatever was tatted on his arm looked like an old-fashioned single-shot, bolt-action weapon. "Mauser?" I guessed.

"Close, but that only counts in horseshoes and hand grenades." He put his cigarette out in the ashtray, already overflowing with butts. "Walk with me." I followed him in through the emergency entrance.

We passed the triage desk, and headed for the bank of elevators. This was the first time I was in the hospital as an employee and not a patient. The Starbucks coffee kiosk was closed, as was the tiny shoppette. The cafeteria was open. Servers in hairnets stacked heated metal trays in the scullery.

We came to the elevator, and Hasford pressed the "Up" arrow. He flexed his forearm. "This, my friend, is a Winchester model seventy-thirty ought six. It's a match rifle, with an extended floating barrel and an eight power Unertl scope."

The elevator car came, the doors opened, and we stepped aboard. Hasford pressed the "8" button and leaned against the back of the elevator. "I been knocking dicks in the dirt since Jack Kennedy got doled his ounce of lead in Dallas." He shook his head, and his ponytail bounced and his neck brace creaked. "No more hurting, though. I'm in the helping business these days."

He whistled a bit of the Jacques Offenbach Marine Hymn. "From the halls of Montezuma to the shores of Tripoli," I said.

His eyes brightened. He stopped whistling and asked, "You a devil dog?"

I shook my head. "Army, regular." That disappointed him. He frowned, and looked away from me, like a father whose son had let him down.

The elevator stopped on the eighth floor and we both got out, him before me. "We've got to get your ass suited up mo ricky tick, trooper. You need a mask, gloves, and robe." We walked to a door, where he flashed his CAC and a lighted panel turned green. He opened the door and held it for me.

"Mask?" I asked. "Is there a TB infection or something?"

"Close." Two nurses' aids in burgundy scrubs passed us. We walked by them, into a sanitary station across from the nurse's window. I walked up to the foot-treadle activated sink and started washing my hands with antimicrobial soap.

There was a bank of lockers behind us, from which Hasford extracted several shrink-wrapped items. He tore through the packages and kept talking, while I washed my hands.

"It's Methicillin-Resistant Staphylococcus Aureus, better known as MRSA."

"Holy shit," I said.

He slid the robe over my arms, started tying it in the back. "I'll help you tonight, but from here on out, you're on your own."

"Got ya."

"It spreads easy person-to-person, so you need to be real careful with your two cares."

"I've only got two patients?"

He finished tying my back, spun me around, and handed me two latex gloves. "Yeah, that's the good news and the bad news. There are only two reported cases up here. We're only going to have one RN dealing with Thigpen and Jones, in order to cut down on communication."

"Those are the two who've got it?"

"The only two as far as we know," Hasford said. "And you've drawn the short straw, because you're the FNG."

I didn't have to ask what that meant, and I knew that arguing wouldn't do any good. Besides that, I didn't have a wife or kids or anyone to communicate the disease to when I got home, which made me an even better candidate for the job. I wondered if I could spread the sickness to my dog. I didn't want to ask that question, since it would mark me as the kind of person whose only friend was a dog. That was true, but I didn't want to broadcast that and make a bad first impression.

"Both of them have been here the longest, which probably explains why they got it."

I pulled on my latex gloves, and they responded with satisfying snaps. "What symptoms will they present with?"

"I like that," he said. "You're talking like a real nurse." He coughed, and handed me the mask. I placed it over my mouth. "Be on the lookout for necrotizing fasciitis, sepsis, necrotizing pneumonia, the works."

"Are their narratives on a computer or-"

He cut me off with a gruff laugh truncating in a smoker's cough. "No, at the foot of their beds. This ain't exactly Walter Reed at its worst, but it ain't the Hilton, either. Our budget's been slashed to the bone."

"Right," I said.

"You know about what happened awhile back at Walter Reed?"

I nodded. I was still on active duty when the scandal broke. It was all over *Stars and Stripes* and *Army Times*. It was the biggest fiasco to hit the Army since the abuses at Abu Ghuraib came to light.

"Black mold on the walls," Hasford said. "They had amputees pulling guard duty. There were even drug dealers hanging around outside those fucking rat-infested buildings."

I felt like saying a packet or two of heroin might be just what the doctor ordered, when you're missing a leg and sitting alone in a room covered in black mold and your girlfriend fucks some other guy a few states away while rats scurry beneath your bunk.

I felt grateful for the moment, thinking about all that. I was happy to have only lost my mind and soul in Iraq. I hadn't lost anything important, like an arm or a leg. "You ready?"

I nodded. "Good."

We walked out of the sanitary station/locker room, and back onto the ward. A doctor, a diminutive Indian woman with a stethoscope draped around her neck, walked past us and smiled. I smiled back at her, and then remembered the lower half of my face was covered.

Hasford walked to the nurse's station, where another RN was monitoring a computer screen and drinking black coffee. I stood on the threshold of the nurse's station and listened to my supervisor while he talked. "This shit colonizes in the armpits, so after you wash up here and dump all your linen, you take another shower when you get home."

He disappeared inside the nurse's station, and then returned a moment later with a pen and stack of ECG paper. "You got a dog or a cat?"

"Dog," I said. I thought about Tiffany, nestling on the unmade bed. After this shift I would go home, pop some Percocet and Ambien. I'd drift off to dreamland and hopefully escape Iraq in my dreams.

"This shit likes to get in the intestines, too. I'm not a veterinarian, and I don't know if it's communicable to animals. Wash your fucking hands again before you feed your dog, and then wash them again after you feed your dog. You dig?"

I nodded. He handed me the paper and pen. "Being as this is your first shift, we'll start you off easy tonight."

Too late for that, I thought. I didn't say anything. "I need you to get PP rhythms on both Jones and Thipgen. You know how to do that?"

"Yeah," I said, and tasted my hot breath as it poured through the mask.

"Good. Jones is in a coma and he's got Alzheimer's." I thought I detected a note of sympathy in Hasford's voice for the first time that night. "He's fading fast, and there's not a lot we can do but keep him comfortable."

The RN sitting in front of the computer, a beady-eyed bald man with glasses, looked up at Hasford as he spoke. "As for Thipgen, check his legs."

"For pressure ulcers or...?"

"No. He's got antiembolism stockings on and his wife keeps putting these homemade socks over them. She knits whenever she's in his room. If she's put those on, I want them off." His jaw pulsed in anger once, and I heard the grinding of teeth. "He's got enough hypertension for a soul food restaurant already, so look around his bed and make sure his wife or grandson didn't sneak him anything else that can make him sick. He's on a restricted diet and he knows it."

"Anything else?"

"Yeah, if he keeps at you about a cigarette, he's authorized lozenges. Just come see this guy here." He pointed at the seated RN.

"And he'll give him one. No way in hell is he going outside for a smoke break. He's highly infectious. He's dying from a lifetime of untreated diabetes, too."

The seated RN spoke up. "Way to stay positive, Kevorkian."

"Facts are facts." He pointed down the hall, toward the end of the corridor, where what looked like a shower curtain hung. It billowed slightly from the artificial breeze of the air-conditioning.

"It's not the most sophisticated form of quarantine, but it at least serves to let people know to keep their asses out of there. Last room on the left, that's your military left. If you don't know your left from your right, the room on the right's unoccupied. That should make it even easier."

I nodded again, turned down the hall, and walked with my pen and paper gripped in my latex-gloved hands. The floor at my feet was sticky, and I almost slipped. Something slimy, like melted paraffin, gripped the bottoms of my nonstick shoes. "What the hell?"

"Nobody knows what it is," Hasford said, from behind me. "It's some kind of mold." I wondered if it had anything to do with the infection in the room I walked toward. I was starting to regret my decision to work, rather than to lay around on disability with my dog and my pain pills.

I passed through the shower curtain and into the bedroom. I heard all the normal sounds one expected to hear in a hospital. There was the painful wheeze of labored breathing, the beep of an EKG counterpointed by the hiss of oxygen. Through the window I could see the blinking lights on a radio tower hovering above the Cincinnati Zoo.

The man lying on the bed directly in front of me spoke. "*Thuoc la co hai cho suck hoe Toi khong hut thuoc lo.*"

I guessed it was Vietnamese, but I had no idea what he was saying. I looked down at him. I thought about something Mathias said back in Iraq, as Sergeant Carter bitched about his sunburn and applied lotion to his forearms. "Black don't crack. I got the melanin, and you don't. That's why your white ass is burning like a lobster."

The man before me was evidence to the contrary, however. He was black, and he had definitely cracked. His skin was ashen gray, the dullness so uniform it looked like he was rolled in dough. Several IV lines and catheters pierced his emaciated scarecrow of a body. His face was a featureless, frozen mask of pain.

He repeated his litany of Vietnamese. I stood there uneasily, listening to the wheeze of the other man in the bed across the room. I looked at the chart at the foot of Thigpen, Claude's bed. I read the narrative report, and the notes left by the last attending nurse. I set the clipboard back in its cradle, lifted the blanket from over his bony legs. I saw the antiembolism stockings, sans the knitted socks Hasford warned me about. I replaced the blanket, and crouched down on the ground.

I glanced beneath the bed, looking for salty snacks or soul food. I felt slightly guilty for doing it. I didn't think I had the right to tell a man not to do something that might kill him, if it brought him a last bit of joy before he left this planet. I was no Kevorkian myself, but I understood the argument of quality-of-life versus quantity. If the man wanted to die eating pigs' feet or fatback, then I thought that was his right.

There was no food. There were only several old magazines, with covers as faded as eight-millimeter home movies. I slid one of the magazines out from under the bed, and held it out to the moonlight so I could get a better look at it. *Sepia Magazine*, it said. The cover featured a picture of the comedian Red Foxx, and the cover story's title was "TV's Unhappy Millionaire."

I crouched back down. I slid the magazine back under the bed, next to a tube of what I saw was Mary Kay extra-emollient night cream. I guessed it belonged to the wife who gave Hasford fits. I had never seen that particular black-oriented magazine before. I guessed it was an out-of-print relic from before the time of *Ebony* and *Jet*, something Thigpen read maybe when he was in Vietnam or Korea, or whatever war he was in.

Claude Thigpen's eyes opened, and he looked at me. I was startled by his eyes. They were yellow and red, both jaundiced and bloodshot. His lips were cracked and dry, and slightly bloody from where their skin had blistered and broken. "Puff," he said, softly.

"You want a cigarette?" I asked.

"Nah." He grimaced, his mask of pain tightening even more. "Nah, Puff."

"You're authorized a nicotine lozenge," I said.

"Fucking new guy. AC-Forty Seven, Puff the Magic Dragon drop heavy ordinance on that ass."

He closed his eyes, the EKG behind him flat-lined, and I dropped my paper and pen. "He's coding!" I shouted, and realized there was no one who could hear me. I looked frantically around the room for the AED set, didn't see it. I ran to the door and turned on the room light, ripped my facemask off, and shouted toward Hasford. I pulled the shower curtain aside as I spoke.

"Code Blue, where's the fucking AED?"

"Shock cart coming!" Hasford spun, said, "Get the code team," to the seated RN, and ran down the hall.

I didn't understand why there weren't paddles in every room in a hospice ward, unless the patients in question had specific DNR orders, but then I remembered what Hasford said about budget problems.

I ran back into the room, threw the blanket off Thigpen, and ripped his shirt open. His chest was as ashen as the rest of his body, sunken and with each individual rib tine looking like a key on a xylophone.

Hasford came to the door's threshold with the case in his hand, and gave it to me. Something else was in his other hand, but I was panicking too badly to notice what it was. "You've got to do it!" He shouted.

"Why?" I asked. "Because of the illness?"

He shook his head, or tried to. The neck brace was in the way. "No, I've got metal in me and I'm a shock hazard."

"Fuck," I said. I remembered that one time we practiced in nursing college and someone had used the shock paddles while their body was in contact with the metal railings of the bed. I remembered how they trembled and did the funky chicken on the floor for about ten minutes after that.

"Alright." I opened the box, turned the machine on, and waited for it to perform its self-test. I tore open the foil containing the two electrode pads. My hands trembled, but I managed to get the cables attached to the AED.

"Hurry up!"

"I'm going!" I shouted, forgetting the guy was my boss and that he could have me fired.

"Power on," the machine said, and I carried it with me to the edge of the bed. I was frankly startled that the VA sprang for the voice-activated jobs, since they were more expensive than the ones with just the readout displays. I peeled the plastic backing films from the electrode pads, slapped one on the clavicle and the other to the left of the heart's apex.

My own heart was beating like mad now. I felt like I was alive for the first time in years. I felt like I was back in Iraq. I was happy and scared of death, rather than depressed and afraid I might live to see another day that was exactly like the last one. I glanced at the face of the machine. It was already at 360 joules; it didn't have to be set, unlike the ones we used in training.

"AED in analysis mode," the machine said. I held the shock pads over Thigpen's naked chest. My hands trembled. This was the first time I had done something like this outside of a training setting.

The beep of the AED machine switched to a steady charging tone. Thigpen still hadn't drawn a single breath since uttering his cryptic words about Puff the Magic Dragon. "Fully charged," the machine said.

I pressed the paddles against Claude Thigpen's naked chest, applying twenty-five pounds of pressure, discharging the current into his body. His wan frame flopped like a fish starving for water, and his EKG resumed something approximating a normal rhythm.

"Fuck," I said. A moustache of sweat collected on my upper lip. I wiped it with the sleeve of my robe. I saw now what Hasford had in his hand, a red little manual ventilation bag. He held it up to me apologetically and said, "I wasn't going to kiss someone who's got something that communicable."

He pointed the resuscitation bag at the AED box he'd handed me and said, "Power that thing down and then bring it to the nurse's station."

"Okay."

"We need to remove and transcribe the computer's memory module and print a rhythm strip with the code data."

"Can do," I said.

"Then we have to check his chest for electrical burns. If he has any, we've got some corticosteroids."

I looked at Thigpen's naked chest. "It doesn't look like it."

"Well, then, we'll hit him once with some lanolin just for shits and giggles." Hasford took a deep breath, coughed once. "I could use a cigarette. You want one?"

"Yeah," I said. I hadn't had a cigarette in years, but I needed one. I lifted the patient's right wrist and felt for a pulse, brushing away first the hospital wristband, and then a knotted tangle of what looked like the black laces from an old combat boot.

Hasford answered my question before I could ask it. "It's a slave bracelet," he said. "Some old 'Nam shit that Bloods did."

* * *

Hasford and I ate dinner after the shift was over, around 8:15 a.m. It took me a lot longer than him to decontaminate, and a part of me was more than a little pissed at him for saddling me with Patients Jones and Thigpen. I was not looking forward to work tomorrow, and something told me I would have trouble sleeping when I got home. My heart was still amped up from the earlier Code Blue. I had bad tinnitus, but I was worried that I wasn't deaf enough to drown out the sounds of the city's hustle and bustle that would accompany my off-time, during which I was supposed to sleep. I made a mental note to pick up some blackout curtains and earplugs, when I got the chance.

"Shit on the shingle," Hasford said, as we entered the cantina. It was called "Patriot Cafe." Steam from the metal cooking trays wafted upward and made the kitchen staff sweat as they heaped plates with fatty food. I grabbed a tray and slid it along the metal railing in front of the bins where breakfast was served.

"How'd you like your first shift?" Hasford left his place in line, went over to the cooler, and grabbed two bottles of Coke. He handed me one and I set it on my tray.

"It was intense," I said. "When Thigpen stabilized, he said he got gangrene in Vietnam. You think maybe that has something to do with the infection?"

Hasford shook his head, and pointed at the greasy mountain of scrambled eggs the lunch lady larded onto his plate with an ice cream scoop. She followed that with several rubbery slices of bacon, depositing them atop the globe of eggs with a set of tongs.

He moved on down the line, toward the cash register. "They're both all jacked up." I let the kitchen staff load my plate down, and followed Hasford over to the register. He held out his lanyard to the woman at the register, who hit his CAC card with one of those little price guns.

"We don't pay?"

"Who would pay for this shit?" He looked at the cashier. "No offense."

She laughed. "None taken, sugar. I eat across the street at Subway when my shift ends."

We walked our trays over to a table by the window. Across from us was a table where a volunteer in a blue vest sold those mesh-webbed trucker hats that announced various campaigns, from World War II to Operation Iraqi Freedom.

"Jones is growing a watermelon in his head," Hasford said, and speared some fluffy egg with a plastic Spork.

I chewed a rubbery slice of bacon. Its texture was so slippery that it resisted me as if it was alive. "Tumor?" I asked.

"Yeah," he said, and then looked directly in my eyes. I stared back. My father, a psychiatrist, once told me that he could tell whether a man had been to war or prison just by looking at him. My old man worked at both county hospitals and the lockup before switching into private practice. He claimed that after a while, it was just something he sensed. It was a vibe he could pick up, as if war or prison were carried in the skin. I understood what he was talking about looking at Hasford right now. Vietnam loomed over him, roughed his skin up like sandpaper, and shadowed his form like both a shield that protected him and a cloud that darkened him.

"You've got your own head problems," he said.

I sat up, on the defensive. I almost spit out my bacon in surprise. I should have probably spit it out on general principal, just based on the way it tasted. "You've been looking at my file?"

"I've been in stockade at Mannheim and LBJ, and I killed the time playing solitaire with a deck of fifty-one."

That puzzled me, so I didn't say anything. He explained. "Some of what I do is legally gray. What I'm trying to say is, if you want to report me and get me fired, go ahead. If you want to sue me, do that, too."

I shrugged. "I don't give a shit," I said. That was the truth, except for one detail, which had to do with my genitals. I had been diagnosed with a hydrocele, a kind of fluid pocket in my testicle, after getting back from Iraq. I was also diagnosed with something called epididymitis, which I think was something like an inflammation of the sperm-producing portion of the testicles. It hurt like a sonofabitch. The only treatment involved needles, so I begged off. After I reported the conditions, for some reason the VA logged them as "complete atrophy of the penis." Every time I got a printout of my medical history from the VA to take to a private provider, I was always too embarrassed to speak up about the mistake and request a revision.

I wondered, as I shared breakfast with Hasford, if he saw that part. Then I wondered why it mattered. It wasn't as if I was trying to date him. Maybe it was a manhood thing.

"I apologize," he said, and burped.

I shook my head. "I don't give a shit," I said, again.

He spoke quietly, not wanting to broadcast the conditions of our patients. Apparently he still sort of respected their privacy, even if he didn't give two shits about mine. "Thigpen's got sickle cell, diabetes, and some evidence of Agent Orange. You can tell from some of his scars that he got gangrene." He uncapped his Coke. "Jones got trench foot in the Pacific, I think. That still causes some problems for him, but he's too out of it to feel the pain."

"War is hell, I guess," I said. It was a cliché, but it was something to say. Nurses, doctors, and patients came to sit at the tables around us. I stared at the neighboring tables. I saw wizened men with portable oxygen tanks, canes, wheelchairs, and mobility scooters. They were sunken creatures, grown gnomish and small from a lifetime of taking orders and absorbing abuse on behalf of an ungrateful nation. I felt anger rising for them. I knew, even though I was tired as hell, that the anger I felt for them was really the fear that I would end up like them. I was afraid it was inevitable.

I thought women could sense my weakness, my brokenness.

Every time I spoke to a pretty waitress or an attractive barista, I was sure that she knew my dick didn't work, no matter how short our exchange was, and that she could also tell I was always one gesture away from suicide.

"I forgot to pray before breaking fast," Hasford said, and I wasn't sure whether or not he was joking. I had tried religion, both before the war and afterward. There was a little chapel in the VA, across from the office of the Military Order of the Purple Heart. There were stained glass windows, patterned with crosses, menorahs, and Islamic crescents. I sometimes went there to try to pray.

"Our DI used to make us pray for war before chow, because war was what marines were supposed to do." He guzzled his Coke, and I opened mine. I stared out the window at the sun rising over Cincinnati.

"You still pray for war?" I asked.

He shook his head. "Once a marine, always a marine, maybe. That doesn't mean I've got a hard-on for killing, anymore." He finished his Coke, exhaled, and leaned back in his plastic seat. Then he grinned. "So what the fuck happened to your head in Iraq?"

I wondered why I didn't dislike him. "I guess I lost my mind."

"No, not that," he said, laughing. "I mean the TBI."

I shrugged. "I can tell you what the doctor told me." I pushed my plate away. I couldn't eat anymore of this shit, free or no. I decided I would go to the Proud Rooster on Ludlow and pay for a proper breakfast whenever we were done here. "I was Medevac'd to the Green Zone, where they did a..." I paused, trying to remember, exactly, "...decompressive craniotomy to relieve the pressure. After that, they sent my ass to Landstuhl. I had a surgery on my left shoulder, for a reverse bankart lesion, a labral tear, and a winged scapula."

Shit, I thought, pausing, *I already am one of those shrunken-up, beaten-by-the-world bitter-ass vets*. I had Medicare coverage and a laundry list of physical ailments so long that I already managed to bore my supervisor/breakfast partner. I hadn't even gotten to the corticated cystic lesion or the traumatic arthritis, not to mention the problems with my testicles.

"Every new war brings a new type of weapon," Hasford said,

philosophically. He pointed the tines of his greasy Spork at me. "New weapons bring new injuries."

"That's what the doctor said, although he didn't call them injuries. He called them 'sequlae.'"

"I'll have to remember that the next time I'm playing *Scrabble*."

"New kinds of explosives lead to new blast injuries. Nobody really understands TBI's, but I do know one thing," I continued.

"What's that?"

"Mine ain't that bad," I said. "I mean, I'm working." I held out my hands, encompassing all of the VA. It had been my domain for a while now, but only as a patient. Now I was an employee. I felt proud, in a way.

"You get your degree at UC?" He nodded in the general direction of the campus, over the brow of the next hill behind us.

"Yup."

"People know you were a vet?"

"Some of them did," I said.

"They ask you that stupid question?"

I frowned. I didn't know to which stupid question he was referring. He leaned forward, so that I could smell his sour breakfast breath. "How many people did you kill?"

"It's a question I can't answer," I said.

"Why?" Hasford asked.

"It's like you said. New wars bring new weapons." I thought about Carter. I saw him in my mind, hefting that SMAW with all of his steroid-infested muscle, before the Frago from higher came down and said no more use of SMAWs or Mark-19s within city limits. They brought too much collateral damage.

I asked Hasford, "You know what a shoulder-launched multipurpose assault weapon is?"

He shook his head. "That's a new one to me."

"It's like a bazooka, sort of. It fires a thirty-pound thermobaric rocket. If you've got a china hutch in your house and we fire it at the side of your wall, some of your plates are going to shatter."

He laughed at my casual sadism. It was a pose, like so much of the indifference we pretended to feel during the war. We made constant gay jokes and called each other "fags" and "pussies" before and after combat. We did it just to take the stress out of that weird attraction we started to feel for each other. You'd look at the back of your friend's neck in the heat and wonder if he was going to die, and you'd want to press your lips to his neck and kiss it and cry.

Hasford laughed, though. He needed to believe the lie of the tough guy bullshit as much as me, at least for the moment. "That's what I mean, though," I said. "If someone fires an AK round at us from a window in a house, then we lay down suppressive fire. Dunfy's unloading his squad auto until he melts the barrel, and I'm pumping M4 rounds. Then someone lobs a couple two-oh-three rounds in there, and then afterwards we go inside and there are two insurgents dead. Who killed who?"

I paused, unsure if my question was rhetorical or not.

"I wish I didn't know who I killed," Hasford said. "As a scout sniper, though, I didn't have that luxury. I know the face and even the fucking shoe size of every notch on my belt." He stood up with his mostly empty tray and I realized I was done.

We walked our trays to the scullery, which was humid with the fog of hot water pressure-washing greasy plates. I followed Hasford outside to the smoker's spot, where old vets and nurses smoked under the Mylar bus stop shell next to the hospital emergency exit. I squinted against the force of the morning sun. The smell of the Cincinnati Zoo carried on the air, along with the pungent mist from the Proctor & Gamble factory in Mill Valley. Fog from the Jim Bean distillery added another layer of tangy acridness to the air.

"Here." He handed me a smoke, and I leaned in as he lit it with his *Non Gratum Anus Rodentum* Zippo, featuring a rat wielding a pistol and a flashlight on the side of the lighter. I puffed and looked up at the blue sky, happy to be healthier than everyone locked away in hospice up there. I felt a stab of guilt over the lack of guilt I felt at my happiness.

Hasford smoked and grinned at me with the crooked edge of his mouth. "You might think this was a rough shift, but you got off easy."

I drank smoke from my cigarette. Smoking in Cincinnati probably wasn't the brightest idea. I'd heard that, due to all of the factories in the city, there were an inordinate number of cancer clusters in our fine metropolis. Maybe if I kept it up, I'd end up languishing in one of those beds upstairs.

"Thigpen's a tough customer." Hasford said. "He doesn't much care for Caucasians. We're an equal opportunity employer, but we haven't found any black RNs willing to work graveyard. It'd make our job easier."

"What's his deal?"

"You weren't in the 'Nam." He didn't say it in a taunting way. His tone was more solicitous. It was as if he half-respected me, even though I was in the Army and not the marines. "Rednecks didn't make life easy on the Bloods."

One of the smokers in OR scrubs, a black man with a flattop smoking a Swisher Sweet, coughed and said, "And what, Has, you ain't a redneck?"

Hasford looked down at the smoker, who sat on the bench and leaned his back against the foggy Mylar shell. "I'm white trash, but I ain't a redneck."

The black man on the bench giggled, yellow smoke pouring from his cheap cigar. "What the fuck is the difference?"

"White trash ain't got no class, but we ain't racist. Rednecks ain't got no class, and plus they don't care for your black asses. My spotter was a Blood, and I cried when MLK got his dick knocked in the dirt, right alongside my spotter."

"I call bullshit," the seated man said.

Hasford gave up on trying to convince the dude in scrubs of anything, and turned his attention back to me. "You know those good ol' boys had so many Confederate flags on their hooches and jeeps in the 'Nam that the Vietnamese actually thought the Stars and Bars was the American flag."

Both the seated cigar smoker and I laughed at that one. Hasford smiled, on a roll now. "Yeah, they thought the Stars and Stripes was just a unit insignia."

The guy on the bench was skeptical. "You didn't fly that Confederate flag?"

Hasford stabbed his chest with the thumb on the hand not holding the cigarette. "I'm an Ohio boy, born and raised. If I was in the Civil War, I'd have been fighting for the Union."

"Let me guess, to end slavery, Mr. Lincoln?"

"Hell no," Hasford said. "For free soil."

I looked away from the conversation, up the hill. I stared toward the apartment, where a shower, my dog, and my pain meds were waiting for me. Hasford sensed me pining and waved the hand holding the cigarette, before taking a puff. "Take off. See you tomorrow night."

"Peace."

I turned and started walking up the sidewalk, which was already hot from the force of the waking sun's rays. Shards of glass were melted into a fossilized wad of gum pressed deep into the cement. I looked up the hill, toward the spread of university buildings there. I looked toward the parking garages and the library, and the College of Arts and Sciences building. I took an elective on ETA Hoffman's classic tale of terror, *Der Sandmann*, there. The instructor was a beautiful German feminist professor. I fell in love with her from my seat in the back of her classroom.

It was worth it to risk and waste my life in Iraq, just to get that GI Bill. It bought me a small hollow in that liberal arts honeycomb, away from all the tough guy homophobic killers and among all of the bright-eyed undergrads who believed in diversity and unicorns.

My German feminist professor would sit on the edge of her desk, cross her legs in those black stockings, talk about the automatons in the Romantic works of Hoffman and how phallogocentrism was a key feature in all the works of Germany's revered titans, from Schiller to Goethe. She would click her high-heels together as she spoke. She educated me into getting my first public erection in years. The night I thought my brother was going to assist me in suicide, I sent her an email in which I told her I thought she was the most beautiful woman I ever met. I figured I would be dead soon, and thus could afford the bravery and honesty. Now I was still alive, and ashamed. I was terrified of running into her at a coffee shop or maybe while walking my dog.

I glanced once back toward the brick fortress that was my former asylum and now my employer. I remembered walking the halls of the VA on an inpatient basis, shuffling on a Trazadone and Abilify and Prednisone high. My assigned nurse came up to me one day and said, "You don't remember me. I'm Max's mother."

And then I remembered, and recognized her. Max was my friend when I was a teenager. We'd started a punk band together. We'd seen our first all-ages show at a venue only a few blocks from where I now walked. We left our Catholic school and went to see Marilyn Manson at Bogarts, before he was really famous. The extent of his costume at the time consisted of a single contact lens and sheer body stockings, and ripped fishnets on his arms and legs. That same Catholic school was the one where I had marched on the night I intended to commit suicide. I had cried, kissing the feet of the Mary statue outside of the church where I could never take communion because I wasn't Catholic. I still loved the church with its stained glass suffering Stations of the Cross and its frescos of painted saints, who'd been burnt and crucified and turned into pincushions with the persecution of Roman arrows.

The neighborhood held too many memories for me, no question about it. I couldn't leave it and I couldn't run away, because I needed the job and the money to live. My world was a haunted house and I was both a ghost and a rube who'd paid admission to be scared.

CHAPTER THREE: BACK TO WORK

German immigrants in the middle of the 19th century chose to settle in Cincinnati because its location along the Ohio River reminded them of the Rhineland valley. At least, that's what I learned in an American-German architecture elective I took at the university.

I lived in Germany for a couple of years. Most of that time was spent training to go to Iraq, and then getting ready to head my next unit. I can still say with some certainty that the comparison between the two regions is apt. Cincinnati does look and feel like a lot of midsized cities in Germany, especially in the Rhineland region. Then again, that could be because the Germans who settled here decided to remake the place in their image after they immigrated.

I thought about Germany as I got ready for the next shift. I fed Tiffany, walked her, and gave her twenty throws of the tennis ball in the park to run her ragged. Her eyes were watery with contempt, and her tail fluttered like a snake's rattle as I left her to go to work. She was used to me loafing around with her all day, and my new schedule was a betrayal of sorts.

It was a moonless night. The only light came from the gas lamps and the occasional car that drove up Ludlow Avenue. If I was a single woman, walking alone in that darkness, I would have felt nervous. As it was, however, I kept my hair in a military high-and-tight and I was fairly certain I still gave off a general air of violence and anger wherever I went.

Most of the apartment buildings in the neighborhood were Romanesque revival manors. They were left by millionaire capitalists who died around the turn of the century, and then sold the buildings that were then subdivided. Many of the buildings looked like small castles, just like in Germany. They were beaux arts fortresses with terra cotta cornices and roaring stone lions nestled in their pediments.

My throat itched for a cigarette as I walked, and I cursed myself for accepting that smoke from Hasford last night. My mind drifted to a trip I'd taken to the Czech Republic with Dondy and a couple of other soldiers shortly after we got back from Iraq and redeployed to Germany. I remembered being drunk, staggering through dark streets that looked much like these, lonely cobblestones echoing underfoot. I'd had several shots of absinthe and also had unprotected sex with a Slovakian girl. She told me in broken English that she was gang-raped by Bulgarian gangsters and forced into a life of prostitution. I'd staggered into the Old Town after our encounter, away from the Jewish ghetto and the statue of Franz Kafka, until I came to an ancient clock ringed with zodiac signs. The hour struck midnight and a skeleton symbolizing Death with a smile on its face came out of the clock like a cuckoo, and I could have sworn it shouted "You've got AIDS!" It was probably just the absinthe and the traumatic brain injury talking.

I had a dream last night in which an insurgent fired a tracer round at Mathias's sappy plates, hitting a smoke grenade. It created a cloudy plume that took on the form of Dunfy's dead face. I missed my friend and I missed that Slovakian prostitute. She had been the last person I had sex with, I realized. That meant I hadn't had sex in years.

I barely even talked to women these days. The last relationship I had with a female that came close to something normal was with my German tutor, Claudine. I was minoring in German studies in addition to history, while working on my nursing degree. She was an exchange student from a small German town called Bielefeld that I'd never heard of before.

She had brown hair and even browner eyes. Even the small explosion of robin's egg freckles on her face was brown. I usually felt insecure, nervous, and borderline terrified around women. There was something soothing and forgiving about Claudine. We met in cafes and coffee shops, and even in an expensive fachwerk restaurant that served German cuisine authentic enough to please her.

They had these black Labradors in Iraq that they kept around the hospitals and morale centers. Soldiers could pet and hug the dogs in order to deal with the pain of the war. I was attracted to Claudine, but I also felt about her the way the war-scarred soldiers felt about those black labs. She was absorbing the ugliness of the war whenever we met. She distracted me from myself while also improving my German.

My greatest weakness in German was conjugation and word order. I could speak the language much better than I could write it or read it. I could get through Kafka's *Der Verwandlung* if I had a *Wörterbuch* handy, and short works of poetry by Novalis or Holderlin were easy enough. Thomas Mann and Gunter Grass might as well have been writing in Greek, though.

I paid Claudine $20 per hour over her objections for the help. I always picked up the tab when we ate out or went for coffee, no matter how hard she insisted on paying. She said that she had a fiancé back in Bielefeld. That was fine with me, since I never flirted with her. I could masturbate, but sex became impossible sometime after I got out of the army. That didn't mean that I couldn't cherish every little accidental brush of her knee, warm beneath the material of her blue jeans as it glanced against my own thigh, or that I couldn't savor the even warmer, callous-free pad of her hand that I felt whenever we shook upon meeting each other each day for lessons.

For a while there, I contemplated becoming a Casanova of cunnilingus in order to make up for my limp dick. I read articles online and even a book on technique called *She Comes First: A Thinking Man's Guide to pleasuring a Woman*. But I never got the chance to try out any of the things I learned from sex therapist Ian Kerner's work. I did learn, however, that the average penis has far fewer nerve endings that the average clitoris. I also learned that while a penis usually has between three and five contractions during orgasm, a female's genitalia usually goes through twice that many.

I gave Claudine one last wistful thought before entering the VA building through the emergency entrance, and walked past the triage station to the bank of elevators. I pressed the "up" button and waited, recalled my mother and one of her favorite questions she would pose each morning upon waking. "What fresh hell awaits me today, Lord?"

I waited on that elevator, knowing that it was all bad on the eighth floor. I knew that neither of my two highly-infectious patience were ever going to get out of here alive. The elevator car came and I got on. I pressed "8" and waited, tapping my foot and playing with the ribbon of my lanyard.

I found Hasford standing in front of the nurse's station, talking with the seated nurse in his swivel chair. "Hey, Kevorkian," the sitting man said. "Your employee is here."

Hasford glanced at his watch. "You're late."

I looked at my own watch. "I'm five minutes early."

He shook his head. "If you're not ten minutes early, you're ten minutes late."

It was one of those stupid sayings we had in the Army. Apparently they'd had it in the Marines back when he was a devil dog. Another one was, "If it ain't raining, we ain't training." Some dipshit noncommissioned officer would inevitably say this whenever we had a field exercise or *an espirit de corps* run to complete, and God deigned to commence with a thunderstorm just when our project got underway.

"Sorry," I said. I looked at the seated RN. "Why do you call him Kevorkian?"

Hasford answered for him. "Because I believe there's some dignity in death. That makes me the bad guy, apparently."

The seated RN shook his head. Hasford continued. "If the patients knew what resuscitation really entailed, like getting pounded on the chest until their ribs broke, I'm pretty sure a lot more DNR orders would get signed." He glanced down the fluorescent-lit hall, toward the shower curtain hung in the corridor that separated my two patients from the rest of the ward. "There are worse things that death."

"Here we go," the seated RN said.

Hasford ignored him. "Keeping people alive for the insurance money should be against the law."

The seated RN glanced up from his computer, and then at me. "Whatever you do, don't let him palm that stupid book off on you."

"What book?"

Hasford said, "Raymond Moody's *Life after Life*. Ever heard of it?"

"Nope."

"It has a bunch of firsthand accounts of near-death experiences, people who were drowning or got into car accidents and had heart attacks."

The seated RN sighed, but Hasford continued, "These people were clinically dead for a short time and then resuscitated, and in Dr. Moody's book they described what they saw."

"What did they see?"

"Beautiful things," Hasford said. He sounded as wistful as I felt few minutes ago, thinking about absinthe and my Slovakian princess and practicing cunnilingus techniques on my German tutor. "They were reunited with long-dead loved ones, they felt a sense of peace." He paused, and then spoke low, *sotto voce*. "The most important part was that they said they didn't feel pain anymore."

"Maybe I'll have to read the book," I said.

His face brightened and the seated RN placed his head in his hands, exasperated that I hadn't heeded his advice. I'd accepted the bait, apparently. A moan came from down the hall, reminding all three of us that we were in a hospital, and we had a job to do. Hasford jerked a thumb toward the room where the supplies were kept.

"Suit up," he said. "You don't need me to help you anymore."

"What am I doing tonight?"

"Suit up." His voice was a little sterner now. "Then come see me, and I'll tell you what you're doing."

"Hooah!" I said.

"I'm a marine. We say 'hoorah.'"

"Hoorah!" I went into the room, changed. I got my mask on, but left it dangling around my neck. I managed to get my robe on and tied in the back, with some minor difficulty. I snapped my latex gloves on my hands. I emerged from the room and Hasford stood there with his hands full.

"You're checking Norman Jones for pressure ulcers."

I accepted everything in my latex-gloved hands. He fixed me with his gaze. "I assume I don't have to hold your hand?"

I did inventory of what I now held. There was a piston syringe, a clear plastic garbage bag, a bottle of saline solution with the dimensions of a large mouthwash bottle, as well as an irrigation container that was kidney-shaped, like a bedpan. There was also a see-through garbage bag.

"I know what bedsores look like." I checked all of the stuff I balanced in my hands. I noticed there was also a foam stoma chart, with various sizes cut out on it. "Am I changing a colostomy bag?"

Hasford shook his head. "No, Thigpen's a big boy and he likes to be independent. He changes his own bags. You can use that there to measure the wounds, if you find any. You shouldn't find anything past stage one, though."

"When's the last time he was in a wheelchair?" I nodded in the direction of the curtain partition behind us.

"Who?" Hasford asked. "Jones?"

"Yeah."

"Why?"

"Pressure points for patients who spend a lot of time in wheelchairs are different than for supine patients."

The seated RN pointed a ballpoint pen he'd been using on a crossword, clicked it once, and said to Hasford, "Your boy is sharp as a tack."

"It's been awhile," Hasford said. "The last time was when they wheeled him down to CT and found the glioblastoma multiforme."

I didn't ask how long ago that was. If I knew when the tumor was discovered, it would be that much easier to predict when he was going to die. The rough answer to that question was "soon," at any rate.

"Alright," I said, and turned. I pulled my mask over my face. Immediately the sound of my hot breath echoed in my ears, like the rush of the surf against rocks. The floor was still sticky, and I cursed myself under my breath as I pulled my nonstick shoes from the mucus-like puddles gripping the traction of my soles as I walked.

Claude Thigpen sat up in his room, with his legs thrown over the side of his bed. Among the patches of ash on his kneecaps and shins were spots of whitish vitiligo. He squirted a bit of Mary Kay TimeWise moisturizer into his palm and rubbed it on his legs. "My wife gives me this shit." He set the tube down next to his knotted shoelaces, the "slave bracelet" Hasford had told me about yesterday. I didn't know what to say to that, so I didn't say anything.

He unbuttoned his hospital gown, exposing the colostomy bag. His hypoallergenic bag was filled to bursting, with yellowish, liquid feces. "You need some help?" I asked.

"I got this," he hissed as he spoke. He looked down at the pouch.

"It's bad business, but it beats diapers."

I turned on the fluorescent light in the corner of the room and then walked over to Norman Jones' sleeping form. "I won't argue with you there."

"Shit," Thigpen said, and squinted. I walked over to my patient's bed, set down my supplies on the dresser next to the metal railings that held the old World War II vet. Thigpen's voice came from behind me.

"You racially hung up?"

"What do you mean?" I asked. His voice was incredibly hoarse. I wondered if he had perhaps been recently intubated.

"Some gray boys had a thing against us Bloods, called us all kind of names. Brillo heads, chocolate bunnies…" It sounded like he could keep going, but he was busy with his colostomy bag.

"No," I laughed. "I never even heard those terms bandied about when I was in."

I gently lifted Norman Jones's frail form, unbuttoning his hospital gown. I wasn't Tom Brokaw with his "Greatest Generation" rap, but I did feel a kind of reverence and awe for veterans of "the Big One." Vietnam still seemed like a sort of private disgrace, and the war in Iraq was just something people wanted to forget. World War II was something mythic, like the Civil War.

"You was in?" Thigpen asked, speaking to my back.

"Iraq," I said, and hoped that would be enough.

"But you ain't hung up, racially?"

I lightly probed the comatose patient's sacrum and coccyx, saw no traces of even slight irritation, redness. "I'd be lying if I said I was color-blind, but I don't walk around filled with hatred all day."

"Good, then." Thigpen limped to the bathroom, with his robe open, exposing his shriveled genitals and the bloody stoma wound knotted in his stomach. He carried the colostomy bag in his hand and the slosh of feces hitting the toilet bowl echoed. He spoke to me from within the bathroom. "I got five-thousand Vietnamese piasters under my mattress. I'll give them to you if you get me a pint of Gilbey's."

I rolled the patient slightly, spotted a stage one pressure ulcer growing on the right greater trochanter. "Gilbey's?" I had never heard of it. I guessed it was something truly bargain basement, like Popov or

Wild Irish Rose.

"It's gin."

I unscrewed the saline bottle and poured half into the irrigation container, going slow to avoid splashing. "I don't even know how much a piaster's worth. The offer's tempting, but I could lose my job if I started bringing patients contraband, especially stuff that can get them killed."

Thigpen continued working on replacing his colostomy bag with a new one in the bathroom. I heard the slap of the plastic ostomy bag hitting the toilet. I felt sorry for whatever hospital staff had to come into this room and clean up. I inspected my patient's wound for necrotic debris, measured the perimeter of the sore with the stoma chart.

I spoke loud enough for Thigpen to hopefully hear me. "Can you eat marshmallows, or is your diabetes too bad?"

"Shit," he grunted. "What you think?"

I depressed the syringe, applying full force to irrigate the pressure ulcer, and what little bit of necrotic debris there was scattered. I felt sympathy pangs of relief for the comatose man. He must have felt some pleasure when the cool saline hit the friction burn and worked its way into the wound, despite his slumbering state. I couldn't gauge the odor of the drainage, since Thigpen's colostomy bag was giving off too strong a reek of its own. The wound didn't look severe, though. The trochanter one was the only pressure ulcer I spotted on his whole body.

Hasford hadn't given me a cotton swab, so I touched a latex-gloved finger to the wound and softly pressed. I assessed for tunneling and wound undermining, neither of which I found. I hoped the old man would sleep better now, no matter how much time he had left.

I carefully removed my gloves, following standard de-contamination procedure. I discarded them in the plastic bag I'd been given. I rolled the sleeping patient back into a comfortable position. I even placed his arms one over the other across the chest, as if readying him for a casket. I noticed a gel foam mattress overlay beneath him, which was ribbed like the bottom of an egg crate.

Thigpen limped out of the bathroom. He glanced over at me and

Norman Jones, he with the tumor the size of a watermelon in his head. My supervisor was right about Claude Thigpen; he'd changed his colostomy bag like a pro. He nodded at Norman Jones' sleeping form. "Dollars to donuts that cracker's worm food in less than a month."

I stood up. I saw one of those canisters of Total Solution Disinfectant that were scattered throughout the ward, and were as numerous as rolls of toilet paper. I picked the can up and pointed it into the clear plastic bag where I'd just thrown my gloves, depressing the trigger. I looked over at Thigpen, who was slowly working his way back into his bath towel-bedecked bed.

"That's not a very nice thing to say about your roommate. Don't you believe in karma?"

He scoffed at that. Thigpen wrapped himself in blankets and towels, until only his feet with their yellow toenails were peeking from the white linen cocoon he made for himself. "Don't tell me about karma. I'm Buddha."

"I'm pretty sure Buddha doesn't talk about people like they're worm food." I tied the plastic bag into a knot, gathering up my supplies.

"That's what Mama San said, that I was Buddha."

I walked to the corner of the room, turned the light out. The moon had finally escaped from the shroud of clouds that had imprisoned it earlier in the night. A bar of light broke through the window, splashed across the ceiling. Thigpen stared at it. He reminisced. As he spoke of the distant Vietnamese Mama San, he might as well have been me thinking about my absinthe visions of the Slovakian prostitute, or my more sober love for Claudine, my freckle-faced German tutor who helped me in coffee shops and made me feel human for a while.

"We'd hit the pipe in Soul Alley. There'd even be a few gray boys toking opium with us, if they wasn't too hung up on race." I stood in the doorway with my trash bag, my saline, and other supplies. I listened. "She had a little gold Buddha statue, and she pointed at me. 'You Buddha, black man Buddha.'" He tried to laugh, and coughed. Then he did actually manage to laugh after a bronchial spasm, and continued doing his Mama San impression. "'Black man has thick lips like Buddha- same hair, same nose.'"

"Goodnight, Buddha."

He shot up in bed. He went ramrod straight, so quickly I wondered if it was possible for someone to sit at the position of attention. He spoke loud enough to wake the dead, but it didn't put a dent in the slumber of his comatose roomie.

"'I have an intuitive feeling that the Negro servicemen have a better understanding than whites what this war is about.'"

Claude Thigpen fell backwards. He plopped back onto his mattress, just as quickly as he shot up. I knew he was quoting someone when he spoke, but I didn't know who. I was only sure that this time it wasn't the Mama San.

"William Westmorland," a voice behind me said. I turned to see Nurse Hasford standing behind me, wearing all of the same safety gear that I had donned. "From a speech given in Saigon."

I didn't know what to say to that, so I said, "I'll take your word for it."

CHAPTER FOUR: MY FIRST DAY OFF

My brother lived with me for a while a few years ago, but things didn't work out. I had my PC and he had his laptop. His laptop was faster, and I sometimes used it to play videogames and look at porn.

One night I came home to the apartment we shared, and saw massive holes in the plaster walls of my bedroom. There was a message written in smudged red that said, "You douchebag, you gave my computer a virus. I wish you died in Iraq."

We didn't live together after that. We didn't even talk to each other for a year or two, but things eventually smoothed out. The message he wrote wishing I'd died in Iraq had been scrawled in the lipstick of a girl he was dating at the time named Sasha.

A couple of years after he and Sasha broke up, I got a call from my mother. She informed me that Sasha had a kid a couple of years back, and had petitioned the court to force my brother to take a paternity test.

My mom gave me Sasha's telephone number. I called the girl and set up a date with her and her son, Daniel, while still awaiting the results of the paternity test. She lived in Northside, where she also worked something like fifty hours per week at a Valvoline. I agreed to meet her and her son in her part of town.

I wasn't sure whether or not the baby was my brother's, and I was technically going behind my brother's back by meeting them without telling him. But I felt I had to see the boy, and I also felt certain that the boy was my brother's son for some reason.

Since getting back from Iraq, I'd had one foot in this world and the other planted firmly in the fresh hell of the afterlife. I had the days to myself because I was living on disability, and I would usually walk to the park, where the moms and their children would busy themselves on the playsets.

I always felt envious, doing my donut on the walking path around the playground, with Tiffany leading me on the leash. The sun would shine and the women with the swollen breasts and pregnant bellies would prance around in their sunglasses like fertility goddesses. They would sway as they walked, aware of the power they held. I felt a force field between myself and the playground, even though it wouldn't have taken much for me to set foot on the mulch bed surrounding the swing sets and jungle gyms.

Tiffany was a cute little terrier, but I was too weird and too much of an obvious wreck to even rope a woman into a conversation with my cute puppy. I felt banished, excommunicated. I'd never had my sperm count checked, but I was sure the environmental contaminants I'd been exposed to in Iraq, like the depleted uranium and radon, had turned my boys into non-swimmers.

I didn't think I would ever have a child, or get married. I didn't even think I would ever have a girlfriend again. I was just taking up space, siphoning dollars from the U.S. taxpayer with my manifold injuries. I got small pleasure from takeout Chinese food and television here, and long sleepless nights of masturbation and pain pills there. So the idea that I might have a nephew was more than a little appealing to me, since it would give meaning to my life again.

I met Sasha and Daniel in Northside for lunch one day. The neighborhood was trendier than Clifton, if a bit rougher and more downscale. There were fewer new age shops and more tattoo parlors. There were also a bunch of eateries with clever names and a really good record shop that sold vinyl, zines, and comix.

I found Sasha and Daniel sitting on the sidewalk outside of the Bluebird Café. It was a grease pit that wasn't as good as the Proud Rooster, my personal favorite spot a few blocks from my apartment.

"Hey." I leaned down, touched the warm fontanel of Daniel's head. I knew instantly that he was my brother's son. He smiled at me, and sucked his pacifier. He had a potbelly and a face that could go from lamblike docility to a mischievous grin in a matter of seconds. His mother had blonde hair that was worn from being dyed too many times, and a torn Dead Kennedys shirt with no sleeves and several safety pins running up and down the length of is worn cotton fabric. Her ears were elven and her eyes were glassy, as if she'd taken too much acid.

"Hello, Daniel," I said. He ignored me, or didn't seem to care that I was speaking to him. Sasha stood, and he took her hand. Then all three of us adjourned to a restaurant with the unfortunate name of Tacocracy. I found out that day that Daniel and his mother were vegans, and a few weeks later I discovered that the boy was my brother's; I was officially an uncle.

My brother didn't sound very happy with the situation the next time I talked to him. "She said she couldn't get pregnant."

"You didn't use condoms?"

"She said she couldn't get pregnant."

My brother was the opposite of me, in that he always had a girlfriend. He wanted to see his son, but he was also worried that having to deal constantly with Sasha would put a strain on the relationship with his present girlfriend.

The next time I talked to my mother on the phone, she began a routine that she would continue every time I talked to her on the phone after that. It went like this- "I'm going to have to end up supporting that baby ... Your brother never has a job. He lives off his girlfriends ... You know you're going to be the only male presence in that baby's life. Joey, that baby needs you-" Etcetera, etcetera, and so on.

I tended to meet Daniel and Sasha at least once a week, either for playdates in the park, or for lunch. I texted Sasha on my first day off work from the VA and asked her if she and the Dirty D would be available for lunch. She texted back, "Yeah," and we agreed to meet at Amol. It was a nice Indian restaurant in Clifton, only a few blocks from my apartment. It was also less than a five-minute drive from where she lived.

I got there early and sat in a booth. I waited, nervously drumming my hands on the Formica and making the vinyl booth beneath me creak as I shifted my weight. I had a new toy for Daniel that I'd bought at an upscale boutique on Ludlow Avenue. It was a pink dump truck made out of soft, pliant rubber. Daniel loved cars even more than he loved dinosaurs, probably because his mom worked with cars all day at Valvoline.

I admired her for being a strong single mother. She would take help if it was offered, like my mom paying the child support or me slipping her money for groceries occasionally. She was also very proud and independent.

"Hello, sir." The waiter stood over me and smiled. He'd been working at Amol for decades, so long that I could remember when he was fat and wore a turban. My father and I used to come here together for dinners, shortly after my parents got divorced.

"Kashmiri Nan, please, and coconut soup while I'm waiting." I pointed at the empty space across from me.

"Of course."

"And they need a vegan menu." I pointed again at the empty space across from me.

"Of course."

He turned and left the table, and shouted something in Hindi to the cook hidden in the back of the restaurant. There just wasn't enough time to learn every language. I was barely fluent in German, more like conversant. Those skills would rust without Claudine. She was now back in Bielefeld, probably for good, with her husband.

I looked out the front window of the restaurant, feeling placid and strangely happy. I watched the people walk by and listened to the clack of distant construction work thundering as jackhammers tore through concrete.

I invented an alternate life for myself, sitting there and waiting for my bread and soup. In this alternate life, I never dropped out of high school and got my GED. I never joined the army. I went from my parochial grade school, Annunciation Catholic, to a Catholic high-school run by the friars. I studied hard, and got into a good college. I majored in premed, and then became a doctor.

My wife and I would be nominally Catholic, but it was more of a social thing. We were there to smell the incense and votive candles, and be surrounded by the stained glass and ceremonies, and to provide a steadying influence in the lives of our children. She would have sleeve tattoos that were easily covered up by her business attire (I hadn't invented a job for her yet). She would have a hairy vagina, to which I wouldn't object, because I was both progressive and somewhat submissive. We would go out to eat two three times per week. We would take long walks with our son or daughter (probably daughter) in tow, and I would go down on her once or twice a week. I'd perfect my technique with new things I learned from blog updates at sex therapist Ian Kerner's website. Sometimes we would eat Thai and sometimes Indian, usually after seeing a quirky indie film at the art deco theater. Sometimes-

"Uncle Joe!"

I turned at the table, and saw Daniel extending his arms toward me. "It's the Dirty D!" I announced. I acted as if he were a rival wrestler, a face about to be reduced to heel status after I broke his back. He smiled and squirmed as I lifted him up, and leaned down on one knee. I hoisted him toward the ceiling, savoring his giggling, and slowly brought him down onto my kneecap, pretending to break his back. His giggling ended in a pleased cooing noise, like a soft bubble popping.

"Hello," his mom said. Sasha shifted her purse and sat down in the booth across from me. The waiter gave her a vegan menu and she mouthed the words "Thank you." She had dyed her hair black and gotten a tattoo of a gorgon on her left shoulder.

"I like your tattoo."

"Thanks." She sipped her water. Daniel crowded in next to her, clinging to his mother so tightly that I suspected he wanted to breastfeed right there. I wondered if vegans breastfed.

"I already know what I want." She scanned the menu, anyway. I lifted the dump truck to Daniel. His smile widened, revealing several small teeth and empty spaces in his baby gum line.

He took the dump truck in his hands and held it aloft, as if it was a child and he a proud parent.

"What do you say?" Sasha closed the menu.

"Thanks, Uncle Joe."

I couldn't hear that enough. I felt like I had some purpose again. I had told myself that I couldn't commit suicide while my mother was alive, because it would cause her too much pain. I planned to blow my brains out on the day she died, however. I couldn't kill myself at all now that Daniel was around. He was keeping me tethered to the world, whether or not he knew it.

"How's work?" I asked.

"About to quit," she said.

The waiter entered our midst, turned our glasses over, and filled them with water. He looked at me, and I wondered if he recognized me from those dinners my father and I had together here all those years ago. I suddenly remembered being a kid and somehow getting into the Esquire to see *Bram Stoker's Dracula*, and how exciting and illicit the R-rated film made me feel.

"Are we ready to order?"

"I'll have the lamb vindaloo," I said.

"Vegetable korma," Sasha said. Daniel didn't speak, just played with his pink dump truck. I knew before even buying the thing that he wouldn't object to its pastel shades. His mom liked to paint his fingernails with whatever polish she used on her own hands that day, and she said she even hoped he turned out to be gay. I figured that, children being defiant by nature, he was likely to grow up to be a total womanizer, a lothario like my younger brother.

"Daniel," I said. I couldn't tell whether or not he was listening. I never could. I wasn't sure at what age children started to process what kinds of information. My brother saw his son from time to time. Daniel never shouted, "Dad!" the way he shouted "Uncle Joe!" when he saw me, but Sasha assured me that Daniel knew my brother was his father. Both she and my brother were heroin addicts around the same time, and both had cleaned up their acts well before the birth of the Dirty D.

The waiter disappeared, and returned a short time later with my Nan and soup. I tore a piece of the bread off and chewed it, savoring the buttery raisins buried in the dough. Daniel didn't look up from his truck when the food came. Getting him to eat was something of a chore.

"So what are you going to do?" I asked.

Sasha yawned, stretched, and then said, "I'm going to be an electrician. I'm joining a union, but first I have to apprentice."

"They pay you for that time?" I dipped my spoon into the coconut soup and slurped up some of the white fleshy shreds.

She nodded. "Yeah, it's an apprenticeship, not an internship."

A siren wailed outside and Daniel perked up. He looked at his mom. "Fire truck?"

She half-turned toward the front window of the Indian restaurant, through which sunlight spilled. "I think it was an ambulance, babe."

"Firetruck," he said, sure of which sirens he'd heard.

"How's your new job?" She asked.

"Good," I said, not sure whether or not I was telling the truth. "It beats laying around on disability. It feels good to be a productive member of society." I tore another shred of the Kashmiri Nan from the loaf and soaked it in the soup, before eating it. I spoke with my mouth half-full. "If I get too productive, though, they'll take away my benefits, like Medicare."

"That sucks," she said, "that they punish you for working. I mean, you earned that money."

"Daniel," I said. He rolled his dump truck along his side of the booth and didn't look up. "Don't ever join the military." Gays were openly allowed to serve. That meant that even if she turned him into a flaming homosexual, there wasn't any guarantee that he might not go to war someday.

I stretched in the booth, and heard my back crack once. "I have to go to the chiropractor after this."

The waiter came back, bearing our food. I was careful to position the hot tray of lamb behind both my bread and my soup. Sometimes Daniel would get curious about non-vegetarian dishes. He would point and say, "What's that?"

"You don't want that," his mom would say. "That's a bird," or "That's a pig." His veganism was a sore point with both my mom and my brother.

"That baby needs protein!" My mother would shout at me when we were on the phone. My brother was a bit more acidulous. "She said she had to go to like five or six doctors before she finally found one who said it was okay for him to be a vegan. It's fucking borderline child abuse, man."

Both my mother and brother talked about getting partial custody of Daniel at some point, taking their case to court if they had to. I thought it was best to leave him with his mother. He was so attached to her that sometimes when she went to the restroom, he would cry harder than when she assured him he didn't want the savory-smelling food on my side of the table.

He was too engrossed in his dump truck now, though, to care

about my food, or even his own. Daniel was a messy eater whenever he did eat, but I was a good tipper. I thought it was only right to tip heavily. It was a bit of karmic realignment and my way of thanking the Gods for giving me a good disability rating when I applied. After I was actually approved, I was given a lump sum backdated to date of injury (when I was admitted to the Green Zone hospital with my TBI). The check was cut for $15,000.

I immediately took one-thousand dollars out of the bank and went to the VA after I got my lumps sum. I headed to the Military Order of the Purple Heart Office and found my liaison, a fat man with gray hair and a walrus mustache.

"Here," I said, handing him the envelope. It was filled with ten crisp one-hundred dollar bills.

"What's that?"

"It's a thousand dollars. Thanks for helping me with my case."

He shook his head. "I'm not allowed to accept that."

I thought for a moment. I don't remember the exact date, but it was late December when I walked into his office. "That money isn't for you helping me. It's a Christmas present, completely unrelated to your work on my case."

My liaison smiled gratefully, pocketed the envelope, and said, "Thanks, brother."

I had no regrets about my act, didn't even think it was charitable. If a bill for lunch was thirty dollars, I'd leave a ten-dollar tip. Fuck it. We all die at some point.

"Here, Daniel." Sasha mixed korma with rice on a large spoon. Daniel set the dump truck down and opened his mouth, wrapping his mostly-toothless gums around the spoon. She didn't even have to trick him with an airplane routine. He chewed, and smiled. Bits of rice and vegetable fell out of his mouth and stained his fat, cherubic cheeks.

A lot of times when I talked to my mother about Daniel, she would say words to the effect that, "You know, you should marry Sasha, just out of convenience, even if you two aren't attracted to each other."

I would usually tell my mother to drop the subject at this point. If she didn't, then I would end the call. I wasn't really attracted to Sasha, as she was too skinny and pale for me. I was also pretty sure I did nothing for her or any woman, for that matter.

As convenient as our potential marriage of convenience would be, it also would confuse the shit out of Daniel. There was no chance in hell that my brother and Sasha would ever get back together. I wanted Daniel to see my brother as his father, and to continue to see me as "Uncle Joe!"

* * *

My chiropractors were out on Beechmont Avenue. It was a nightmare commercial strip of billboards and yardarm signage. Telephone and traffic light wires clogged the skies. The streets were choked with gridlocked traffic. It was a land of fast food restaurants and laundromats. The neighborhood of Anderson held as many memories for me as Clifton. The memories were almost all bad here, unlike in Clifton.

My father and I moved out to Anderson after my parents split up, and we lived in a bachelor's complex just off Beechmont Avenue. I was never any good at making friends, so I smoked weed before and after school every day. I got terrible grades and hung out with a pothead named Greg who used to occasionally beat the crap out of me when he was drinking as well as smoking weed.

I googled Greg shortly after getting out of the Army and returning to Cincinnati. I discovered from a local crime blotter that he was arrested for importuning two minors under the age of twelve in a park. Another link on Google said he now worked as an employee at a warehouse that provided kindergartens and elementary schools with supplies, things like crayons and notebooks. I ran into Greg once at a bar, since getting home from Iraq. He was so messed up on either meth or crack that he didn't recognize me when he asked to borrow a dollar to get on the Metro bus. I gave him a five-dollar bill, and then he hugged me and cried.

I went to two different chiropractors who were located only a few blocks from one-another. I wasn't sure whether the two doctors were in competition, so I never mentioned to one that I was seeing the other. I was always afraid that one doctor would spot me going to the other's office and feel somehow cheated or betrayed.

I went to Anderson Township Chiropractic first. I parked in the lot, next to a local bakery that smelled of strong coffee and donuts. I got out of the car and walked into Doctor Milland's office.

"Good morning." His assistant in blue scrubs smiled at me, from behind her desk.

"Hello."

"Mr. Sullivan," Doctor Milland said, from inside his office. "I'm ready when you are."

I walked into his office. "How are you, Doctor?"

"I'm good. How's school?"

I lay face-down on the table, with my head nestled in the cradle. "Oh, I graduated. I've got a job."

"Good to hear."

Doctor Milland was a meek, mildly overweight man with silver hair. He had a red face and a gentle voice, so soothing that just hearing him talk seemed to give me as much relief as the manipulations he did. He pressed on my back with his hands and there was a loud crack, after which I sighed. Then there was the sound of his spring-loaded activator instrument, pulsing up and down my spine like a miniature jackhammer, delivering about one-thousandth as many joules as the shock pads I'd administered to Thigpen's chest a few days ago.

"Okay, Joe, you can turn over now."

I flipped, and the tissue paper on the bed rattled beneath me. I tried to remain as loose as possible, bracing in spite of myself. He tugged my head to the left, and another series of relieving cracks rippled through my neck and shoulders. I turned my head in the other direction, and he cracked me once more.

"Okay, Joe, see you in two days."

"*Danke*," I said, and stood. I walked out into the waiting room. I thanked his assistant and then headed back to my car.

I was rated as seventy-percent, service-connected disabled, according to the VA. That meant I got something like $1300 a month from them. I got another $930 dollars or so per month in Social Security. This might sound like enough for me to scrape by without working. Aside from the chiropractic, though, which was covered by

Medicare, I also saw a private practice mental health therapist at a "Spiritual Wellness Center." I also went to a shiatsu massage therapist, who charged eighty dollars an hour. None of that was covered by my insurance.

The shiatsu massage therapist was a tiny brunette with thick tortoise-shell glasses who had great taste in music and movies. I didn't experience much social anxiety when I was with her, since I kept my face down during our session and I was paying her for her time. I usually talked up a storm.

She would work her feet up and down my back, rubbing oil into my sore joints with her toes. I had her listed under "Contacts" on my cellphone as "Foot Goddess." My "Spiritual Wellness Coach," was a bit older, but equally attractive Jewish woman with curly hair and an effervescent smile. I'd had terrible panic attacks before seeing her. It got to the point where my vision would cloud and everything would break apart before my eyes, as if the world was composed of nothing but pixels.

My coach taught me some techniques that were objectively silly as hell, but were quite effective at banishing the spots and tunnel vision. I would press my hand to my head, and tap my fingers against my skull. Then I would begin what she called "aforemations," rather than affirmations. I wouldn't lie to myself with the mantra of "I'm getting calmer and calmer." Instead, I would phrase the mantra as a question, "*Why* am I getting calmer and calmer?" I essentially tricked myself with the slight tweak in phrasing.

I would also tap my skull and say "Even if you have a panic attack, I will still love you unconditionally." This was to help me with the self-loathing, the feelings of weakness and failure I felt whenever the panic attacks happened. Before seeing this therapist, I'd get panic attacks so severe that I'd pull my car over on the side of the road and literally lay down on the lawn of the first house I saw. I even had a breakdown at school, and I fell down on the cobblestone path in front of the university library. I shivered and cried. I screamed, "I'm blind!" until the paramedics arrived and calmed me down.

I waited for the traffic to abate a bit, and then pulled out. I drove across the street to the cruciform parking lot where my other chiropractor was located. I drove between the FedEx and McDonald's buildings buttressing the strip mall, and I parked in a handicapped space. I got out and walked through the entrance.

"Good morning, Mr. Sullivan!" Both of the assistants were attractive females in their early twenties. One had dark eyes and jet hair. The other had red hair with the perky manner of a cheerleader. To make matters even worse, the chiropractor was female. It wasn't that I was sexist; it was that I knew women hated insecurity. If they saw my hands trembling or heard my voice shake, they were unlikely to make the distinction between a man who shook because he lacked confidence and a man who shook because he'd been in too many explosions. Women despised weakness, and I was all weakness. Thus, I tried to avoid women whenever possible, in order to avoid being reminded of how weak I was.

The doctor was professional, though. She gave me the same smile she gave everyone else who came into her office. "Hello, Mr. Sullivan."

"How are you, Doctor?" I had an unspoken rule in all of my interactions with women, from waitresses to masseuses. I would agree not to insult them by flirting, if they would reciprocate by not showing too much disgust at my "beta" status or general creepiness. It usually made interactions go smoother, and my rule about tipping karma went double when it came to being waited on by a pretty server.

I assumed the position, laying facedown and placing my face in the leather cradle of the table. This chiropractor's touch was softer, and felt more like the auscultation techniques we'd been taught in nursing school. I remained quiet, and motionless.

I remembered once, during one of my classes at the university, raising my hand to answer a question the professor had posed. I'd overheard a girl whisper to another girl next to her, "That guy is *so* creepy." Not only did her words hurt, but they had a chilling effect on my participation in classes. I never answered another question after that. I was terrified of being seen as "creepy" by women. That gave me even more reason to avoid them, unless my brother accidentally happened to impregnate them or I was paying them to either bring me food or to end some of the physical or psychic pain the war had caused.

"Okay, Mr. Sullivan. You can sit up now." I sat up, and the doctor used her acupuncture gun to laser my metabolic points on my head. I'd told her I gained a lot of weight, after which she decided to concentrate her acupuncture gun on those areas.

"Thank you," I said. My heart beat double-time and I held my breath. I yearned to get out to my car and away from the three attractive women, so that I could deflate like a balloon and allow the tension to leave my body. I got back in my car, and headed back downtown to complete my last errand of the day. I was on my way to the VA.

After I got done there I would head home, pop some Percocet, and lay in bed with my terrier. I'd watch my *Simpsons* bootleg that I still had from Iraq, on my laptop. I might also order some takeout from China Kitchen.

I thought about Matthew the Interpreter as I drove back down to Clifton. He was the one who had found the bomb in the computer with all the diagrams, PowerPoints, and porn windows open on it that day we raided that house in Iraq.

Matthew had been with a couple of other interpreters and he had sidled up to me cautiously one day. "Yosef," he said.

"What?" We were about to go on a convoy and I was up in the turret of my Humvee, checking its action to make sure it was well-oiled.

"I have heard that in America, people sleep with dogs in their beds. Is this true?"

"Yep."

He had let out a loud roar of disbelief. To the Iraqis, a dog was the lowest creature there was, and they had a hard time believing that we would allow the beasts to snuggle up to us in bed. Matthew often spoke of moving to Detroit, where he already had some family. If he ever made it stateside, I wasn't sure that it would be a good idea for us to meet up. How would he react, for instance, when he saw Tiffany licking my nose and I not only didn't object, but called it a kiss?

It was daytime, so the VA parking lot was filled with cars whose bodies were baking in the sun. I drove into the five-level parking garage and lucked into a space on the first floor. I got out and headed to the series of trailers housing the Operation Iraqi Freedom/

Operation Enduring Freedom Centers. I walked inside, went up to a bald vet whose head shined like shellac. His cubicle was ringed with photos of him in his halcyon days as a ranger. In one picture, he was covered in camo paint and he wore a ghillie suit of faux lichen and moss that made him look like a swamp monster.

"Here to see Doctor Berman," I said.

"He's waiting for you."

I walked back farther into the trailer, feeling the weak floor of the mobile home groan beneath my feet. I wouldn't be surprised if someone hitched the trailer to a cab and drove us all away in the middle of a workday.

"Mr. Sullivan." The doctor's door was open, and he swiveled in his chair.

"How are you, sir?" I entered his office, and closed the door. I needed confidentiality for this. I was ashamed of my TBI, even though it was only mild, according to the Gloucester Scale.

Doctor Berman had a uni-brow as white as spider silk, and he wore foggy bifocals. He wore an ugly tie from the Garcia collection that looked like the exploded, waxy detritus of a lava lamp accident. "The real question is how are you?"

"Good," I said. "I've got a job."

"That's good," the doctor said. He looked at his computer monitor, but spoke to me. "Studies show that increased motor use, like playing an instrument, can help enlarge or maintain those parts of the brain associated with TBI. Staying active is important."

"Yeah," I said. "I think it's helping."

The doctor looked away from his monitor, and at me. "How old are you?"

"Thirty-three." My body felt older than that, and my soul felt even older than my body. I couldn't kill myself, though, because I had a nephew who needed me to break his back with my knee on occasion.

"Good, you've got more cerebral plasticity than the older TBI patients. But ..." he clucked his tongue and spun in his swivel seat and looked at the monitor of his computer again, "your blood tests show low testosterone, and progesterone is important for the brain. Conversely, estrogen can interfere with recovery."

I thought about something. "Soy has estrogen in it, doesn't it?"

The doctor pursed his lips. "Some types. Why?"

"Nothing," I said, but I was thinking about Daniel and his vegan diet.

"I'm going to prescribe you Androgel. It's a pump-activated testosterone supplement. It's topical, so you'll squirt it out and rub it into your shoulders and chest muscles." He pulled a prescription pad and pen from a pocket on his white coat and scribbled.

"Now, going back to the actual trauma…"

"The explosion," I said.

"The explosion. How long were you unconscious? Did they tell you?"

I shook my head. "No. They had bigger problems to deal with in the Green Zone." I laughed as I remembered the chilly reception I got after being Medevac'd in a chinook, whose lurching evasive maneuvers to avoid ground fire woke me up out of my concussion before we touched down in the Green Zone.

I was ambulatory when we got to the Emerald City. I walked with two doctors, one a major and the other a captain, both in chocolate chip fatigues. One of the men had looked at me and said, "We're a lot less worried about your problems than you are."

We passed a ward where an insurgent cuffed to the handrails of his hospital bed shrieked and his intestines dangled from his open stomach like loose, uncooked haggis. There were pools of blood on the ground. The blood was red, venous, and thicker than the mud puddles children play in.

The Green Zone doctors led me into a room where an X-Ray technician munched a banana. I was used to being told to rate my pain on a scale from "one" to "ten" whenever I saw a military nurse or doctor. I was also used to getting nothing but Naproxen, no matter what the illness. When I began my sentence, "My pain is-" the X-ray tech cut me off and said, "No one gives a shit about your pain here."

My laughter at the memory confused Doctor Berman, and his cottony uni-brow bunched above his humid bifocals. I said, "I think I was out for less than an hour, after Dunfy stepped on that pressure plate."

"You show no signs of PVS or PTA."

I waited for him to explain what those were. He said, "Persistent

Vegetative State and Persistent Traumatic Amnesia."

"Good," I said. I had many fears, but my greatest one was that I would become one of those comatose vets who just stared out into space. I didn't want to be the kind of vet who gets shuffled from one place to another by an orderly who treats the man in question as if he were an inanimate object.

"Alright." The doctor's face flushed with mild embarrassment, and red blotches appeared in his ruddy skin. "I have to ask you these questions, even though they're silly."

I nodded. He asked, "What month are we in?"

"September."

"What time of day is it?"

I lifted my wrist and his voice grew sharper. "Don't look at your watch. Just generally."

I shrugged. "Early afternoon."

"Who's the president?"

I laughed again. "Barack Obama."

He didn't seem to think that was funny. Neither did I, but the question reminded me of the time when I was seventeen years old or so and I had slit my wrists (horizontally, the amateur way) and my father the psychiatrist had me committed to an inpatient facility for teens. This was during the Florida recount when there was some dispute over who had won the 2000 Election. When the admitting physician asked me "Who is the president?" I had to answer him honestly. I said that no one was really sure whether Gore or Bush had won.

"Alright," the doctor said, and handed me the script for Androgel. "You're good to go."

I took the piece of paper and stood. "So, am I getting better?"

He shrugged, which was more honesty than I wanted from him. I walked out of his office and down the hall. I didn't bother to get the Androgel prescription filled. I was comfortable being a pussy, had no desire to be a real man with a raging libido. Someone else would have to kiss the girls and make them cry. I would kiss no one, and cry for myself.

CHAPTER FIVE: FROM IRAQ TO VIETNAM IN LITTLE MORE THAN EIGHT HOURS

My dreams that night must have been bad, because I split a molar in half in my sleep. I ground my teeth until the enamel cracked. It hurt like hell. Tiffany followed me around the apartment while I hopped around, stomping my feet on the hardwood floor. I ran to the fridge, got an icepack, and put it to my face. I thought about putting in a call to my brother.

I'd first discovered his heroin addiction while home on leave from the Army, around Christmastime. We were at my mother's house in Columbia, South Carolina. I'd barged into the bathroom where he was shooting up. The look of guilt and shame on his face hurt me deep into my stomach. Beneath that look he'd given me was a different expression, a queasy one of fear. He was afraid I would expose his addiction to the world and force him to suffer the pains of withdrawal. Walking in on him using heroin was the worst experience of my life. I include everything that I saw in Iraq, even Specialist Dunfy stepping on that pressure plate while we did foot patrol through the Third Infantry Division's old kill zone.

It turned out that my mother was subsidizing his habit, through a form of blackmail. My brother said he would prostitute himself on the street if she didn't give him the money to get at least enough heroin to avoid being sick. She said that she and her husband were planning on putting a pool into their backyard, but that the pool ended up going into my brother's arm.

He told me the stuff he was getting in South Carolina was too weak to OD on, but, years later when he finally got clean, he admitted that was a lie. He told me he was almost dead when I came home from the Army on leave that Christmas and found him shooting up in the bathroom.

I used to drive him to the clinic where he got his heroin substitute, Suboxone, back before he had his own car and was enrolled at Cincinnati State. The stuff was supposed to be a lot less addictive than methadone; it was also supposed to be great for pain relief. I'd talked to Doctor Berman at the OIF clinic about trying something stronger than Percocet. He said the next step was a transdermal, time-release patch. Now that my tooth was broken, it was more than a little tempting to call up my brother and ask for one of his Suboxone strips.

I decided to soldier on, though. It was way too early in my tenure at the VA for me to skip a day of work or be late, broken tooth or no. Medicare didn't cover dental, but there was a dental sick call at the VA that began just as I got off shift in the morning. I thought I would go in after work.

I got dressed, kept the ice pack to my face, and walked downstairs with Tiffany. Tamika was standing there, outside, under the glow of a gaslight. She ran the Third Eye Boutique, the Afrocentric shop that had the ground floor space of the apartment building.

"You were stomping around up there," she said.

I smiled with the half of my mouth that didn't hurt. Tiffany did her business on the concrete. It was only a number one, so I didn't go for the plastic dog poop bag in my pocket. "Sorry." It hurt to speak.

"It's okay. We were just doing our *Namaste* chant." She pointed through the shop window. There was a circle of people gathered around a statue of the Buddha, who meditated with a smoking stick of incense between his hands tented in prayer. I'd never been in her shop before, thinking my vibe of ex-military might somehow come off as racist. Her Buddhist group seemed to be multicultural, though. There were Afrocentric books on display in the front window, like Dr. Jawanza Kunjufu's *Conspiracy to Destroy Black Boys*. There were also more race-neutral books on ESP by Edgar Cayce, and Von Daniken's *Ancient Aliens*.

"I got to get ready for work," I said. I pointed up toward my apartment on the second story.

"Don't let me stop you."

I looked at her in the glow of the gaslight. Tamika's skin tone was copper with a red undertone, like an Egyptian goddess. She had knots in her hair as thick as eighties rope gold chains, what the kids uncharitably called "dookie braids." She was chunky, but I liked big women.

I left her there, and by the time I was dressed for work and downstairs, I found her storefront was dark and the Buddhist chanters had dispersed. I made sure to get to the VA fifteen minutes early in order to keep Hasford off my ass. When I got to the eighth floor and found him, he was too engrossed in whatever he was working on in his moleskin notebook to pay me much notice.

I stood there for something like three minutes. His cervical collar gave a little squeak, and he looked up. He moved his neck awkwardly, like a dog with its head trapped in one of those anti-scratching lampshades.

"I'm working on a biodegradable, odor-free colostomy bag that needs to be changed half as often as the most durable model now available on the market." He slapped the book closed. "Patent-pending."

I went into the changing room and suited up for the shift. After that, I stood before my supervisor, awaiting further orders. "I need you to do two things," Hasford said.

That made sense, because I had two patients. "Yes sir."

"You okay?"

"Mmm-hmm. Hurt my tooth."

"Go to dental sick call in the morning."

"I plan to."

He pointed the pen he previously used to diagram his new colostomy bag, toward the shower curtain separating the quarantined patients from the rest of the ward. "Assess Jones for turgor and make sure Thigpen's wife isn't killing him with saturated fats, sugar, and salts. She can slip him all the Mary Kay age-defying moisturizers and revitalizing creams she wants. No pigs' feet, ham hocks, or purple fizzy sodas."

"Got it." I pulled my mask over my face and walked down the hall, my feet catching in that waxy paraffin-like slime afflicting this section of the corridor.

"Hey man!" A voice called from one of the rooms before I reached my own private ward.

"Yes sir."

It was a young black guy with a pharisaic beard and a tricolor Kufi. He was built like a linebacker and muscles bulged beneath his white-striped velour Puma tracksuit. He pointed at the man in bed behind him, an ancient black man whose skin was basalt grey from the nearness of death.

The man in the Kufi spoke of his dying relative. "You put a grown-ass man in diapers, that shit's embarrassing."

I nodded. "I understand your concern. The patient is suffering from incontinence, I mean bowel trouble-"

"I know what incontinence is!"

His voice got louder, and I lowered my own in the hopes that it would have a calming effect. My tooth throbbed like a raw nerve. I said, "Okay, well, the diapers are not easy to see through clothes. They're easier to conceal than an infant's diaper. I haven't seen his chart, but I think the diapers are probably saving him from a greater embarrassment he might suffer without them, if you understand."

The man in the Kufi smacked his lips, as if he thought I was trying to run a transparent con on him. Hasford's voice came from my six, saving me. "Mr. Sullivan, go tend to your patients and let me worry about mine."

"Yes sir," I said, grateful for the excuse to escape. I walked down the hall, pulled my mask over my face, and passed through the curtain into the quarantined area.

I walked into the room, where an older woman with froglike features sat in a chair next to Claude Thigpen's bed. She wore a seersucker cloche church lady hat. The hat was gray and gripped her head tightly, with a peacock feather sticking up from the back. The feather rippled violently from the force of the hospital's AC blasting through the vents in the ceiling. She had a Mary Kay bag opened on the floor, each of the plastic compartments in the pink interior filled with beauty supplies.

Thigpen spoke hoarsely to me. "I never thought I'd be happy to see you. Please, rescue me from this woman."

"Stop it, Claude." She slapped him lightly on the chest. She reached into the grey jacket she wore that matched the hat, and held out a black combing pick with steel tines. She ran it through the tangle of her husband's hair and sang quietly about laying her burden down.

Her husband suddenly shot up in bed with such surprising force that Mrs. Thigpen scurried backward. Her chair scraped against the floor as she shimmied away from her husband.

"Fuck these teeth!" He removed the dentures from his mouth and flung them across the room. The false ivories shattered from the force of his throw. *Not bad*, I thought, *for a man who Code Blued only a few days ago.*

"I won't need 'em where I'm going." His gums were spotted, as if he had a bad case of untreated gingivitis. He may have had the disease for all I knew, but his gums were the least of his problems at this point.

"You ain't going anywhere." His wife no longer ran the comb through his hair, but stroked slowly. She combed in loving swats, as if trying to shoo flies from the crown of her king's head.

"Wake up, woman," Thigpen said. "I'm dying."

I didn't imagine he had an advance directive. A woman who wore a church hat like that probably thought planning for death would invite it. I knew a guy in the Army who refused his $250,000 SGLI life insurance policy, because he thought that if he planned for his death, then he would die in Iraq. I made my mother my beneficiary. A lot of times during the war when I was sure I was going to die, I would imagine my mother prancing around in a fur coat and rolling in wads of newly-minted cash. It somehow lessened my feelings of fear of my own death, and the guilt I felt over making her relive the pain she felt as a teenager when she said she would watch the news every night-She said she was watching to see if her brother was listed among the KIA.

The war in Iraq was a hell of a lot different than the one in Vietnam. The death existed for the soldiers and their families, but for everyone else it wasn't real. Not even images of coffins draped in flags were shown on TV during the Iraq War.

Mrs. Thigpen stood up out of her chair and walked over to the remains of her husband's scattered dentures. She wore white linen gloves. She picked the individual teeth up and pocketed them with much ceremony, as if they were scattered jewels or family heirlooms that desperately needed recovering.

"My baby has some problems, Doctor. Can I talk to you about them?"

"Sure," I said, and walked over to the woman and stooped to help her pick up the broken choppers. Tonight was a bad night for teeth, apparently. "But I'm not a doctor."

"No, but you're a nurse, so maybe you can help."

"Maybe." She reminded me of someone, a writer whose works I'd read when I was in high-school, during Black History Month. It hit me as she picked up the last of the white teeth in her hands. Zora Hurston Neale, *Their Eyes Were Watching God*. Maybe it was the hat.

"My baby's been having headaches."

"Not like that old cracker over there." He pointed at the sleeping form of Norman Jones and laughed.

"Don't let Jesus hear you talking like that."

"Ugh," he said, but I could tell he wanted to say a lot more.

"Claude's been having real bad headaches."

I handed her the teeth I'd found on the floor. "Have you been giving him any supplements?"

"Just the ones my pastor recommended."

"Which might be?"

She looked up toward the ceiling, struggling for recall or perhaps divine intervention. "Saint John's Wort and ginseng."

"Both of those will do it."

"I'm about to go on a hunger strike." Claude crossed his arms. "I'm ready to die. I ain't got no teeth, anymore. They say what I want to eat will kill me. Fuck it. Let me meet my maker." He shot his wife a dirty look. "Who ain't Jesus."

"Oh, Lord," she said. "I hate to ask you who your maker is, but I can take a guess." She sat back down in the chair. "Probably Satan himself."

"Nope, Black Buddha." Claude sunk down into his bed. He grew meek, all fire sapped from his loins. I had a pretty good idea of why his mood suddenly changed. The Mama San in Soul Alley back in Vietnam told him Buddha was a black man, and thinking about that reminded him of the women with whom he'd cheated on his wife. If he kept talking, or quoted a source to lend credence to his Black

Buddha belief, he might mention a woman with an exotic Asian name and that might make his wife curious about his exotic Asian past. Then a can of worms would get opened on the eighth floor. He was in no position to fight his wife, lying there in that bed lined with the bath towels. He probably looked forward to these visits, the doting with the pick comb. Not just anyone would be bothered to pick up his teeth and ask the VA staff about his headaches. Claude did what all smart men eventually do around their women. He shut up, at least for the moment.

"What will they do if he doesn't eat?" His wife fixed me with her tired eyes, milky with fog and bloody as spider angioma.

"Probably a parenteral feeding."

Her face gathered enough energy to register horror for the moment. Her skin was almond-colored, except the area around the eyes, which was darker. "You mean like they'll stick a tube down his throat."

"No," I said. "Just a needle in his arm."

"Shit," he said. "That ain't no thing. I've got more needles than a porcupine. Poke me with one more, see if I give a crippled crab crutch."

"Hopefully it doesn't come to that," I said. I prepared to walk over to Norman Jones, but the Harlem Renaissance author lookalike walked to the foot of her husband's bed, lifted the blankets, and said, "What about this, Doctor?"

I didn't try to disabuse her of the idea that I was a doctor again. My mouth hurt too much to keep talking. If she wanted to promote me, I wasn't going to fight it.

The big toe on Thigpen's left foot was bluish-black, darker than the others. "It's gangrene," I said, not knowing how to sugarcoat it.

"I know," she said. "He had it in Vietnam, but it went away. Now it's back." She shook her head, and the peacock plume on her hat wavered as if it were the quill with which someone furiously composed. "It's not going away, is it? It's here to stay now?"

"He's not getting adequate circulation," I said. "Massage might help, but probably not."

"Could it fall off?" Her eyes watered. If she batted her eyes a few more times, I thought she might cry and stain those almond cheeks with little crystals.

"If they do," I said, "he won't be able to feel it." That was the truth, and it felt good not to have to lie about something not hurting. I turned from the Thigpens and walked over to the bed of the ancient World War Two vet who fought in the Pacific and now fought a tumor in his dreams.

I picked up the chart at the foot of the patient's bed. I scanned down until I saw the last log entry, and began mine with the pen attached to the chart. "PT unconscious. Turgor Assessment. Joseph Sullivan, RN. 0102."

I set the pen down and walked around the bed, avoiding the lines and wires feeding into the array of machines and dripping solutions around us. I decided not to grip his forearms, since turgor decreased with age and we'd been taught in nursing school that the forehead was usually a better bet. I gripped the skin and was surprised by how edematous and spongy it was. I looked at the half-filled bag of solution hanging beside his bed, and wondered if he wasn't being overhydrated.

I released his skin. The man's mouth opened, although his eyes remained closed. "*Gyokusai.*"

I jumped back. Thigpen laughed. "He ain't waking up. He's talking in his sleep."

"I wonder what he's talking about," his wife said, a fearful lilt in her voice.

"I know what he's saying."

"How you know?" His wife chided him, unbuttoned his hospital gown, and ran the pick comb through the kinks of his chest hair. "You was in Vietnam. That man fought the Japanese, you said."

Thigpen's anger returned, and he propped himself up on his elbows. He winced. I could tell he wanted to lie back down, but he was too pissed to brook his wife's sass without defending himself. "You act like Japanese people can't live in Vietnam. *Everybody* been through Vietnam, from the French to the British."

"Alright, then, genius. What did he say?" The churchy patina was wearing off, and his wife pointed the comb forcefully in the direction of me and Mr. Jones.

"It means something along the lines of 'broken jade'. It's what they say when they kill themselves, you know. They run their planes into an aircraft carrier or do a bonsai charge." He giggled, marveled at the madness of a foe he never fought but whose tenacity he admired. Claude Thigpen slowly lay back down, folded his arms over his chest. His next exhale ended in something wet enough to be a death rattle. "You don't ever give me credit, woman. You get your nephew to help you with the computer. Look up *Nam Bộ kháng chiến*, or if that's too hard for you, try Operation Masterdom."

"Where'd you hear about this?" Her tone made it sound as if she was asking him about a shade of lipstick on his collar that didn't come from her Mary Kay line.

"Soul Alley," Claude said, weakly. It was clear that he was remembering opium and those nights when he was disabused of the rumor that Vietnamese pussy was slanted differently than the American kind. He discovered in the hell of Vietnam a paradise where he was celebrated as an incarnation of Buddha, rather than being treated as someone who could barely drink at the same water fountain as white men. There was an expression on his face, a mix of guilt and pleasure that was especially contorted because he now lacked the dentures to give his features solid form.

I tried to carry on like a professional, and wrote on the narrative chart that I believed Patient Jones, Norman to be overhydrated. I just finished that when the janitor came in. He brandished the mop head-first. The custodian was an old black man whose arms were thin as fence posts but roped with muscle. Claude's face brightened upon seeing another black man, but his wife was apparently serious about the universal nature of Christianity. She didn't register anything like the kinship that her husband did upon the man's entrance.

"That's it!" The janitor gripped the mop by the wooden handle and stabbed the ground. Foam poured from the gray tangle of the mop head and dripped onto the cold tile floor. "What's it?" I asked, puzzled.

"I'm tired of mopping up that slimy shit in the hallways!" He rattled his mop again, and more suds flew in every direction. His gesture was so forceful that a bit of soap actually made its way across the room and stung me in the eye.

I lifted one of my nonstick shoes, glanced at the sole. The strange, plasmatic gunk was stuck to the traction treads. I looked at the janitor and asked, "What is that stuff?"

The janitor shook his head. "I don't know, but I'm tired of mopping that shit up!"

* * *

It was overcast that morning, which made it easier to get to sleep. I was awakened by a voice that made me scatter the sheets from the bed, scaring my terrier until she ran across the room.

"Why ain't you go to dental sick call?"

I looked across the bedroom. Claude Thigpen was sitting in my wicker chair draped with my mother's afghan. He drank from a clear, plastic bottle filled with cheap liquor that sloshed when he took a swig.

"I was too tired." Then I thought about how bizarre the situation was, and asked, "How'd you get here?" I didn't see how he got out of his bed, much less how he got off the eighth floor. It was a secured ward controlled by an access panel one needed a CAC to enter or exit. Then there was the idea of a dying man with gangrene walking a half mile to my apartment and somehow getting through both the front door of the building and my apartment door, both of which were locked.

"Never mind that." He capped the bottle, which smelled like mouthwash even from this far across the room. He pointed at the peeling red paper label. "I finally got me my Gilbey's."

"I'm glad to hear it. Now, do you mind telling me how the hell you got in here?"

He was still in his hospital gown, open at the chest. Claude Thigpen shook his head and spoke with a mouth still empty of dentures. "I thought what those crackers did in Nagasaki and Hiroshima was pretty cold-blooded, when I learned about it at as a young buck at George Washington. It wasn't personal, though." He ran his tongue around his liquor-stained gums. "Vietnam was *personal*."

"What do you want?"

He did his best to fix me with his gaze, which was hard when his eyes were foggy from drink and imminent death. "I want to go to Vietnam. I want you to go with me."

I shook my head. "I don't want to go to Vietnam"

He smiled. "You ain't got no choice."

We both stood in a dense bamboo thicket. The jungle was so clogged with the sharp, tall reeds that not even a Bengal tiger could have clawed its way through. I was in my t-shirt and boxers, and Thigpen was still in his hospital gown. We were both shoeless.

"I never did so much as smoke a cigarette 'til I got to Vietnam." Thigpen tilted his head back, poured the rest of the Gilbey's down his throat. He tossed the empty plastic container into the jungle understory at our feet.

"I used to let An Han blow smoke in my face when we'd lie on her cane mats and I'd watch her burn opium. That was more for the smell." We broke through the thicket and came to an opening where a group of about twelve men in rain-stained and mud-covered tiger stripe fatigues stood around in small groups.

"After that day, I needed a little something to get me through."

He walked up to a group of three black men. One carried an M60, another hauled a spare barrel, and the third carried a gun I didn't recognize. The tip of the M60 barrel was covered with a fully-extended latex condom.

"The pig," Thigpen said. I turned my head, so I wouldn't have to smell his breath.

"I know what an M60 is," I said. "What's that?" I pointed at the third black man, who held a weapon I didn't recognize.

Old Claude Thigpen smiled at young Claude Thigpen and let out a "Shit" so elongated it lasted five seconds. "That's me and my old grease gun. It was just like in my uncle's mechanic shop, except that one greased gooks, not cars." He looked down at his bare, ashen feet. "I shouldn't say 'gook.' An Han would beat my ass." Thigpen whispered, "I left her with a little black baby, or half-black. I never went back. I was afraid Ida would find out."

"Ida?"

"My wife. You met her at the VA."

I walked closer to the three men, who took no notice of me. There was a terracotta pagoda in the distance. It reminded me of a giant version of one in the lobby of a Chinese restaurant I used to go to, a water feature that dripped while I waited for the hostess to seat me. The building was topped in a finial depicting a lion wrapped in ivy growth, as if the beast was chained to the summit of the house of prayer.

To the right of the Pagoda there was a woman in a blue silk tunic, lying on the ground. Each of her arms and legs were pinned by a different white soldier. A fifth man lay on top of her and pumped away. He was fully clothed except for the front of his pants, which were unbuttoned.

"She was already dead," old Thigpen said. "What kind of man gets his rocks off with a dead girl?" I didn't answer his question. He asked another one. "What kind of man shoots a girl in the back of the head while she's praying?" He pointed at the soldier who was humping the lifeless Vietnamese girl in the silken Ao Dai. I couldn't understand why the other four men held her hands down if she was dead. Maybe she was convulsing.

The white man finished humping away, went through several spasms on top of the woman, and then stood. Another one took his place, this one wearing a dusty flak jacket with the collar turned up and no shirt underneath it. His muscles sweated and his helmet fell off his head as he had his way with the woman.

Old Thigpen pointed at the white man with the flak jacket. "That was Sergeant Beecher. He had a John Wayne complex like you wouldn't believe. He got us through the shit, but at a high price." He shook his head, watched the rape as if it were an old rerun on television. Then he looked over at the three young black men, and I looked with him.

The one holding the M60 spoke. "I ain't doing it." He had sharp features and a reddish tint to his skin, as if his African blood was cut with something like Cherokee.

"Which?" The one holding the spare barrel asked. He wore no helmet and had a length of parachute silk wrapped around his head like a bandana.

"Neither." The one with the pig pointed the condom-tipped barrel at the men around the woman on the ground. He then swiveled toward the pagoda, where I now noticed a man was lashed tightly to the front of the temple with telephone cord. "Them brothers will go along with it." He didn't use his weapon to point, but nodded at three black soldiers in tropical combat ponchos. They stood a few paces away from the raping white men, under an ancient tree.

"'Bamas," Young Thigpen said, scowling. The expression on his face was bitter, but I thought he had a ways to go before he reached the stage of terminal darkness I found him in when I first started work at the hospital. "Geecchie-ass, no-good, boot-licking Gullah types want to get in good with the white folks. They don't care how many yellow folks they got to fuck over to do it."

Young Thigpen held up what the older version of him called the "grease gun." The knot of black shoelace that Hasford called a "slave bracelet" slipped along his thin wrist as he brandished the gun. "What we do out in a shootout in the boonies is one thing, but this shit ain't fair game."

Old Thigpen spoke up. He tried to touch the gun the younger version of himself held, but his hand passed through the cold metal like it was made of air. "The official name is an M3A1 Submachinegun, if you're curious."

"I'm not," I said. "I had a weapon in Iraq, but I don't care for guns in the real world. I had a little Walther I used to keep under my bed, but I sold it. I was afraid I might shoot myself in the head."

He pointed at the group of gang-rapists. They alternated positions, moving clockwise as a new man straddled the woman. "You do anything like this in Iraq?"

I shook my head. "No, I'd have killed myself by now if I had. We did what we could to follow the Geneva Convention, the Escalation of Force protocol. I never did anything this bad."

Old Thigpen grinned. "It gets worse." He pointed at the younger version of himself. "I wish I hadn't been so hard on them 'Bamas, but I didn't grow up in the South. I couldn't listen to those cats' music." He shook his head. "It was almost as bad as honky-tonk."

He pointed at the two men rallied around the crew-served weapon tipped with a condom. "They was from the city like me. Cyrus was from Chicago and Milton was from somewhere around the Bay, either Oakland or 'Frisco. I can't remember which. Probably Oakland, because there was more Bloods there." He cast an eye back toward the bamboo thicket, where he dropped the empty bottle of Gilbey's. He probably wished he had more right about now.

"I could talk with them about music. Cyrus liked Miles more and Milton was more of a Coltrane cat. I kept telling them both they cut a platter together in '58. Nobody had that particular wax, even in the rear. You couldn't get bebop on the AFN. The closest you could come was soul music, like the Temptations or the Supremes. That ain't bad, but it wasn't really my bag."

"Thigpen!" The white sergeant shouted.

"Shit," both the younger and older version of the man said, at about the same time. The older one looked at me and said, "It begins."

The younger one muttered to his two cohorts. "I ain't going."

"Thigpen, get your ass in gear!"

"I'm short," the young man said. "Too short for this shit."

The Indian-looking soldier holding the M60 pig asked, "How short?"

Claude shook his head. "I ain't got my short-timer's calendar, but I'm too short for this." He looked at Sergeant Beecher. "Fuck your three chevrons, Sarge. Article fifteen my ass. I'll go be a civilian. Fuck up my file all you want."

A light rain fell. The sergeant walked away from the woman on the ground being raped, and the man tied to the pagoda. He held something that looked like a duct-taped pipe in his left hand, and what I knew to be a bolo knife in his right. The knife looked to be over a foot long.

"You got something against lifers?"

Young Thigpen shook his head, and blanched grey as the sergeant in the flak vest got closer. Claude finally worked up the nerve to speak. His voice was lower, and his two comrades kept their eyes down at their shoes. The other three black men, "'Bamas," as Thigpen called them, watched from beneath the ancient tree. The rain grew harder and I understood why they were wearing ponchos, but I didn't understand why the other men weren't. The rain had a chill to it, and I wasn't sure whether or not it was a harbinger of monsoon. I only wished to be away from here and underneath the covers of the bed in my apartment back in Clifton, with my little wire-haired terrier coiled at my feet. I had my own dreams and nightmares of Iraq to contend with, without having to deal with Thigpen's own memories crowding into my mind, like the tumor that ate away at the brain of old Norman Jones back at the VA.

"If you bust me down, that's another...what the shrink calls a 'disincentive' to me re-upping for another term."

The sergeant pointed the sharpened tip of his bolo blade at Thigpen's nose. The knifepoint grazed the cartilage of his nose, pressed close enough now to pop a blackhead on the young black man's nose. "Fuck that egghead Jew and fuck you too."

Thigpen grinned, didn't budge. "That ain't the way to make friends, Sergeant." Sergeant Beecher spun and waved his knife toward the three black men in ponchos hiding from the rain beneath the tree.

"You need to be more like your friends over there. They seen what can happen when a bunny gets too uppity with a grey boy." He looked back at Thigpen. "You know what a Mississippi Wind Chime is?" Thigpen looked sick, and the sergeant smiled. "I'll give you three guesses."

The smile disappeared from the sergeant's face, and he pointed at the NVA tied to the front of the terra cotta pagoda. "You're busting your cherry, right *riki tick* now. Or we ain't moving from this valley."

Thigpen looked to his two friends for support. He got none, since their eyes were still on the ground. He slung his grease gun over his shoulder. "You a real tiger, sergeant."

"What you mean by that?" The white man twirled his knife.

The black man with the M60 answered that for him. "A pussy with stripes."

Sergeant Beecher tugged the collar of his flak jacket, where chevrons would be on the lapels if he'd been wearing a shirt. "Yeah, but I got the stripes. Now get your ass over there and bust your cherry."

Old Thigpen leaned into me, as if explaining the details of a movie whose plot I might not be following. "Beecher had his own way of torching a village. Most crackers would just use a Zippo." He shook his head. "He'd load his M16 with nothing but tracers and fire at the thatch 'til he sparked the hut. I never saw anything like him before. Never wanted to," he added.

"You win, Sergeant." Young Thigpen sagged, his heart broken. "I got to get something from the 'Bamas before I break my cherry."

One of the Southern blacks in ponchos said, "We're out of spaghetti and meatballs." Everyone laughed at that, except for the pack of rapists looming over the dead Vietnamese girl, and the man lashed to the tree; I suspected he was related to the woman being raped.

"We still got some ham and lima beans, though." One of the poncho crew held up a C-rat. Thigpen shuddered, the Army food almost as nauseating as the brutal scene before them.

"Nobody liked ham and lima bean C-rats," old Thigpen said. He walked away from his two partners and followed his young self and the sergeant in the direction of the temple.

"We didn't have C-rats," I said. "We had MRES. Meals-ready-to-eat." I remembered living off nothing but MRE cheese and crackers for two weeks, and how I wallowed and writhed in agony on a stretcher in the troop medical clinic at Camp Victory with the worst case of constipation in the world. When I did finally pass a stool, it felt like a hardened wad of gum packed with jagged glass was trying to move through the tender pink mouth of my sphincter. That was the worst day in Iraq for me, aside from the one when Dunfy stepped on the pressure plate.

Young Thigpen walked over to the three Southern blacks. "I need a bit more than ham and lima beans to get me through this one, Bloods."

One of the three 'Bamas took that as his cue. He dug into a bag at his feet, the wet rubber rustling like gutta percha as he extracted something that looked like a toothpaste tube capped with a plastic top.

"You know what that is?" Old Thigpen asked.

"No," I said. "I can guess." I'd remembered Carter digging into the platoon's combat life saver supplies, shooting himself with atropine and sucking on a fentanyl lollipop. I looked closer at the little toothpaste tube the Southern black medic held. I was invisible to them, so my curiosity hurt nothing. The little tube said, "Half-grain per 1.5 cc Syrette solution of morphine tartrate."

The medic uncapped the toothpaste, poked Thigpen in the vein, and squeezed. "Come on!" Sergeant Beecher shouted from behind them. The medic's hand shook as the white man barked. "We ain't got all day. Let's puncture that hymen!"

"Thank you," Thigpen said.

"You'll be alright," the other soldier whispered, and squeezed the rest of the solution into Thigpen's arm. Claude's wrist relaxed completely, and the slave bracelet on his right arm slid further down toward his wrist.

"I'm sorry about calling y'all 'Bamas. We're all bloods."

The medic smiled, pulled the Syrette from Thigpen's vein, and tossed the tube into the bamboo thicket behind them. The rain was coming in slanted sheets, and the Southerner said, "It's alright. Don't everybody dig on Lightning Hopkins or Howlin' Wolf."

"I can't do blues but for John Lee."

"It's a start."

"Come on!"

Thigpen turned. He walked over toward Sergeant Beecher, who was standing in front of the Vietnamese man tied to the pagoda. "I'm being reasonable," the sergeant said. He twirled his knife again, this time more theatrically, as if he were a professional thrower ready to put on his act at the midway. "I ain't asking you to go Apache on him. I already did that."

Sergeant Beecher pointed the tip of his blade at the space where an ear once was on the Vietnamese man's head. The weather was hotter now. The rain became fog when it touched the ground, but the mist wasn't thick enough to shroud the scene. I stared where the ear had been, into the cochlear hollow. It was now just a bloody spiral that looked like a coiled Fibonacci symbol.

"Shit," I said.

"Damn, Sergeant."

"It's a souvenir." Sergeant Beecher held up the length of duct-taped pipe he had in his other hand. "He had it coming." He smacked the one-eared Vietnamese man with the pipe, which echoed like an aluminum bat making contact with a softball. The man didn't utter a sound, and his lack of noise angered the noncom. "I'll give it to the little bastard, though. He managed to make a shotgun with a little bit of water piping he stole from our base camp."

The sergeant flung the improvised weapon toward the wood line of the bamboo thicket. "Cleaning the Quonset by day, and attacking the wire at night. Ain't that right, Charlie?"

The man was defiant, despite being sliced and bludgeoned. He spit blood and shouted something in Vietnamese. "What's he saying?" I asked old Thigpen.

"'Fuck you,' or words to that effect."

"I can't say that I blame him."

Sergeant Beecher leaned down to the ground, where an ancient military telephone was. At least, the phone was ancient to me. My MOS was in the Communication field. I was what they called a "commo geek," so the instrument held a bit of fascination for me, apart from whatever use the Sergeant was about to get out of it.

"What is that?" I asked. "I know about PRCs and SINCGARS, but that shit is Stone Age."

Old Thigpen smiled while young Thigpen shook like a leaf, despite the shot of morphine he just took. "That there's the EA 3-12. They don't make 'em like that anymore."

"I've done all the heavy lifting," Sergeant Beecher said. He held out the phone to Thigpen as if there were an incoming call the private needed to take, maybe a Red Cross message from home. A ground and a hot wire were attached to the terminal block of the phone. I noticed the wire wrapped around the man bound to the tree actually terminated in exposed copper sticking in his bloody nostrils.

"It's raining," Claude said, weakly. "I might shock the shit out of myself, too."

"Private," Sergeant Beecher said, and the quiet tone of his voice was somehow more menacing than all the barking he previously did. "It's Bell Telephone Hour. Time to ring." He held the phone's cranking mechanism out to Young Thigpen. "I ain't asking you to party with the peckerwoods." He nodded toward the soldiers, who were finished raping the woman and were now covering the body with moss and mud. "I need you to have some skin in the game. You can either go back to the rear with some dirt on your hands, or your ass is getting buried out here with her." The NCO jerked his head toward the woman's body surrounded by the four white GIs. "Crank it!"

Young Thigpen looked at the Vietnamese man's eyes, which widened as the black man's hand touched the phone crank. Old

Thigpen watched his younger self and I watched along with him. He turned the crank and sparks popped in the poor Vietnamese man's nose as if his head were a light bulb that just shorted.

The man made a sound that begged for pity. Thigpen kept turning, cranking for dear life. It was as if the motion wasn't torturing the man, but was propelling some magic ship that could take Thigpen away from Vietnam and get him back to the bars and pool halls of Chicago, a world away from here.

The man shivered, danced, and writhed. Sergeant Beecher and the peckerwoods laughed easily, while the Southern blacks laughed uneasily. The two men in the rear with the crew-served weapon remained silent. Smoke and blood poured from the Vietnamese man's head, eyes, mouth, and nose, until his body went limp. Thigpen stopped cranking, his hand trembling.

I rolled on my side in the bed, shouted "Tiffany, help me!" My terrier responded by sitting up and jumping into the bed with me. I stroked her wiry beard and kissed her gray, warm head. Her coat was even warmer than usual, on account of the sun finding its way through the clouds. Its light poured through the window of my apartment, creating yellow bars that sunned the hardwood panels and would give Tiff a place to sit and soak up vitamin D throughout the day.

I hugged my dog, pulled my pillow over my head. I tried to get some sleep, of the dreamless kind if at all possible.

CHAPTER SIX: STILL GOT YOUR SAFETY PLAN?

A panic attack was unavoidable. I'd set my alarm clock for 3 p.m., since I had a four-thirty appointment at the Fort Thomas PTSD Clinic. That meant I would have only had five or six hours of fitful sleep, if the Vietnam nightmare hadn't happened. But now I was truly fried after the rainy afternoon spent under the pagoda with Private Thigpen and Sergeant Beecher.

I had a quick breakfast at the Proud Rooster. I scarfed down a Western omelet and some Goetta sausage, a Cincinnati specialty. I ate underneath an old black and white photo of a junior-high basketball team mounted on the knotty pine wall, between two flimsy league trophies covered in spray-on gold. The bill for breakfast was $6.85. I left a ten, after which I walked to the bus stop and waited for the Metro to Fort Thomas.

I spotted a childhood friend walking toward me as I waited. He'd been in a band with me and my buddy Max. I could tell that time had not been kind to him and I wasn't in the mood for a reunion. I kept my head down, my eyes gazing at my feet. He passed without comment, leaving an alcohol scent thick as aftershave in his wake.

The heavy smell of carbon monoxide preceded the bus, and I called bullshit on the advertisement on the side of the Metro that said their fuel source was green. I got onboard and found a seat near the back. There were no transfers between here and Fort Thomas, so I set the alarm on my phone to vibrate and wake me up in thirty minutes. That would give me five minutes or so to compose myself before I got off the bus.

I started blinking, settling down to try to sleep. The spots appeared. Rippling tendrils of lightening streaked across my vision, and I felt like shouting, "I'm blind!" The people on the bus would laugh at me or look at me like I was crazy. Maybe I shouldn't have held back, since busses were filled with crazy people. Still, there was a good chance that I was the craziest on-board this morning.

There was a hiss and a jerk, and the driver pulled out. We passed by the old library, a couple of Indian restaurants, and an expensive clothing shop called Hansa Guild that sold merino wool gloves and eiderdown pillows well outside my price range.

I thought of Renee, my spiritual wellness coach. Sometimes I called her when these attacks happened. Her voice would soothe me. She was much more helpful than Dr. Barker, my counselor in Fort Thomas. He was free and her services cost more than one-hundred dollars an hour.

I held my breath, bracing against the profusion of spots and the terror of blindness. The more I held my breath, the worse it got. I got back to my old breathing routine finally, five seconds in through the nostrils, holding it in for two seconds, and then seven seconds of exhaling out through the mouth. My own breathing rhythm sounded like the crash of surf on the beach in my ears. I closed my eyes and the spots followed me. They mocked me, terrifying me, like my conscience given form. It was a wash of electric snow telling me that even though I hadn't taken part in individual war crimes, like Thigpen and his "Bell Telephone Hour," I had been part of the war machine. That alone was crime enough, and so now I was going to be blinded like some Greek man in an ancient tragedy.

"Fuck," I said, and the single word surprised me. It escaped my lips without my planning to say it.

"You've got sleep apnea," a voice said. It was Claude Thigpen. I looked around. All of the seats directly around me were empty. The closest passenger was an attractive brunette with pale skin and sharp bangs, wearing thick Skull Candy headphones and staring out the window. I wondered what kind of Indie / shoegazing playlist was carrying her away from the humdrum day she had ahead of her working as a barista in Fort Thomas.

"You're not here," I said. It was one thing to have Thigpen invade my dreams. If I was having auditory hallucinations while awake, then I was finally crazy.

I looked out the window, hoping the scenery could distract me. We passed Burnett Woods, a yoga studio, Skyline Chili. That cinnamon-tinged chili was another Cincy specialty that out-of-towners didn't always enjoy. "You're just my TBI. Maybe it's not as mild as Doctor Berman says."

We passed my apartment and the Third Eye Boutique, and Thigpen said, "I like to astral project."

"I'll bet you do. Where did you learn to do that?"

"I've been floating out of my body on nights at the VA. I learned how to do it from Norman Jones, my roomie."

"That was nice of him to teach you."

"That cracker ain't teach me shit. I rooted around in his mind and found out how to do it on my own. It ain't like we go projecting together. Why the hell would I want to go visit his niece in Indian Hill? I like hanging around Clifton."

"Tamika has some interesting books in her shop," I said. I looked over at the pretty girl nearby. I was grateful to see her eyes were still fixed outside the window, and that the oversized earphones still gripped her head. I didn't want her to see me talking to myself.

"Speaking of Tamika," Thigpen said, "You keep your pink fingertips off my Nubian queen."

"You can relax." I lowered my voice. "I've got erectile dysfunction. I've been studying how to please a woman with my tongue, but my chances of going down on that brown sugar are slim to none."

"I'm old-school," Thigpen said. "I don't lick carpet."

"Your loss." I shrugged. "Do you want to tell me what you want? I mean, aside from chit-chatting about astral projection and pussy-eating." It occurred to me that not even the most discombobulated Ronald Reagan-era schizophrenic ever uttered words as bizarre as what just came out of my mouth. Even Thigpen laughed. I thought that was an accomplishment of sorts, since he struck me as loath to engage in any act with a white man that might be mistaken as friendly.

His laughter came in hot, bitter spurts. "Your dick works alright when you're alone."

"Now, you're getting too personal," I said.

"It ain't like I got any privacy."

"Yeah, but you're in a hospital. You should expect less."

I thought about the first public erection I'd had in years. I was taking a course on German 20th century writers with my feminist professor over at UC. We came to Kafka's *Der Verwandlung* and I remembered a comic book illustrated by Robert Crumb about Kafka, which I ordered for her. I paid the expedited fee to get it faster, just so that I could get it into her hands quicker.

The book came and I walked with it to her office, my hands trembling. She was an adjunct professor, and so had a smaller office than the tenured staff. She was wearing black stockings, and a headband that pushed her barely-graying hair back from her forehead.

I handed her the book and she asked, "How much?"

"*Sonst, ein Geschenk.*" The VA was paying me $1300 a month BAH (Basic Allowance for Housing) while I was in school, in addition to the disability I got from the VA and Social Security, all of it tax-free.

My professor smiled and took the book. "Joseph, you are making me very happy today." I went home that night, got on my knees, and closed my eyes. I imagined myself wallowing with my nose and tongue on the sensitive button of her clitoris, slicked from the pleasure I was giving her as a slave. "Joseph," she said. "You are making me very happy today." That orgasm gave me as much relief as I'm sure Thigpen derived from his morphine Syrette that steeled him for what he did that day beneath the pagoda.

"If you want to fuck with my dreams, fine," I said, to Thigpen, wherever he was. The bus hit a speedbump. "Please don't fuck with my memories, especially not the good ones."

"You mean like this," he hissed. The panic spots flew from my vision and I was walking down the street with Claudine, my German tutor. It had been a perfect day. I had made a mistake by joining the Army and going to Iraq. I had destroyed my mind, my body, and my soul. But at least thanks to my injuries I now had a lot of extra money, and I didn't just spend it on books for my professor whose pussy I desperately wanted to eat. I took my tutor out for meals, lunches and dinners. I showed her the record stores around the neighborhood, and paid her twenty dollars an hour to help me translate my papers from English to German.

She lived on a pittance she got as a teacher's assistant, and probably made two or three times that a month just helping me with my papers. I wanted nothing from her, except to catch the scent of her hair when she walked. I loved to just hear the trill of her heavily-accented English as she struggled to speak without umlauts, as she thanked a waitress or leaned across the table to tell me that she was uncomfortable with me paying for everything.

Her objections meant nothing to me though, and when she told me she had a *Verlobter*, I felt relieved to hear she was engaged. It meant I could relax, and that I didn't have to pretend I was man enough to fuck her. Thigpen saw through my eyes now, as I saw through his last night in my nightmares. Claudine and I had worked on my paper on Edgar Allen Poe's *Der Doppelmord in der Rue Morgue*. We crowded together around her laptop in a coffee shop with throw pillows scattered around exposed brick walls. An acoustic guitarist played in a corner, on an ottoman where a cat slept curled in a ball. I drank coffee, she drank tea, and I felt human for a while.

Then we went to dinner, and I feared my hands would shake. I prayed that God or karma or the Fates- whatever tortured me and brought the spots before my eyes- didn't harass me that day.

It allowed me to eat sushi and Peking duck and the house soup at a Thai restaurant. I even sounded like a normal man when I talked to Claudine, and my voice didn't waver.

We walked through the neighborhood after dinner. Families came out onto their porches, wives and husbands with their children. Claudine saved me at just the moment where my heart was about to sag and I was ready to torture myself. "It's not as nice as it seems," she said. "My sister had a baby. When kids come into the scene, it can get very complicated."

She was right, of course, and I felt better about not having children or being married. I thought that maybe I had avoided a trap that looked lovely from the outside, but was not so wonderful once you were in it. I sang Lou Reed's *Perfect Day* under my breath. She heard it and said, "I know this song. I *love* this song."

"You didn't fuck her," Thigpen said. We were back in the bus, about fifteen minutes from the Fort Thomas VA. I wanted to cop a few minutes of Z's, and chose not to dignify his remark with an answer. If he had such unlimited access to my war-torn cranium, he could answer his own damn questions.

I closed my eyes, drifted into a fitful sleep. I watched as Thigpen's tiger-striped platoon walked toward a group of moaning ARVN they had come across. The Vietnamese regulars had been hit with napalm on accident, in a close support fire mission meant to nail the Cong who had already ghosted.

Steam rose from the jellied wounds on the men. They glistened like Vaseline, and their flesh fell from their bodies as easily as cooked rib meat from a bone. The sound of a vomiting soldier came from Thigpen's six, and strong sunlight broke through the triple-thick canopy of treetops. The steam from the napalmed bodies was joined by smoke from shells that popped as the soldiers walked through the kill zone. They fired into the heads of the moaning men at their feet. Even Sergeant Beecher used his sidearm, a Luger he'd bartered with an Aussie, to put the suffering soldiers at his feet out of their misery.

The ranking NCO looked back at the black soldier holding the pig, and the ammo carrier by his side. "Rip 'em from asshole to appetite. Double-tap 'em and don't stop shooting until you see the white meat." He coughed, on the smoke from the gunfire and the steam from the melting flesh. The chemical broke bone in its journey to eat everything hollow.

"Let this be a lesson on the limited benefits of close fire support. Think twice before you call in Puff."

"Puff," Thigpen said in my ears, with the same weakness he'd uttered the single syllable the first time I found him in the hospital. I was awake again.

"Are you going to do that every time I try to sleep?" I asked. "Because, if you are, I'll just go ahead and put a bullet in my head." I looked out the window. We were on the highway, crossing the bridge from Cincinnati into Newport, Kentucky.

Claude Thigpen laughed hoarsely. He asked, "What makes you think you can escape your nightmares after death?"

"You mean *your* nightmares," I corrected him. "I don't give a fuck how many books you read when you astral project. You haven't died yet. You don't know what happens after death any more than I do."

"Really?" Thigpen said. "I've coded. I've been officially dead before. That's more than you can say."

Fuck it, I thought. *Maybe I'll take that copy of Raymond Moody's* Life after Life *off Hasford's hands. I'll read up so that I can be even with Thigpen, or at least not let him gain too much of an edge on me. If my brother had come through with the heroin when I'd asked him to help overdose me, I probably wouldn't be having this conversation right now.* I thought for a moment about contributing some money to Hasford's patent-pending, long-lasting, odor-fighting colostomy bag. Maybe I would get rich.

"Hasford should be my RN," Thigpen said. I wondered if he was reading my thoughts, since I just happened to be thinking about the old scout sniper.

"Why's that?"

"He's a devil dog, like me."

"Yeah, and I had a soft MOS, too. Communications. I was a commo geek."

"I don't know why I'm proud. The Marines was the last service to integrate. Maybe there wouldn't have been so much racial shit if I'd been in the Navy or the Army. Who knows?"

"Why didn't you try the air force?"

The bus lumbered toward the Fort Thomas VA's parking lot. "My ASVAB numbers wasn't good enough. Took it in Sixty-Eight and was a bolo."

The bus hissed to a stop just beside an old Civil War memorial. That was another war I was glad to miss out on. "I got two Bronze Stars, a good conduct ribbon."

I shook my head. Awards were a sore subject for me. My chain-of-command had written their own awards. They'd given themselves Bronze Stars for sitting in the air-conditioning. They looked at porn on the Internet, and gorged themselves at the dining facilities. They played ping-pong and foosball in the morale centers. The highest award I got was an ARCOM (Army Commendation Medal), and it was never even reflected on my ERB (Enlisted Record Brief).

As unsavory company as Thigpen was, I figured he got his Bronze Star for actually doing something, unlike the FOBBITS (Forward Operating Base Hobbits) that comprised my chain of command. They'd had no qualms about sending twenty-year old kids outside the wire to get mutilated and killed, while they played volleyball and talked to their cheating wives on webcams.

"Why did you get your Bronze Star?" I asked. I was sorry for asking a moment later. I found my foot on something that looked like a rusty, spiked mace as I took the last step down from the bus. "What the fuck is that?" I asked. For some reason I knew not to move my leg. I looked around and saw myself surrounded by rubber trees with trunks as hard as tortoise shells. Marines slowly walked backward, putting as much distance between them and me as they could.

"What?"

"Don't move, Sarge." It was that chocolate bunny Thigpen, whose arm I had to twist to crank the phone back there. Now was his chance to get even. Hell, he wouldn't even have to frag me. He could get my ass blown to bits and write it off as a true-blue mistake. Maybe I shouldn't have bragged about being a card-carrying member in the Klan.

I watched the Brillo head fill a jump boot with rocks until it bulged to bursting. I was sure one of those little arrowheads was going to tear the canvas of the shoe. He held the boot in one hand, reached onto the webbing I kept over my flak vest. Thigpen extracted my bolo knife that was a foot long and some change, the same one I'd put to his nose so close it could have popped a blackhead.

I was sure at this point that he was going to get his revenge, maybe slice my ear off and leave me standing on the Betty. Those psi op leaflets the Cong dropped had finally worked their magic on old Brillo Head. *Black man go home, this isn't your war. They kill your Martin Luther King and your Malcolm X.* He didn't like the way I cut the ear off his yellow soul brother at the pagoda, so now he was going to prove he wasn't a 'Bama doing the buck dance and Tom act for Massa with his stripes. He was going to cut my ears off and leave me here to die on this piece of unexploded ordinance.

I looked down, both as Sergeant Beecher and as Joey Sullivan the RN. I marveled at how little changed between Vietnam and Iraq. The bouncing Betty looked a lot like the mortars and UXOs (Unexploded Ordinance) we found in Iraq. It looked rusted and harmless. Many times bombs and mortars were duds, and they could be laughed at as pathetic Soviet relics. Something that looked broken and fit to be mounted in a glass case in a museum could also have devastating power. It could open like an ancient, rusted Pandora's Box and make your ass mince.

The bunny didn't stab me with the knife. Instead, he used it like a bayonet to dig around the Betty. He slid the boot next to mine with his other hand. He slipped the three-pronged primer from the Betty in between the cleats of my jungle boot and replaced the weight of my own foot with the shoe filled with rocks. He pulled me backwards, and away from the bomb, whose plunger I'd depressed. It didn't rise and we ran toward the tree line. There was no explosion, and I lay with my back against the hollow of a rubber tree. I uncapped my canteen and poured all my Gilbey's over my face. I forgot in my panic that it was gin and not water. I coughed and my eyes stung.

"I owe you one, Hollywood."

I left the redneck's body and stood beside young Thigpen and the sergeant in Vietnam. Old Thigpen stood beside me in his hospital gown, shoeless but unconcerned.

"Why did he call you Hollywood?" I asked.

Old Thigpen answered, because the young one still holding the knife couldn't hear us. "'Cause I did my basic at San Diego. It was a hell of a lot worse at Parris Island, I heard."

I did my basic training at Fort Benning. We were the first non-infantry brigade to train there. The cadre was all infantry. They were not much enamored of us. The drill sergeant lined us up in company formation in the quad near the end of the training cycle, and announced we would be visiting the National Infantry Museum in the following way. "Now we will visit the home of the infantry, and see what none of you had the balls to be."

"Sounds like Sergeant Beecher was grateful you saved his ass," I said. He had switched from calling him Chocolate Bunny and Brillo Head to calling him Hollywood.

"You think so?" old Thigpen asked, his tone bitter as dirt.

Things grew so bright for the moment I was afraid we were about to be strafed in a white phosphorus attack. A few times of rapid blinking allowed my eyes to adjust and let me see we were on a beach. The sand was sugar-white, blending with the foam on the crest of the incoming tide. Both old Thigpen and I squinted against the bleached expanse of the strand catching rays from the sun. The only color came from the rich blue ocean, hemmed by a rose-colored coral reef. It looked like a massive flower that petrified the moment it bloomed, turning to ruby stone. Half-naked, bronzed soldiers on leave balanced on what looked like giant banana peels.

"Them white boys loved to surf," Thigpen said, and then grinned like I never saw him grin before. "There I am."

He walked alongside his younger self, who was strutting with the confidence of a pimp who owned a stable the size of a shah's harem. Young Thigpen wore a grey fedora pulled at a rakish angle. His checkered Guayabera shirt had a few buttons undone, exposing muscles rippled from humping in the bush and taking turns with the other two Bloods on the M60.

"It ain't a fedora," Old Thigpen said, and now there was no question he could read my thoughts. His bare feet left no prints in the white sand, and his hospital gown did not billow in the wind.

"What is it, then?"

"A Chi-town Borsalino."

"And where are we?" I was tempted to say it was Heaven, that maybe the Metro bus driver had fallen asleep behind the wheel and drifted into oncoming traffic. Now we were free, from life and war. If this were in fact Heaven, I would feel some guilt for the pain my death caused my mother and my nephew.

"Uncle Joe!" I could hear Daniel's voice in my ears, like the wash of the tide trapped in the pink-ringed nautilus of a seashell.

"You ain't dead yet. You ain't that lucky." Thigpen walked after his younger self. "We're in Vung Tau, on R and R."

"Oh," I said. "I took some of that in Iraq. They sent me to Qatar." All that trip did was enrage me. I spent my leave at an air force base with swimming pools, restaurants, and an Orange Julius stand. There were massage parlors and a thousand other amenities that it pisses me off now just to recall. I walked up to an airman in chocolate chip fatigues on my last day of R & R. He drank a fruit smoothie beneath an umbrella-shaded table that faced an azure swimming pool and hot tub, where two women in conch bikinis splashed each other. "Fuck you," I said, not caring about the airman's rank or the consequences. He just smiled and said, "Have a lovely air force day," before tipping the parasol in his drink toward me and taking another sip of his smoothie through the straw.

I tried to let my rage cool, walking behind the Thigpens. We passed Tiki-themed bars. The smell of sizzling T-bones charring on grills wafted through the straw and thatch, mixing with the foamy scent of beer and the vapor of sea salt. Soul music pulsed from transistor radios and honky-tonk twanged. The music sounded like pain to me. It was the pain of a knife fight breaking out in Detroit after a craps game gone bad, or the pain of a drunken Pentecostal beating his son with his belt in a barn while a train roared on past. The small town didn't promise a circus to join, but at least it offered an out in the Marine Corps.

We left Lefty Frizzell and Smoky Robinson. We came to a hut where young Thigpen stopped, and the draft beer mugs were shaped like the stone heads of Olmec gods.

The man on the barstool had his back to us, but I knew enough now to know it was Sergeant Beecher. He wore a Hawaiian shirt patterned with marlins and pineapples falling in a tacky pattern across his back. Thigpen planted a hand on the small of the noncom's back.

"Hey, Sarge, let me buy you a beer."

The NCO turned, chomping a fat, wet cigar in his mouth. He said, "Fuck off, nigger."

"Yeah," old Thigpen's voice followed me off the bus, drifting on the exhaust of the departed Metro. "He was grateful, alright."

I walked toward the Fort Thomas VA. My phone vibrated in my pocket. It had been vibrating for I couldn't guess how long. I turned the alarm off and walked toward the red building in front of me. This VA facility was smaller than the main one on Vine Street, where I worked. It housed a long-term inpatient PTSD program, and there was also a nursing home inside.

"I should have left his ass on that Bouncing Betty."

"I can't say that I would have blamed you." I walked through the automatic doors of the VA. I pressed the "up" button on the elevator.

"Those Betties go off at about three feet in the air, perfect for blowing a man's balls off. I don't like the idea of a bunch of little Beechers running around out there."

"Maybe he had Agent Orange," I said. The elevator car came and I got on. It was empty, aside from me and the astral-projected spirit of Thigpen. I kept talking to him after pressing "2" and waited for the elevator to take us up. "That shit can cause all kinds of problems, from cortical blindness to microcephaly."

I'd heard that some soldiers in Iraq had lost their balls. They had to take daily testosterone supplements and were even fitted with prosthetic, silicone-based testicles. I guess there were worse things than having to take a couple of squirts of Androgel per day.

The elevator opened on the second floor, and Thigpen asked, "How'd you get complete atrophy of the penis?"

I sighed. "I didn't. The VA fucked that one up." I decided to stop talking out loud to Thigpen. I glanced at my watch. I was ten minutes early. I would kill that time in the waiting room, reading *Entertainment Weekly* and *Time*. I'd learn about the doings of people who were intelligent, rich, or just fortunate enough to have never been thrown into the snake pit that was the average man or woman's life. Oh, to be one of the beautiful people! Then again, sometimes even they self-destructed. Starlets overdosed on heroin and hunks crashed their Bugatti sports cars. Pain was everywhere, apparently.

"Shit, I miss Vung Tau." Thigpen smiled and sat down next to me. "Fuck that peckerwood. I shouldn't of let him fuck with my stride. I was looking sharp that day." I settled into my foam-backed chair and picked up a copy of *Entertainment Weekly* that had the cast of *Harry Potter* on the cover. I didn't know how old Emma Watson was. I prayed she was at least eighteen, or things were worse than I thought.

"Fashion can change a lot in a couple of years," Thigpen mused. "A couple years before blue jeans was just for mechanics like my uncle. Next thing you know, everyone's wearing them."

"Joseph?"

I looked up at my therapist. He was a thin middle-aged man with chiseled, angular features. He reminded me of a hero who would grace the cover of a Golden Age SF mag. His hair was slightly gray, and his face always betrayed a certain worry and shock. I figured that happened to a man when he absorbed the horror of several hundred ruined vets per day. Private practice would have been a lot easier. There would be a lot more minor sex life problems and a lot fewer problems relating to the nasty business of killing and watching people die in jungles or deserts.

"Yes, Doctor?"

I half stood in my foam chair and set the copy of *Entertainment Weekly* back in the wire cage where it previously sat atop a copy of *Time*.

Doctor Barker glanced at his watch. "I can see you a couple minutes early if you want."

"Thank you."

I stood and left old Thigpen in the waiting room. I went into Doctor Barker's office and sat down. He handed me a sheet attached to a clipboard. A pen hung in a hole punched in the clipboard and dangled by a dog tag chain. The sheet was filled with questions like, "How often have you had recurring thoughts of the most stressful event you experienced in the war?" and answers ranging from, "Never" to "Constantly." I would hand the clipboard back to Doctor Barker after I answered the questions. He would tally up my score and tell me whether the pain in my soul that day was a "ten" or a "forty," or somewhere in between.

I worked my way down the questionnaire with diligent speed. I decided I would tell Doctor Barker about my broken tooth and my new job. I would leave out the trivial detail that a psychotic, black Vietnam vet who hated white people had astral projected into my dreams and now into my waking life.

I finished with the questionnaire and handed it back to Doctor Barker. He counted the numbers and did the math in his head. I thought that this orderly system did as much for him as a therapist as it did for me as a patient. If it allowed him to feel like he logically processed that which I knew could not be logically processed, then I would not begrudge him his vice.

I tried to ignore the framed photos of his family he kept on his desk, knowing the daughters and wife would only hurt my heart and make the regret increase. Instead I focused on his matted and framed PhD from Loyola University. "So, Joe, you still got your safety plan?"

I nodded. My safety plan was a list of steps to take in the event that I felt like committing suicide. The list was stuck to the front of my refrigerator with a "Wounded Warrior Crisis Center" magnet featuring a soldier in silhouette, gripping his head in apparent agony. "It takes the strength of a warrior to admit you need help," the magnet said.

That may be true, but I don't think anyone or anything short of God could have helped me with my present problems. I sensed that if God truly did exist, he was waiting on the other side. The only way to get there was to scrap the safety plan and commit suicide.

I didn't mention that to Doctor Barker because I had no desire to be involuntarily committed to the hospital or to make his job harder than it already was.

CHAPTER SEVEN: PINK FINGERTIPS PERILOUSLY CLOSE TO NUBIAN QUEEN

It was my first time in the Third Eye Boutique, even though I had lived above the shop for some time now. A Buddhist chant came through Bose speakers mounted in the four corners of the main room, and a haze of incense obscured Tamika as she talked to two customers standing over a glass case.

I looked around the shop. There were hardwood drums with geckos and tropical frogs patterned on their sides. They were very expensive, authentic *Djembe* drums. African masks were nailed to the walls. Their hollow eyes gave me the uneasy sensation I was being watched by something far more judgmental than convenience store surveillance cameras. Some of the masks were realistic enough to look like the severed, shrunken and dried heads of conquered enemies. Their dreadlocks were made from dried palm fibers, and ritual scars were cut into the hollow wooden cheeks. Other masks were more elongated and surreal, shaped like miniature canoes. Their mouths were wide in the surprise of an unwanted death at the hands of an enemy tribesman.

I walked up to the counter where Tamika stood over a case filled with pipes. There were bubblers and steamrollers laid out on a velvet cloth. I used to own one of those types of pieces back when I was in high-school. I'd marvel at the way it changed color and soaked up the resin, contemplating the wizardry of the thing with my stoned mind and open mouth, marveling at the rainbow of colors.

Her customers were two young men in cargo shorts and lacrosse-T-shirts, who both wore open-toed sandals. I guessed they were from the local university. They probably walked down here from the fraternity to replace the bong they threw off the roof and shattered last night.

I felt less nervous, since I wasn't the only white person in the shop. The boys turned from the case and thanked Tamika. They walked past me and out of the shop. She looked up from the glass case, at me.

"Hey neighbor."

"Hey," I said. She wore golden stud earrings that featured Nefertiti on them.

"You've lived here too long for this to be your first time coming in my shop." She smiled.

"Yeah, I was nervous." I put my hand on top of the glass case. I pulled my palm away, fearing I would smudge the glass.

"Why?"

I waved my hand, struggled to come up with a satisfactory, dishonest answer. Her smile grew larger as she saw me floundering. "Oh, Yakub." I winced from my words.

She broke out laughing, and leaned forward. I took a look at her soft cleavage, Thigpen be damned. "Where did you hear about that?"

"This dude in my unit, Mathias."

"Are you in the service?"

"Was," I answered.

She closed and locked the case before her. She walked over to the corner of the room, turned down the Buddhist chant. Then she adjusted the volume on her stereo, switching to the radio. The sound of a call-in show replaced the *Namaste* mantra. An expert on military weapons spoke to the rapt host about the Nazi *Wunderwaffe*.

Tamika walked back over toward me, played with a braid that tapered in a dentalium shell. "Why do you keep your hair like that?" she asked.

"Habit," I said. "You don't like it?"

She shook her head. "I don't." Then, "Who was Mathias?"

I shrugged. "Some dude in my unit."

"Black?"

I nodded. "NOI?" She asked. I squinted, so she said, "Nation of Islam?"

"I don't think he was serious about anything. He just liked to fuck with us. He said Yakub the Big-Headed Scientist was an evil doctor who created the white man. He said he created the genetically inferior devil to torment the black man, the original man."

She leaned her elbows on the glass case. I suspected she didn't hear white people talk honestly about race often. I felt I didn't have much to lose or gain, either way. I was too far outside of regular society to worry about taboos. "Do you believe it?" she asked.

"No, I'm not powerful enough to be the devil." She laughed again. I thought I was doing alright. I think I was too tired to feel my normal level of social anxiety. I might be a mess around her the next time we met after I got some sleep, if we met again.

"He used to play this song by the rapper Rass Kass, *The Nature of the Threat*, because it pissed Sergeant Carter off. You ever heard it?" I asked.

"American Islam's like radical feminism. It's a young person's game. You'll burn yourself out with hatred. I believed in it when I was younger, and I keep my mouth shut around the Muslims who come in here." She looked around at her cozy fiefdom. "Arguing is bad for business. The Nation is better than nothing for some black men. It's better than the military," she added.

"Were you in?"

She shook her head. The subject on the radio call-in show segued to Nazi parapsychology experiments, or rather Hitler's interest in suppressing the research before it got out of hand. Tamika said, "My dad was a Navy steward on a submarine."

"Did he like it?"

She moved around, stacking items on the shelves.

"He knew every job on the ship, but they only let him be a steward. He washed dishes, served officers food, did their laundry."

I thought about something. If her dad had served long enough ago to endure Jim Crow, then she was probably older than I initially thought. I almost asked her about her age, but checked myself in time.

"He stayed in long enough to see the service desegregate. Harry Truman signed that Executive Order in '48, I think." She stopped arranging things behind the counter. Her golden earrings shined in the light. "Was there something you needed, or did you just want to stop by and say, hi?"

I paused. Her interest grew. I took a deep breath. She licked her lips, and a natural gloss hung there. "What?" She giggled.

"I think I'm being contacted by a spirit."

She rushed over to her stereo and turned it down. Then she glanced through the storefront to make sure no one else was in the store, or coming in. "No shit?"

"No shit. One of my patients at the VA."

"When did he die?"

I shook my head. "No, he's still alive, but..." I trailed off. "He's bedridden, in palliative care. He's a Vietnam vet. He can't walk, and he's in my dreams. He won't leave me alone."

"Hmm." She didn't question my assertion at all. I felt I'd made the right choice by coming here. She disappeared through a beaded curtain into the back of her shop, and came back with two books in her hand. Their covers were mottled, the paperback jackets yellowed and peeling. I guessed they were from her personal stock, and not for sale. She handed the topmost copy to me. It was *Ghost Hunting: A Practical Guide* by Andrew Green.

"It's not a ghost," I said. "It's his...spirit, or something."

"No," she said. "But the same rules apply."

"He said he's been here." I turned the pages, and the smell of decomposing paper and frayed glued binding hit my lungs. Old books were my favorite smell.

"Really?" She leaned close enough to kiss me, and I was afraid that Thigpen would materialize now to slap me. I felt the slight stirrings of an erection, but nothing more. "Don't get offended by my question," she said. Tamika leaned back, away from me. I was surprised by how much her absence hurt, and I wanted her face close to mine again.

"Shoot," I said.

"Do you have anything strange going on with your brain? Like, maybe you were in an accident?"

I nodded. This wasn't information I usually divulged, but she was being forthright with me. She didn't mock my initial claim, and she was even sharing her private stock of books with me. "My buddy stepped on a massive explosive cache, and I got a TBI. Traumatic brain injury," I added, just in case she wasn't familiar with the acronym.

She nodded, her excitement growing. She tapped the book I held, the clear varnish of her long nail somehow arousing me further. I was half-erect. Tamika said, "He says ghost sightings are caused by the brain's electrical fields. Injuries, seizures, and things like that can make you more sensitive to their presence."

"Thigpen has seizures," I said. "Maybe his seizures and my TBI are causing the link."

"Thigpen?" Her tongue snuck out of her mouth again. Tamika licked her upper lip.

"The vet," I said. "He's a Vietnam veteran."

"Black?" she asked.

"Yeah. Does it matter?"

"No," she said. "Just curious."

We both stood there, thinking for a moment. She spoke first. "Maybe you should find out the history of the VA, like if it's built on an ancient Indian burial ground or something like that. That might explain the psychic stored energy."

"You mean like *Amytiville*?" I asked, and smiled. Her expression didn't change.

"I'm serious," she said, and the smile dropped from my own face.

"Okay," I said. "If I remember, I'll check."

She pointed at the book I held. "You know wartime does tend to increase the tendency to see ghosts. More apparitions were seen in World War I than at any other time. Were you in Afghanistan?"

I shook my head. "Iraq."

"It was still a war."

"I know," I said. I knew.

The bell above the door chimed and someone entered. I went tense and moved to the side to let her conduct business. It was the two university students, back with a handful of cash they got from the ATM across the street. One of the two boys pointed in the glass case and said, "Let me get the Sherlock bubbler."

"A most excellent choice." Tamika used her key to unlock the case and slid it open. She walked the blown glass piece over to the register and checked the boy's ID. She rang the sale up, and gave him his pipe in a brown paper bag. Then she looked back over at me and asked, "Are you getting any weird signals on the radio in your car?"

"I don't have a car." I immediately regretted saying that. I didn't think she was superficial or shallow, but a man without a car in America's car-centric culture was advertising something about himself. "I have a bike," I said, and that was the first lie I told her. I winced from it, but at least now she might regard me as bohemian and environmentally conscious, rather than a broke loser or perhaps an alcoholic who got a DUI and was suspended.

She walked away from the cash register, came around the counter, and stood in front of me. She took the book she'd given me, and placed another hardback in my hands. "What about ectoplasm?" she asked.

I tried not to laugh, but couldn't help it. "You mean like in *Ghost Busters*?"

She laughed with me this time, but didn't appear to take offense. "It doesn't have to be a fat little green man like Slimer, but yeah."

"Wait," I said, and lifted my nonstick shoe. "The janitor just quit because there's this weird sludge all over the eighth floor in the hospice ward."

"Bingo!"

It was starting to make sense now, or at least parts of it were. "What exactly is ectoplasm?"

"Pseudopods of real matter that come out of the orifices of the mediums, or the spirits."

I wondered if Thigpen's spirit was dripping some kind of spiritual flotsam from his spectral ostomy bag when he went roving and projecting over the hilly streets of Cincinnati.

"What religion are you?"

I dug inside my shirt for my dog tags, held them out to her. She clutched the beaded chain. "No rel. pref.," she said. "No religious preference."

"Agnostic," I said. "There's got to be something spiritual if all of this is actually happening, if I'm not just crazy." There was a chance that I was really being contacted by spirits, but I was convinced that even if that was the case, I was still crazy in addition to being some kind of unintentional medium.

"What were you raised as?"

I pointed my hand at wall. I motioned in the direction of the old Catholic school I attended as a boy. "I went to Annunciation

Catholic."

"The Catholics have a much stronger belief in ghosts than Protestants, who tend to be skeptical."

"What about Buddhists?" I pointed at her golden statue, with its eyes downcast and prayerful hands securing a stick of patchouli. "Of course." She touched my shoulder with her right hand, and an erection braced against my checkered boxer shorts. "You should feel lucky."

I wasn't so sure about that. "Why?"

"There are a lot of believers who spend their entire lives trying to contact spirits, and they never have any success. One just fell into your lap."

"Yeah, but he's showing me horrible things. I'm seeing images of war, torture, rape- all the worst war crimes in Vietnam."

"There's got to be a reason he's showing you this stuff." She withdrew her hand from my shoulder. I looked down, at the next book she placed in my hands. It was *The Devils of Loudun* by Aldous Huxley.

"What's this?" I asked. I knew *Brave New World* and *The Doors of Perception*, but that was as far as I got with Huxley.

"It's about a tale of possession in 17th century France, in a town called Loudun. A Roman Catholic priest named Urbain Grandier supposedly went and made a pact with the devil about some Ursuline nuns, and they all became possessed."

A queasy feeling shot through my body. So far Thigpen had only harassed me and intruded into my sleep. What if he took the next step suggested by the book held in my hands? What if he commandeered me like a parasite, possessing me? It would make a strange sight, to see a white male with a high-and-tight military haircut getting onto the Metro bus and rotating his head three-hundred and sixty degrees like Linda Blair in *The Exorcist*. People would be further confused when I started shouting "Fuck y'all crackers!" or words to that effect.

Tamika sensed the source of my unease. "He might not want to possess you."

"Well, then," I said. "What does he want?"

"Ask him." That sounded simple enough. Only, what if the waking Thigpen was unaware of the doings and wanderings of the nocturnal spirit that floated around Ludlow Avenue? He might look at me like I was crazy. I might say "What do you want?" to which he would respond with a prosaic demand like, "A nicotine lozenge would hit the spot right about now." That would leave me feeling like a right fool.

Tamika walked back up to me, squared herself to me so that her amber eyes penetrated my own. Her locks fell in thick knots over her ears, covering the golden Egyptian queen earrings she wore. She placed one hand on each of my shoulders. Everything in my body slackened, relaxed until the blood rushed to my penis like a coursing army rushing to storm a castle keep. My hands reflexively went for her wide hips, and I loosely touched her ass. It felt like a fertile swollen basket, as comforting and maternal as the Venus of Wallendorf draping her belly and breasts over the weak men beneath her form who feared crop failures. She didn't fight me, or look as surprised by my action as I did.

I leaned into her and was sure she felt my erection touching her belly as I moved forward. I hugged her and placed my head on her shoulder and drank in her smell of cocoa butter and talcum powder and roots and herbs, of a healing black woman. "I'm sorry," I said.

"It's okay," she whispered. I didn't think it was possible for my dick to get any harder, but when her hot whispering breath reached my ear, it caused warm nettles to pass through my body.

"You've got a big dick," she said. "Not just for a white guy." She withdrew from me, stood back, but kept her hands on my shoulders. Tamika looked in my eyes to gauge my reaction.

"I know," I said. "I usually can't get hard with a woman, not since the war." This was the first time I'd told a woman this information. I don't know why, but it made me feel stronger rather than weaker, maybe because it was the truth.

"Do you want to borrow that?" She nodded at the book I held in my hands.

I shook my head. "I don't think I have time to read." I handed it back to her.

"I want you to do something for me. This is something I know you'll have time for, because you'll be at work when you do it. Okay?"

"Yeah."

"I want you to try to harness your power. First, I want you to find out what Thigpen wants from you. If you want to be free from him and his bad dreams, that's step one."

"What's step two?"

"I want you to recognize that what you have is a gift, not a curse. I want you to try to consciously use it while you're at work, and then I want you to report back to me. You got it?"

"Sure." I liked how forceful she was being, commanding me. I'd always been submissive with women, and I liked the feeling of working for one.

"Good," she said.

"Alright." I turned, smiling. I pointed toward the ceiling, where my apartment was. My pain pills, terrier, and my warm bed were waiting. I'd had to wake up early to go to Fort Thomas and I'd killed some time here, but I still had a few Z's to cop before my next shift. It was going to be doubly hectic, now that I had to work my "gift" that I frankly considered a curse. That was in addition to whatever chores Hasford had waiting for me when I got to the eighth floor of the VA.

"I've got to get some sleep," I said.

"Go get some sleep."

I headed toward the door, walking backwards so that I could maintain eye-contact with her as I went.

"Do me a favor," she said.

I opened the door, and the bell above chimed. "What?"

"Don't cut your hair for a few weeks." She smiled one last time. "See what happens."

CHAPTER EIGHT: HARNESSING THE GIFT/CURSE

Chewing two 325 milligram Oxycodone tablets on my way to the VA had me walking on air. I wondered why I couldn't feel this way all the time, why the happiness and lack of pain contained in the little pills couldn't last forever. It barely lasted twenty minutes. That happy feeling was mostly gone aside from a residual buzz by the time I was on the eighth floor.

Hasford still wore his cervical collar, and it apparently irritated him. He scratched his neck with a penlight, saw me, and then handed me the tool as if he didn't just used it to scratch his neck. The pen was warm from where it had dug beneath his collar.

"You look like stir-fried shit."

"Thank you," I said. I twirled the penlight in my hands. It was light as carbon fiber. It had a nice balance to it, as if it was a gold fountain pen. "This is high-speed."

"Yeah, it's one of those Welch Allyn Professional jobs. I went online and did my homework. I'd put it in a request order at the last meeting. Christmas come early to the eighth floor."

I looked behind the glass wall of the nurse's station. The fat, bald RN drank orange soda from a Styrofoam cup and looked at his computer monitor. He could be playing Minesweeper or Solitaire for all I knew.

Hasford pointed at the pen. "It's got multiple lumen settings, just in case Thigpen bitches about it being too bright. Jones won't bitch about anything."

"How is Jones?" I walked into the changing room, but left the door open while I suited up.

"He's on his way out. He's got new nerve sheath tumors. I forget the exact name, but it's on his chart."

"Malignant?" I struggled to tie my robe in back and slipped the latex gloves over my hands. The air filled with a fine powder.

"Nothing but. They're in his peripheral nerves, metastasizing."

"Will there be any radiation therapy or surgery, do you think?"

I finished suiting up and walked back onto the floor. Hasford said, "I think they've done all the aggressive medical therapy they're going to do." He pointed toward the curtain down the hall. "Go speedily to thy work."

I started down the hall, thought about something, and stopped. "Hey, I think I have sleep apnea."

He squinted. "Did you have a sleep study performed?"

I stifled a smile as it rose to my lips. "Something like that." I wondered if he had some sort of patent-pending device in his moleskin notebook, a sleep machine to go with his colostomy bag.

I carried on down the hall and found the floor was even stickier than usual, heavily coated with the melted paraffin goop. I thought about collecting a sample to bring back to Tamika, but Hasford was still watching me. I wasn't sure how that would look. "Fuck," I said. "It's worse."

"The last janitor quit," Hasford said. "We're still working on getting a new one. In the meantime, guess who's doing double-duty as night nurse and custodian?"

"Yours truly?"

"Yup."

I parted the curtain, walked into the quarantined area of the hall. I planned to test the direct responses of both my patients, but there was something else I needed to get out of the way first. I had let myself be used by Thigpen like a puppet. I felt powerless, at least until I met with Tamika at Third Eye and she helped put things in context. Now I wanted to see if I had any power, if I could control this thing rather than letting other people and their nightmares steamroll over me. I parted the curtain again, this time from inside the quarantine area looking out. I glanced at Hasford. I thought with every fiber of my being, begged to be shown his soul, or at the very least the memories that he carried with him in his skin.

Things were grainy but rich, like a home movie of a childhood

Christmas. The colors were simultaneously robust and faded, the worms of dust slicing through the celluloid and creating little Rorschach blobs inside the mind I now entered.

"Doesn't look good," I said. The DI in his Smokey the Bear hat looked at me staring into the punji pit with its razor-sharp stakes, like teeth in the mouth of a giant monster waiting to devour our young, green hides.

"Even a squirrel as blind and dumb as you can find an acorn every once and awhile, Hasford."

I went to the position of attention, my thumbs touching the seams on the sides of my pants. "Sir, yes, sir!"

The DI leaned in closer to the pit. When he spoke, it wasn't just to me. "Something else to take into account, shit birds. This is just a training scenario. The real thing will be covered in shit."

The camera was in shaky hands, the home movie rumbling along on a dusty road where we'd done battalion *espirit de corps* runs. We jogged past a wooden fingerboard painted in blood-red, aimed toward the Pacific: "Vietnam" it said. "Ten-thousand miles."

My balls rattled, the sperm in my testes danced like Mexican jumping beans, and my teeth clicked like castanets. I was still Hasford and I was now in Vietnam, but I might as well be Joey Sullivan in Iraq. This ride felt even bumpier than a C-130 or a Chinook, worse even than the rumbling wooden plank that served as a bench in the back of the deuce and-a-half I once rode in with a water buffalo hitched to the trailer.

I looked around. We were in a chopper with no seatbelts or seats. Everything smelled of that damp canvas odor that reminded me of the Army. It was the smell of the constant wetness of ponchos and canteen covers that never really dried, surplus from the Korean War moldy and handed down to Vietnam-era soldiers, and Vietnam gear kicked down to raw recruits training for Cold War exercises in Germany, ad infinitum.

The UH-34 screamed like a dying dinosaur mired in hot tar, and the chopper shook as if every bolt might come loose and the entire bird might fall apart in midair. We picked up altitude and speed. The chopper banked. I saw the same blue ocean and white sand I saw while on leave with Thigpen when we got rebuffed by his racist NCO.

Patchwork grids of watery squares I guessed to be rice paddies reflected in the mirrored sunglasses of the door gunner, who wasn't fazed by either the noise or the speed of the chopper.

Beauty, I thought, *wasn't much of a problem in Iraq*. Most everything there looked like a brown and grey wasteland. It looked like Akron or Chillicothe, Ohio, if crop dusters dropped tons of sand from the sky and turned everything colorless. There were some spots in Iraq that were beautiful, like that ancient Ziggurat of Ur at Tallil Airbase. The sacred relic had stood just a few clicks away from where the infidels erected trailers filled with Burger King and Subway food. I lived in a trailer close to the ancient temple that was built in honor of a Sumerian god for a few months in Iraq. The ziggurat was the supposed home of the Bible's Abraham. And then there were times, especially when we convoyed along the Tigris-Euphrates, where a bit of greenery would sprout along the water's edge and startle my eyes that had been bored for miles. There was nothing in Iraq to rival the beauty of Vietnam I saw with Claude Thigpen, though, or what I now witnessed through Hasford's eyes.

I felt a soaring power, something like what a bird must always feel but takes for granted. Somebody or something took that power away from me in the next moment. The greens and golds of the elephant grass were like jewels, bending from the force of the helicopter's rotors. The sky above was an ocean blue enough for the white boys to surf, if only they could reach it.

I ran out into the open to get Morris, feeling Hasford's pain. It was worse than the pain I felt for Dunfy. At least Dunfy was there one moment, stepped on the pressure plate, and was gone the next. Morris was going to live for a while in my arms. Dinks were still laying down fire, but it was the suppressive, susurrating mist of ghosts making their retreat. I was a sniper and I knew when shots were aimed. They could still get lucky and hit me, but it wasn't the Marine Corps way to leave a man lying out there in agony. It made more sense for me to risk death myself to get him and bring him back to cover, even if he was going to die.

"Fuck, it doesn't feel like more than a bee sting."

"Ain't much worse, either," I said.

Morris tried to look at his arm, but I wouldn't let him. I held his head in my lap. I took my compress from my belt. I tried to apply it to his wound, and my hand went inside his arm. His arm bent and dangled by a joint, coming off in a break that gave cleanly.

He didn't scream, couldn't feel or think. I thanked God. The grass around us bowed. My hands were burning from shrapnel cuts, gray spots that stuck out as if I'd been poked repeatedly with a Number Two pencil that left little blobs of graphite in my skin. I couldn't tell how bad I was bleeding, because my dripping blood was covered in my buddy's shower of blood.

Voices rose and sank beneath the sound of the helicopter's whapping rotors. I was experiencing this moment for the first time as Joey Sullivan, but there was also the sense that this moment was frozen for Hasford. It was moving in slow motion, some kind of film strip rather than something that was actually happening even as it happened. Beneath that there was guilt. The sun was sneaking up. It was showing me that it was alive, that it was a god, and also that death was the most beautiful thing there was. I was grateful to be witnessing it this close- to be a part of it- but I was also grateful that it was my friend who was dying and not me. Thus the guilt and the joy, and too many emotions to count or understand, even decades later. The only way to count them would be to die and have God explain why the worst moments in life were also secretly the best.

I ripped my bro's M79 bandolier from his chest, and saw where one of the Soviet rounds the Dinks fired had primed one of the grenades, maybe half-exploding it. That might explain the shrapnel in my hands, which burned me.

I moved the bandolier up the stump of my friend's arm and ignored the severed hand and forearm on the ground. A horrified vision of the hand crawling off like a spider made my stomach somersault, and I made sure not to look at that hand again. I would rather watch the life leaving Morris's eyes than look at that hand on the ground anymore. I made a tourniquet with the bandolier and twisted. His blood stopped pumping as if from a high-pressured spigot.

"You having fun?"

I looked up. Hasford was behind the quarantine curtain, with me. He saw the guilt in my eyes, but I wasn't sure that he knew until he spoke.

"You've got the gift," he said, pointing at the side of my head. "That TBI is worth its weight in gold." He removed his fingers from my temple, and pointed at his cervical collar. "Pity my injury's too low. A few inches north and maybe I could have spent some more time back there with Morris."

It was hard to hide the disbelief in my voice. "But you saw what I just saw?"

He nodded. "Yeah, but only because you saw it here with me. I can't recall it on my own." He held out his hands, still gray in spots from the remnants of shrapnel. "Got my first Purple Heart that day."

"I didn't get any in Iraq."

Hasford shrugged modestly. "They were giving them out like candy in the 'Nam."

"I doubt that." Then I said, "Sorry."

"For what?"

"For poking around in your head like that."

He waved away my concern. "Fuck it. I read your file without your consent. We're even now."

I didn't think we were, but I didn't argue. "I thought..." I paused, wanting to tread carefully and not offend.

"You thought what?" His eyes narrowed to pinpoints.

"I thought you were a sniper?"

"I was." He went rigid as a cornered cat, as if I was questioning his professionalism.

"That was some mighty close contact back there."

Hasford nodded, understanding what I was getting at now. His posture relaxed. "I've got kills, notches for everything ranging from three-hundred to a thousand meters. But sometimes you kick the hornet's nest and you're right on top of them." He tapped his tattoo of the single-shot, bolt action rifle. I was sure it was done to commemorate the death of the soldier I'd just held in my arms. "The Winchester is your best friend when you've got some distance between you and Charlie. It's not as good up close and personal."

He turned, grabbed the edge of the curtain, prepared to go back to the front of the hospital. "You going to read that book?"

"Which one?" Between him and Tamika I was going to acquire a pretty large pile of recommendations. "Raymond Moody," he said. *"Life after Life."*

"I don't know. I'm not sure if there is life after life."

"There is." There was no doubt in his voice. "I know what it's like to be a ghost." I thought he was going to talk about how 'Nam vets were treated when they first rotated back to the world, but he said, "Uncle Sam can't do shit right. He'd fuck up a wet dream if you let him." He laughed. "They mixed up mine and Moody's telegram, sent my mom one stateside saying I died from wounds suffered in combat." Hasford laughed louder, had to check himself. He stifled his giggles with a closed fist, lest he wake the patients sleeping on the ward.

"I called my ma and it took me twenty minutes to convince her I was still alive." He took his fist from his mouth, pointed at the door to my patients' room. "Get back to work."

"Yes sir." I spun and walked into the bedroom. The lights were off, the only illumination coming from the moon as it crept through the metal slats of the blinds over the window. Its white light was counterpointed by the crimson wink of a radio tower in the distance.

I walked over to Norman Jones. I came around to the foot of his bed and picked up the clipboard. I wrote the time and my name, and the action to be performed. I also glanced at the newest condition added to the narrative. "Malignant nerve sheath/ multiple neurofibrosarcomas." It didn't sound good.

I turned the penlight on, opening the patient's left eye. I swung the penlight from his ear toward the midline of his wrinkled face. I let the light linger on the pupil and then removed it. The pupil neither constricted nor dilated as it should have. I guessed that had something to do with the tumors. I pulled my latex glove up over my watch and waited for twenty seconds to elapse. Then I held both of his eyes open, shined the light in his other eye. There was no constriction in either pupil, nil nerve function. He was dead to the world, and close to literally dead.

I allowed his eyes to close and turned the penlight off for a moment. I wrote my name, the time, and the findings on the space provided on the clipboard. I didn't see the point in testing his doll's eye reflex, but I knew Hasford wanted me to go by the book. I held the old man's waxen eyelids open and turned his head gently from side to side. The eyes did not move in the opposite direction in which I turned him.

I released my hold from his head, gently stroked the remaining gray hairs atop his head, and walked over to Thigpen's bed.

"I'm awake."

I jumped, startled from the way his croaky voice broke the silence. "In that case," I said, and walked to the corner of the room. I turned the light on.

"Don't touch me!" Thigpen blinked against the brightness, squinting and pursing his lips. His skin was as dry as one of the mahogany masks that hung in Tamika's shop.

"I can't," I said, "without changing gloves. I don't want to communicate between you two more than I have to." I wouldn't want to touch him, anyway. I felt he had a sinister power over me. I really didn't trust myself not to strangle him for forcing his way into my mind and my life, whether or not he was conscious of invading my dreams when he himself was asleep. I had seen horrible things inside Hasford's head, but that was my choice.

I held up two fingers of my right hand. "How many fingers am I holding up?" He glanced at the latex-gloved digits.

"Rabbit ears."

"Can you give me a number?"

"Peace sign."

"Good enough," I said. "Follow the rabbit ears." I moved my two fingers from left to right, in front of his gaze. His eyes tracked the fingers well, and I guessed he complied because I was using his term rather than mine.

"Good," I said. "No extraocular movements, and your conjugate gaze is good. No oscillating movements, no nystagmus."

"I'm surprised," Thigpen said. I gripped the pen anchored to the chart at the foot of his bed, and wrote my findings.

"Why's that?"

He grinned from ear to ear. "I've been drinking Gilbey's like a mother."

I decided to take a chance. If he reported me, it was the word of a delirious dying man against a professional. I wasn't anymore lucid than he was, but I could at least present that front to the world at large. "Can you get the fuck out of my dreams, please? I need my sleep to work. If I don't get enough sleep, I can't do a good job. If I don't do a good job, that results in inferior care for you." I walked closer to him, felt like slapping him with the glove covered in the germs from the eyes of Norman Jones.

"Don't talk to Tamika anymore," he said.

"Is that all you want?" I liked her, but I'd dodge her for the remainder of my life if that was what it took to get Thigpen off my ass. It would be a difficult task, though, since her shop was just above my apartment. But I was willing to do anything short of murder to get away from his memories of Vietnam, and to have my head to myself again.

"No. There's something else."

"What?" I almost added, *I'll do anything but murder*, but I didn't want him to know he had me over a barrel.

He opened his mouth wider, as if he were a boa about to unhinge his jaw and make way for a mouse. Claude Thigpen removed his new set of teeth from his mouth and set them on the end table next to him. A trail of drool dripped from his mouth, as thick as the ectoplasm coating the hospital corridor's floor and the bottoms of my nonstick shoes.

"I want you to go to Arlington National Cemetery."

"That's in D.C."

"I know where it is." He looked over at the dentures resting on his nightstand. "They gave me new teeth, but they took a couple of my toes."

"I'm sorry you had to part with your toes. Now what do you want me to do at Arlington?" I guessed he wanted me to put flowers on the grave of one of his Bloods he left back in the bush, perhaps one of the bebop cats who lugged the pig and ammo around with him.

"I want you to piss on the grave of a white man, and then I'll leave you alone."

"What?" I took a couple of steps toward him. I was ready now not to slap him, but to punch him with a closed fist. He'd taken his dentures out so there would be no risk of screwing up his teeth. "I'm not pissing on the grave of a veteran."

I'd been to Arlington only once in my life, to pay respects to Buck Sergeant Steven Dunfy. He was killed in action and buried in Section Sixty, beneath the shade of white oaks and red maples.

"Not just any white man," he said, ignoring me. "I want you to piss on the grave of a racist-ass cracker."

I didn't mention the irony of the phrase "racist-ass cracker" to him. His lifelong anger was bone-deep and too strong to accommodate anything subtle as irony. I couldn't say that I blamed him. I'd only witnessed a sliver of his past in Vietnam. I'm sure there were even worse memories, stronger humiliations and pains going back to childhood. Then there were more hard days when he rotated back to the world, got off a Greyhound, and started life as a mechanic in his uncle's bay on the south side of Chicago.

"How am I supposed to tell who's racist or not?" I asked. "They're fucking dead."

"You can read me. You can read him." He nodded weakly toward the hall where Hasford had stood before the shroud separating the quarantined area from the rest of the hospital. "You'll be able to read the graves." He propped himself up in his bed, gripped the hand-railings covered in bath towels there to protect him from bruising like a grapefruit when he seized.

"I ain't asking you to disrespect a man who served his country with honor. I'm asking you to piss on the grave of a man like Sergeant Beecher."

"Why not his grave?"

Thigpen shook his head. "That cracker ain't dead yet. He runs a marina in Florida."

I put my head in my hands, massaged the bridge of my nose. I felt the spots, the panic attack coming on. I wondered if my TBI was going to flare up, wondered if this all wasn't one mass hallucination.

"Alright," I said. "If it will make you leave me the hell alone, and if I can find someone buried in Arlington who is beyond a shadow of a doubt a subpar specimen of humanity, then I will piss on his grave. You've got to leave me alone after that." I pointed a threatening finger at him.

"Scout's honor. You're number one, G.I."

"First day off I get, I'll buy a ticket." I shook my head. I couldn't believe I was doing this.

Thigpen sagged into his mattress. He stared up the ceiling, but spoke to me. "You ain't got to buy shit."

"What do you mean?"

"You do me this solid," he said, "and I'm fin to do you a solid." He sang a few measures from one of the old songs by the Delta bluesman his wife quoted when she combed her husband's chest hairs with the afro pick, stroking the fibers like guitar strings with a Mississippi bottle slide. "'Follow me,'" Thigpen said, "'and I will turn your money green.'"

CHAPTER NINE: THE RETURN OF AN OLD FRIEND, OR SOMETHING LIKE IT

There was a metal-grated box in the foyer of the apartment building's rear entrance, with strips of tape listing the current residents and glowing little doorbells adjacent to each name. Someone rang me, which was a first. I walked over to the intercom and pressed the "talk" button.

"Joseph!"

"Claudine!"

It was my tutor from Germany. I wanted to ask her what she was doing back in America, but I buzzed her through first. I could ask her when she got upstairs. I should be sleeping, getting ready for my next shift at the VA hospital and my trip to D.C. I could make some time for an old friend from out of town.

There was a knock at my door and Tiffany ran in little circles. She picked her toy up in her jaws, a once-stuffed squirrel that was flat as roadkill now that she had torn the cotton innards from it. She waited by the door with the toy in her mouth. I opened the front door, and there was Claudine.

She was as beautiful as ever, dark brown eyes and light smattering of freckles. Her hair was tied in a bun piled in a tight knot on the back of her head, and a few brunette strands fell from the bun and onto her exposed shoulders.

"What are you doing back in America?"

"Things did not work out with my man."

"Es tut mir sehr leid, das zu horen."

"Oh, you are still learning German? That is good to hear."

She leaned down to Tiffany, whose tail wagged. It had been a long time since she last saw my tutor. Claudine reached down and grabbed the tail of the squirrel my dog kept in her mouth. A low roar filled Tiff's tiny belly.

"Ah," Claudine said. "She is a ..." She searched for the correct English words, and came up with a mixture of English and German. "...*sehr* dominant girl." She picked Tiffany up, toy dangling from the dog's mouth. She carried her toward my bathroom. Claudine had been up here before, a long time ago. She knew the layout of the apartment. She placed a rather confused Tiffany in the bathroom and closed the door on my terrier.

"*Was hat mit ihr Mann passiert, oder sollte ich das nicht fragen?*" I wasn't sure whether or not I mangled the German, especially the word order and conjugation. I was never sure where to place my subjunctive verbs in a sentence. I had one German professor who was quite pleasant when she taught her elective on *Hausmarchen*- that is, the fairytales by the Brothers Grimm and other associated German myths, many of them actually Scandinavian in origin- but she was quite the bitch when she taught language. She had a list of "capital offenses," that is, mistakes one could make that would earn them a zero on their papers. It is safe to say that without Claudine's assistance; I would have failed that course.

"I'm sorry," Claudine said. "Tiffany cannot be here for this."

"For what?"

Her brown eyes glowed like flaming amber, and the freckles on her face seemed to crawl as if they were living insects. "I am a dominant girl, also." She shoved me backwards, and I stumbled from the hardwood of the apartment and fell back-first onto the linoleum floor of the kitchen. Whoever built this place was somewhat lazy. The cold and hot taps were reversed in the shower, and the linoleum was cut wrong. It curled around the edges of the room like cheap, industrial carpet. I had bigger problems than linoleum right now, however.

"Claudine..."

Her face hovered over my pajama pants. "No," I said, weakly. On top of my erectile dysfunction, I hadn't shaved in months. I knew that would be a turnoff with a younger girl like her, since it was a veritable jungle down there.

"I never told you that..." I paused.

"Was?" She said. *"Was ist das problem?"*

Her bun came undone and spilled in a violent coil. I looked down at my penis, engorged with blood. *"Kein Problem,"* I said. She pulled my pajama bottoms down until the elastic band of the checkered cotton pants gripped my ankles.

Tiffany barked in the bathroom. If this blowjob took too long, one of the neighbors might call the cops and make a noise complaint. Claudine gripped my testicles in her left hand.

She giggled. "Your dick is so big, but your balls are so small!" I couldn't explain that my balls were shrunken in terror-or at least surprise, since I definitely felt some pleasure. *"Mein Mann* had a small penis."

I laughed dumbly. I was a fairly intelligent man by most rights, but with my cock in her right hand and my balls in her left, I was essentially an idiot for the moment.

"Is that why you left him?"

"Shhh. *Kein mehr Quatsch."* She tickled what little bit of testicle hadn't retracted into my body in fear, and licked the mushroom-shaped tip of my penis. *"Du bist die Meisterin,"* I said. *"Und ich deine Sklave."*

"Rechts hast du. Genau."

She bobbed forward until her lips pressed flush against the nest of pubic hair that made me so self-conscious. I liked performing cunnilingus more than I liked getting head, even before I had studied the art of pussy eating as a consolation technique to apologize to women for my limp dick, but this was a heavenly blowjob. It was like she was delivering Percocet to my body through the suctioning of her lips and tongue. Relief washed over me in waves, and the premonitions of an orgasm were already there, an orgasm as deep as the discovery of the sex act itself.

"Claudine ..." I wasn't sure if I was just saying her name in praise, or trying to get her attention. She paused, removed her mouth from my erect penis. A stream of spit trailed from her slicked lips to the puckering tip of my cock, which was leaking pre-cum.

"Can you stop?"

"Es gefällt dir nicht, oder?"

"Nein, es ist aussergewöhnlich, aber... "

"*Was?*"

"I want to eat your pussy and jerk off. I want you to stand up while I'm on my knees. Or I want you to sit on my face and let me lick your clit like a dog, like a slave." She slapped my balls with the fingers of her left hand a little too hard, which was just right, the pain perfect.

"*Nein,*" she said, and gripped the veined base of my dick so the shaft grew as if inflated by a bicycle pump. "I told you, I am dominant girl tonight. I suck your cock and you shut up."

"Works for me." I placed my hands over my eyes, opened my mouth, and she continued. She tongue-massaged my penis, lapping and bobbing. I imagined her sitting on the edge of my bed naked, with my German professor naked on top of her. My feminist professor held a riding crop in her left hand.

"Joseph," she said. "You will make us both very happy today. This is your initiation into the feminist matriarchy, where women have all of the power. You will lick us both like a slave until you come, and then you will obey us forever after. *Verstehst du, Sklave, oder?*"

I imagined myself licking two tiers of hairy pussy, the pubic hair on the vaginas as much a turn-on for me as my own hair was a thing of self-conscious doubt for me. "Yes," Claudine said, lying beneath my professor in the fantasy, jutting her pussy toward my face to ensure that I did not neglect her on my rounds. "We are very dominant girls."

I thought about the time my professor folded her stockinged legs one over the other in class and said that studies showed "women are smarter than men," and I came in spasms deep enough to feel like the thrashing death throes of a dying beast. Claudine sat up with a mouthful of my sperm, and then stood.

I looked on helplessly as she walked from the kitchen into the living room. I frankly didn't care what she did with my sperm. I wasn't one of those blowjob aficionados who cared if a woman spit or swallowed, so it was fine with me when she let my seed drip from her mouth like cracked egg yolk into a frying pan. It landed on the hardwood floor.

I tried to breathe, as my thudding heartrate slowed. I reached down for my pajama bottoms, doing a crunch in the process and feeling the spare tire of fat around my waist. That was another point of insecurity with me. Or it would be, if she hadn't sucked the insecurity out of me. The orgasm was over, though, and now I could think and worry again.

I pulled my pajama bottoms on and tied them. "I gained a lot of weight since we last saw each other."

She shrugged. "Some girls like hard bodies. I like men *mit ein bischen* extra."

"*Verstandlich.*" That made sense, as I liked big girls quite a bit. Tamika was thick, and I was as attracted to her as I was to Claudine or my German professor. I'd forgotten to incorporate Tamika into my heavy fantasizing a minute ago, but maybe it wasn't a good idea to mix German femdom fantasies with race play scenarios. It was sort of like mixing incompatible cuisines. Maybe when I fantasized about Tamika, I would imagine her jamming my face into Michelle Obama's chocolate pussy to initiate me as a white boy slave in the cult of the African goddess.

"*Jetzt muss ich gehen.*"

"*Warum*? You just got here."

"*Ich war nie hier. Danke.*"

Claudine disappeared, and I stood. It wasn't a dream. It couldn't have been. I'd heard that people sometimes sleepwalked on Ambien, but she and the whole experience was too real. Not only that, but the puddle was there in center of the hardwood floor. I'd never had a wet dream in my life, either.

I leaned down to inspect the pile of semen. I saw that it wasn't white, but was rather clear and plasmatic. I thought maybe that had something to do with my hydrocele and epididymitis, the testicular inflammation conditions I'd brought back with me from Iraq. Maybe I was shooting blanks and couldn't have kids. I would have to be content with being "Uncle Joe!" to the Dirty D, my little brother's son, Daniel.

It finally hit me when I touched the sperm with my forefinger. It wasn't sperm. It was that same weird goop that was all over the floor at the VA hospital, the stuff that got stuck to the bottoms of my supposedly nonstick shoes. It was the ectoplasm that caused the old black janitor to quit in an exasperated huff.

"Shit." I wondered what it meant, that this stuff was coming out of my body in general and my penis, specifically. I stood up, wiped my hands on my pajamas. I didn't worry much about getting semen stains on my clothes, since I did all of my own laundry and didn't have to deal with a drycleaner. I was heading toward the kitchen to get a paper towel to wipe up the goop, when I heard Tiff barking from the bathroom.

"Oh, crap. I'm sorry, Tiff!" I ran toward the bathroom, opened the door. She stopped barking just long enough to grab the stuffing-free squirrel in her jaws and rushed between my legs, on into the bedroom. She would run to the comforter, create a nest for herself, and burrow beneath the warm blankets.

I had quite a number of unanswered questions, but they would have to wait. I had to get some sleep for now, and then I had to go to work. I'd stop by Tamika's shop and see if she couldn't maybe help me with my problem after my shift at the VA.

CHAPTER TEN: EVERYTHING'S COMING UP THIGPEN, AND NOTHING'S COMING UP SULLIVAN

My terrier's favorite spot to throw the ball was just at the edge of the park, where the water fountain was. I would use the ball launcher to wing her slobbery tennis ball down the hill, and she would run after it. I felt somewhat guilty about locking her in the bathroom, so I gave her more than the normal number of throws that night.

A light rain fell. The raindrops pelted the water fountain, and the ripples looked like tiny shockwaves produced by goldfish surfacing for feed. There was a naiad statue in the center of the fountain, with copper lily pads covering her naked breasts and stigmata flows of water shooting from the holes in her bronze hands. It was humid, and the rain created dew when it hit the grass. A fog shrouded the girl statue in the fountain and made her look like she was really alive and dancing.

I finished throwing the ball with Tiff, and took her back upstairs. Then I got ready for work and headed out.

Most of the stores were closed this late. The Indian food market was still open, and the smell of dried beans and curry wafted outside on the wind as I walked toward the VA. I passed the Corinthian, one of the oldest and crappiest institutions in Clifton. It had the ambience of a VFW hall and the food was worse than that served from the carts downtown in front of the courthouse. It had nothing but bad ratings online, and no one I ever talked to understood how the place stayed open for the last few decades, while shops that actually served the community folded one right after another. It could have something to do with location, but a lot of people were convinced Corinthian was a front for some sort of Aegean drug smuggling operation or human trafficking ring. I'd been the only customer in sight the few times I'd eaten there.

I passed new condominium developments, luxury brick big boxes that sprouted up overnight to challenge the nineteenth century Victorian mansions. These new complexes served rich engineering and IT students, who treated the more historic Clifton like their playground and the residents like their servants. Expensive mountain bikes were chained up in front of one of the apartment buildings, beside which there was a new hookah bar whose window was fogged with flavored smoke from vaporized e-cigarette cartridges.

The blues and reds of police squad cars pulsed up the block, and the entrance to the tanning salon- laundromat was cordoned off with yellow police barrier tape. A dead black man lay sprawled in a pool of his own blood, surrounded by homicide detectives and EMTs. The helicopter from the top of the UC Medical Center tore through the foggy air and headed our way.

I'd heard that the trauma center at the hospital served as the training ground for surgeons preparing to deploy to Iraq and Afghanistan to deal with the war-wounded. Cincinnati's ghettos gave them an apparently endless supply of bodies to practice on.

It was weird how the three communities lived side-by-side, and never really intersected. The hipsters and bohemians ignored the privileged college students, and both ignored the ghetto dwellers passing through Clifton in their old hoopties and LTDs with dark tint and candy-paint jobs and spinning Dayton rims. I guess all three groups ignored a fourth group, the vets and the hospital staff employed to keep our crazy asses from committing suicide or otherwise imploding in a public and inappropriate way. If that happened, it might remind people that we and war still existed.

I passed the exit of the laundromat-tanning salon. There were two cop cars staggered in a herringbones formation, like the one we were taught to use in Iraq for certain rallying maneuvers. A lot of guys in the Army thought they would become cops when they got out, but apparently it was harder to go from "green to blue" than they thought. I'm pretty sure those doing the hiring wouldn't come right out and say it, but they probably thought we were damaged goods.

Most of the VA parking lot was empty, but there was some night construction going on. Vapor lamps with the power of kliegs lit the pit where men in hardhats worked, making the area look like some strange lunar excavation. I walked toward the emergency entrance, and saw a man with one leg sitting in a Rascal mobility scooter and smoking beneath the Mylar shell. He held an oxygen tank in the hand not clutching the cigarette. There was a sign posted saying patients with oxygen tanks were not allowed in the smoking area, but I didn't think anyone was going to try to stop him.

I walked into the VA hospital through the emergency entrance, passed a glass case display dedicated to the achievements of women in the military through the ages. There was an exhibit on Louisa May Alcott, and another dedicated to women who fought in drag during the Civil War, passing themselves off as men. Both the Patriot Café and Patriot Store were closed. The framed photos of President Barack Obama and the Honorable Robert McDonald, the Secretary of Veterans Affairs, looked down at me as I made my way to the bank of elevators.

I pressed the "Up" button and waited. I stared down the hall, toward the pharmacy and its empty waiting room, and the automated machine that dispensed numbers to the waiting veterans during normal hours. The elevator came and I got on. I pressed the "8" button and waited again.

I whistled to myself, and thought of my mother's words. "What fresh hell awaits me, Lord?"

The elevator opened on the eighth floor. I walked down the hall, and waved my CAC card attached to my lanyard over the sensor granting access to the closed ward. Hasford stood in front of the sliding glass partition fronting the nurse's station, like always.

His cervical collar was removed, and a raised mass of scar tissue rose from the side of his neck. "Good news."

"What's that?"

He pointed down the hall, toward where the partition curtain was yesterday. It was gone. "Quarantine lifted. I want you to focus exclusively on Thigpen tonight."

I went into the changing room, got into scrubs. I put on my latex gloves, but didn't bother with the extra precautions of the robe or mask. I walked back over to my supervisor. He said, "Thigpen's getting the VIP treatment tonight."

"Is it his birthday or something?"

He didn't laugh or smile. "He seized during the last shift."

"You want me to note aural data on the narrative report?"

Hasford shook his head. "Nah, he's well past the two-hour window. You might want to read what the day nurse wrote on the chart about somatic, auditory, and visual warnings."

"Anything else?"

"Yeah, the attending physician says he doesn't have DVT, but he's getting there. He thought the stockings Thigpen had on were too tight, so you need to milk his legs and then measure him. Then write the measurements on his chart."

"What if I see or feel a clot?"

"Stop milking immediately, note it on the narrative. Measure him regardless of what you find out."

"Did he lose anymore toes?" I winced from how offhand my words sounded. I always despised insensitive nursing staff, people who'd grown fatted like ticks on death and lost the ability to feel sympathy because it made things easier for them.

Hasford was unfazed. "Nope. He's still got three piggies going to market on the right foot, and five on the other."

I thought gangrene was more of a World War One thing, but it wasn't mine to reason why. I walked down the hall. I'd been doing this long enough already to sidestep the ectoplasmic trail left on the ground, moving with the mincing step of someone who was superstitious navigating the cracks in a sidewalk.

The lights were off in the room, and I turned them on. I walked over to my patient. I felt especially weak, as if I'd just given blood.

"I think I'm getting Alzheimer's." Thigpen covered his eyes with the backs of his bony, ashen hands.

"What makes you say that?" I pulled the blanket off his legs and draped it over the padded metal railing of his bed. I didn't see any bruises on his body, which meant the bath towels and pillows had done their job when he seized.

"I can't think. I can't even remember my wife's name."

I walked around the bed, removed the antiembolism stocking from his left leg. The material whispered as I pulled the cloth off. "It's called the postictal period. It lasts for about twenty-four hours after you seize." I wadded the stocking into a ball. "You don't have Alzheimer's. You'll be good as new in no time."

I walked over to his other leg, removed the stocking. It gave as easily the skin on a shedding snake. I ignored the portions of his right foot that were missing.

"Want to know how I got gangrene?" Thigpen removed his bony hands from over his tired eyes, and smiled at me like he'd just managed to homebrew something better than Gilbey's.

"If you want to tell me, that's your right. You also have a right to privacy."

"I ain't gonna tell you. I'm gonna show you."

That color-rich Kodak vision appeared before me, the fronds of the Vietnamese palms bright as the scales on jade dragons. Nha Trang wasn't the world, but it wasn't Vietnam, neither. I owed that yellow soul brother my life, since he saved it by shitting on that sharpened stick that went through my foot and got me out of the bush and into this new REMF supply unit.

I couldn't believe what I was seeing, or feeling. Someone opened the door on one of those Quonset huts and I got hit with a blast of air-conditioning that felt like the breeze from a cooler filled with Pabst Blue Ribbon. The streets were paved with macadam, or some kind of hard-packed shells from the Vietnamese shoreline. They might as well have been paved with gold, the way they felt underfoot after being in the bush for so long.

I pulled my tiger-striped boonie low over my eyes, happy for the attention it got me. I was part of something elite, not a lemon-lame line unit. At least, I had been part of a wild outfit up until this moment. Now I was going to sit my black ass in the rear with the gear. I was going to do it with a soul patrol, too, not a mixed outfit. Someone hipped Uncle Sam that there would be less fragging if Blood stayed with Blood, and we were allowed to pick our own hooches now. That meant I was heading toward Blackstone Mau-Mau, the black quartermaster's tent next to the basketball court.

I saw the Stars and Bars flying over Peckerwood Central, but didn't let it slow my roll. I thought about what Claude Brown said in *Manchild in the Promised Land*, that even grey cats who thought they was white negroes couldn't say "baby" the way a black man could. Even if one of the 'woods was watching me ditty-bop down the paved macadam, he wouldn't be able to copy my walk verbatim, no sir.

I spotted the Garvey flag, the two crossed spears on the shield surrounded by a wreath with the tricolors behind that. That flag meant war if the 'woods wanted it, but peace if they were smart enough to leave the black man alone.

"Hey, shit bird." A white full-bird colonel in the passenger side of a jeep addressed yours truly. His driver was a peckerwood with a uniform too starched to ever have so much as touched a blade of grass. "Yes, sir," I said, thinking *Die, you fucking pig.*

"You don't salute your superiors?" The bird raised himself up to his full height, which wasn't much.

"Sorry sir." I shot him a crisp salute, anything to get him out of my face so's I could get on with my day and get in where I fit in. "I been in the bush. You know they don't like us to salute, 'cause it draws sniper fire, sir."

His look relaxed. Sometimes even white men would give a Blood pass if he had that fighting spirit. "You're in Camp Cupcake now, soldier." He smiled, and his face reddened. It sickened me to do it, but I smiled back. I would rather him be mean to me than try to be my friend. It was as if he expected me to break out in song at any moment. "The worst thing you've got to worry about is sunburn at Camp Cupcake. And you coloreds won't have that problem."

"No, sir." I said, smiled. I thought about that mimeo'd poem from the Harlem cat, about rape, and I imagined raping that full bird's daughter in front of him while I saluted and smiled. The colonel settled into his seat, and motioned for his driver to carry on.

"I-

The vision of Vietnam dissolved. I left it against my will. "What the hell," I said.

Thigpen laughed weakly. "Boy, you remind me of Esau out the Bible."

I blinked rapidly, wondering why I was pulled from the vision when I wanted to follow it. I wanted to see what happened when young Thigpen finally made it to the black quartermaster's Quonset.

"I didn't know you were religious," I said, wadding the two balled antiembolism stockings up and depositing them in a wastebasket operated by a foot treadle.

"I ain't, but Ida is. It ain't like I can just get up and walk away when she's pouring that white man's religion into my ears while I lay here."

"Esau sold his birthright, or something like that. Right, for a bowl of soup?"

He pointed a weak finger toward me, and his hand dropped. "You got it."

"You think I did that?"

"You did something." He shrugged. "Something to make you lose your power."

Panic shot through my body, because I knew he was right. I stifled my fear. A squeaking sound came from my six, and I turned to see a new janitor working his mop obstinately over the ectoplasm in the hallway.

I massaged Thigpen's legs. I moved upward, toward his heart in wavelike motions. "The fuck you doing?" He glanced down at me, his chin on his sternum. "You getting a little too familiar for my taste."

"Doctor's orders. It's called sequential compression therapy. It's totally safe. It will keep you from getting deep vein thrombosis." I released my hold as I got to the tops of his legs with my stroke. We had been taught not to stroke back and forth, as it would undermine venous return. "Your life's in expert hands," I said, which wasn't a total lie. "You don't want to know what deep vein thrombosis feels like."

"Oh, you had it?"

"No, but I knew guy in Iraq who sat cramped in a Humvee too long with his legs folded under him. It killed him. You can even pass out if you lock your knees when standing at the position of attention for too long."

"Sorry to hear that." I couldn't tell if he was being sarcastic or not.

"I need you to do something for me," I said.

Thigpen glanced down at me, shock written across his face. "While you doing that?"

"No. The next time you get up to empty your colostomy bag, I want you to walk around for five minutes or so. That will help empty the femoral vein and prevent blood pooling and clotting. You got it?"

"Alright. Now I want you to do something for me."

"I am doing something for you." I nodded at his legs, which I was deep massaging. I felt no clots thus far.

Hasford knocked on the door, interrupting us. I looked up, took my hands off Thigpen's legs. "Yes sir?"

He handed me a tape measure. "Thank you," I said, and looked back at Thigpen. Claude Thigpen waited until Hasford was out of the room before speaking again. Then he said, "Whatever you did last night, I need you to cut that shit out. You hear me?"

It felt strange to let myself be talked down to by the elderly man, but his tone had me nodding as if it was a reflex and he was my parent issuing a stern warning. Maybe I was eager to agree, because secretly I felt ashamed for giving in to the mirage of Claudine or whatever it was. I planned to talk to Tamika about it after this shift.

"Done," I said, and stopped massaging.

"You need to preserve your juices for Arlington."

"That's right," I said. "I almost forgot." I wasn't looking forward to the case of jetlag I was going to get from going to D.C. "Can't say I'm looking forward to it." I extended the measuring tape and placed the distal end under Thigpen's thigh at the gluteal furrow.

He squirmed. "That shit's cold."

"You want me to warm it up for you?"

"Nah, I just wasn't ready for it is all. You ever read *The Autobiography of Malcolm X, as told to Alex Haley*?"

"Yeah."

"Did you dig it?"

I nodded and gave him a short summary. "He started out as Detroit Red, hustling and selling drugs and pimping and burning his hair with lye. From there he became a bean pie slinger like Captain Bowtie."

"Captain Bowtie?"

"Farrakhan."

He chuckled. "Some people say he helped kill Brother Malcolm."

"I've heard that," I said. "I think from John Henrik."

He squirmed again, although this time not from the coldness of the metal end of the measuring tape. "You're kind of conscious for a grey cat."

I ignored him, wrote my actions, name, and time on the chart. I also wrote the correct sleeve size for whoever relieved me and would put on his next set of antiembolism stockings. "Malcolm gave up the Nation of Islam and converted to Sunni, I believe. He made the Hajj and stopped hating white people."

"Yeah," Thigpen said. "That's when Brother Malcolm lost me."

"It's also when they killed him."

He shot up in bed, galvanized as if he'd just been defibrillated with one too many joules. "You keep your hands off Tamika!"

"I will, "I said, "but I plan on talking to her."

"You know how you win a war?" Thigpen asked, apropos of nothing.

"Read a lot of Sun Tzu and Von Clausewitz?" I wasn't too interested in the question, or the answer. If life was a war, then I had lost. I also frankly didn't care that I'd been defeated, which made me doubly pathetic.

"You have more babies than the enemy." He stared at the stucco ceiling and spoke to it. "It was already mixed babies when I got to Vietnam. I went to Khanh Hoi and you could see the babies left behind by the Senegalese troops who got it on with the girls there during the Franco-Vietminh War."

If my sperm was in fact ectoplasm, I wondered what my progeny would look like, if I were able to find a willing female and I managed to get it up. I glanced down at the man before me, wondered why I helped him if he hated me so much. The only answer I came up with was that it was my job. I would go to Arlington for him, too. I wanted him to get him out of my head, and to stay out.

"Shit," he hissed. "I miss chitterlings and Cambodian pussy."

I walked to the front of the room, and turned the light off. "Your days of sowing wild oats are over, I think. If you get your hands on any more genuine soul food, you can kiss the rest of your toes goodbye, too."

"It's worth it," he said, weakly. I found it hard to argue with him. War, heroin, women, chitterlings- something eventually killed us all.

* * *

The poor bastard caught me on my way home from work, walking in the rain. "Joe!" I looked over my shoulder. I had ducked him at the bus stop, but now it was too late. I tried to remember his name. "Brook?"

"Yeah, man." He extended his hand and I shook as we walked in the rain. He wore an Army field jacket. I guessed he'd never been in the service, and that he'd gotten it from a surplus store. It was covered with an inordinate number of unit patches sewn indiscriminately all over the coat. There was everything from the Indian head of the Second Infantry Division to the Screaming Eagle of the 101st Airborne.

"How've you been?"

"Good," I said. "You?"

He reached in his pocket, pulled out a plastic strip. "I'm on Suboxone, but I don't think it's working. I've got to wait for it to wear off before I cop. I won't get the effect if I try to shoot while it's still in my system."

We walked past the tanning salon-laundromat, where the crime scene had apparently been scrubbed in the last eight hours. It was impossible now to tell that someone was murdered here a little while ago.

Brook sniffled. "You seen Max?"

I shook my head. "I ran into his mom when I was inpatient back there." I nodded toward the red brick tower that was the VA.

"Yeah, she's retired. She gets bored and still goes to work with 'her boys.'" He reached in his pocket for a pack of cigarettes and lit a Marlboro with a shaking hand. "So, you were in the Army?"

I nodded. He pulled on his patch-covered jacket. "I wasn't. This is just something I wear."

"They make good equipment." I thought the new digitized ACU Gore-Tex jackets were better, but I doubted there were many of those in the surplus stores yet.

"We should get the band back together again." Brook laughed. I thought about all four of us together, nearly twenty years ago. I remembered how Max liked punk music a lot more than me, and our lead singer Burt liked heavy metal. Brook liked funk. We were a weird mix, at cross-purposes and different levels of talent and dedication.

We had band practice in Max's parents' basement. Brook would slap his bass like a white, twelve-year-old wannabe Bootsy Collins, while Max scraped out simple chord and harmonic progressions. Meanwhile Burt roared inscrutable, Cannibal Corpse-caliber lyrics. I struggled as the drummer to keep time with three very distinct and different personalities. I was never the greatest on the drums, and I got lost in the sauce. They eventually sacked me and replaced me. They recorded one demo, and then disbanded.

We stayed friends for a few years. The first time I smoked weed was with them in Burnett Woods, the same park across the street from my present apartment. We all got arrested together for running around in the United Jewish Cemetery in Clifton, and we got busted by the same cop for throwing snowballs at the Metro bus when school was cancelled one day due to heavy snow.

I'd tried to get into the music Max liked, but I could only pretend for so long. I got an Operation Ivy shirt even though I'd never heard the band, and I could even listen to mainstream punk groups like The Ramones or The Misfits without having to pretend to like it. But I quickly got bored with the underground stuff. I remember going home and tearing my Operation Ivy shirt to shreds one day after Brook and Max called me a poseur and sang Television Personalities' *Part-Time Punks* to mock me.

I also tried to get into the music that Burt listened to, but it was even worse. I hated bands like Morbid Angel and Deicide, whose album covers had titles written in inscrutable font. The singers always growled and couldn't be understood without a lyrics booklet handy.

Brook suddenly stopped, looked queasy, turned up the collar of his jacket. "You think I could borrow like five bucks?"

I reached into my back pocket, opened it, and dug into my wallet without taking the billfold out. I had a couple hundred bucks in twenties in my back pocket, and I didn't want Brook to see it. I dug a twenty out, the smallest denomination I had. His eyes went wide and his mouth opened when he saw the Andrew Jackson.

He nodded toward the laundromat. "I can break it and get four fives."

I shook my head. "It's cool, man." I tried to smile. "Just let me know when you want to put the band back together again for a reunion."

He squeezed my right shoulder with a shaking hand. "You were always cool in old Brook's book." I thought about mentioning that it wasn't true, that he called me a poseur and kicked me out of the band. As bad as things were for me right now, though, I knew they were even worse for him, and I didn't feel like guilt-tripping him at the moment.

"Peace." He puffed his cigarette, took the twenty, and turned on his heel in the other direction. I wondered how people found their first heroin connection. I wouldn't know where to look, if my brother wasn't an ex-addict.

I continued walking down Ludlow, more than a little shaken by the impromptu reunion, hating that I had to live and work in a place filled with so many memories. It didn't matter whether they were good or bad, since the good ones hurts as bad as the bad ones, or maybe even worse.

There was a psychedelic-painted Volkswagen Transporter parked in front of my apartment building, and a white guy with dreadlocks carrying a cardboard box. He wore a Rasta Baja that was unzipped and revealed a t-shirt patterned with a falling cascade of weed leaves. I pegged him as a "trustafarian," an upper-middle class white kid pretending to be a Rasta man, and maybe even teaching a few seasonal courses at the Naropa Institute in Boulder on horticulture. Now *there* was a poseur. Still, that was a nice panel truck.

I got closer to the VW and admired the paintjob. There were colorful paisleys and amoebas, dye swirls surrounding an airbrushed painting of Bob Marley smiling the same smile of contentment that Buddha and Gandhi wore, as if he'd found the secret and wasn't going to lose it anytime soon.

"Hey, Joey." Tamika held the door to the shop open for the white Rass, and smiled at me. I shifted my weight from foot to foot.

"Can we talk?"

"Yeah, just let me handle a little inventory." She wore a crocheted lavender head wrap that wasn't meant for rainy weather. The pile on her head was somewhere between the sizes of the ones worn by Nina Simone and Erykah Badu. I stayed outside and watched as Tamika and the Rasta man settled accounts. He left the cardboard box on the glass counter and walked out of the store, and past me. I almost thought of saying "One love," but held my tongue. He got in the Transporter and started it up.

Tamika said, "You can come in for a minute. I'm not open for a few more hours, but we can politick. What's up?"

I walked inside, closed the door behind me, and the bell above the door rang. "Who was that?" I asked. I thought I sounded like a jealous boyfriend. "Sorry. It's none of my business."

"That?" She opened a Band-Aid tin and pulled out a joint wrapped as tightly as a mummy. "That was Jason." She looked at the joint. "Do you mind?"

I shook my head. Tamika took out a long-stemmed lighter and sparked the joint. She sucked in a volume of smoke and held the joint out to me. She spoke with the smoke still chambered in her lungs. "You want a hit?" I shook my head. She blew the smoke away from me, walked over to a sandalwood incense holder and lit a patchouli stick with that same long-stemmed lighter. Then she walked over to the stereo in the corner of the room and turned it on. An old Deep Forest album started.

"Sorry," she said, and pointed the lit end of the joint toward the front door. I could see the VW pulling out through the glass. "His name's not Jason, anymore. It's 'Jah Son.'" She laughed and coughed, made a fist and gave herself one CPR jab to the sternum to clear the phlegm from her throat. She was still sexy, or even sexier, when she was smoking like a pro.

She opened one of the boxes Jah Son brought her. "I don't mind when white guys are Rass, but I hate it when they get more Rass than thou. It's like with hip-hop. A white guy's always got to know about the most underground, next level shit just to prove his bona fides."

Tamika pulled brown paper-wrapped glass pieces from the box and set them on the counter. "I can't front on him, though. Jason blows the best glass and the price is always right. He's mellow about business, always does consignment." She continued to pull the pieces out of the brown box, and spoke without looking up at me. "What did you want to talk about?"

"I think I lost my power, or at least some of it."

That got her interest, and she stopped pulling the pieces out of the box. She continued smoking, though. Tamika searched around for an ashtray. "What makes you say that?" She grabbed a carved statue of Legba, the African God. He held a plate in his hands. She set him down on the counter and ashed into the gold platter shaped like the offertory plate at my old Catholic school.

"I tried to do what you said, harness the power. It worked the first time, but tonight things didn't go as smoothly."

She squinted, and I wasn't sure if it was from the harshness of the smoke or from the force of thinking hard. "What changed between last time and when you tried to harness your gift last night?"

I paused. I didn't want to tell her. I blushed. She said, "You know, that's one reason I'd never want to be white."

"Why?"

"Blushing. It's like you carry your emotions in your skin. I don't know how white boys keep winning those World Series of Poker tournaments."

I laughed.

"You said you wanted to talk," she said. "Now you don't want to talk."

"I want to tell you, but it's embarrassing."

She pointed toward the beaded curtain separating the front of the store from the back. "I do palm readings for customers. I read lifelines. I listen to their life stories. I help a lot more than a psychiatrist, and I do it for a lot cheaper."

"My dad's a psychiatrist."

"Behaviorist?"

I shook my head. "Freudian."

"It's worse than I thought." She tugged on her joint and blew smoke out through her nostrils. "Try me," she said. "I'm good at keeping secrets."

"I've got this German tutor, she helped me when I was at UC." Tamika nodded. "We were just friends. It was low-pressure, platonic. It was perfect for both of us. We went out to eat, worked on homework together in the coffee shops, took long walks together."

"You never had sex?"

"Nope."

"Okay." Tamika's joint went out, and she relit it with the long-necked lighter. "Go on."

"Last night, she shows up out of the blue. The last time I saw her, she was about ready to marry her *Verlobter*. Now she says she left him, rips my pants off, and gives me head on the floor of my apartment."

"Doesn't seem like something she would do, does it?" Tamika's joint was down to a roach. Her long lacquered nails were sharp and served as a makeshift roach clip.

"No, it doesn't."

"It wasn't her," Tamika said.

"Well, I don't think it was anybody."

That confused her. "What do you mean?"

"She didn't leave my apartment. She just disappeared. But I think it wasn't a dream."

Tamika removed her damp head wrap, revealing her braids tipped in dentalium. "It wasn't your tutor, and it wasn't a dream."

"I don't know. I take Ambien. Weird shit happens on Ambien."

"It was a succubus."

"Do you have any books about that?"

She shook her head. "You can get ancient, historical texts on succubae. If you go online looking for books, you're just going to get a lot of second-rate erotica." I thought my own erotic experience was first-rate, but I didn't want to share the details. I had a rich fantasy life, and the irony was that I went deeper into my mind when I was having sex with someone than when I was alone and had nothing but my mind and my hand.

"It sapped your psychic energy," Tamika said.

"It?" I could be pretty progressive and open-minded, but I didn't like the idea that I had sexual contact with something whose gender I didn't know. I didn't even know "its" species.

"A succubus is a female spirit that drains a man's potency, either sexual or creative."

Great. "Who would do this to me, and why?"

Tamika gave up on the roach and ground it out in the golden tray that Papa Legba held. "Someone who's trying to stop you from accomplishing your mission, whatever goal you set for yourself."

I thought about that. I wasn't important enough to have enemies or be on the radar of anyone worth a damn. *Who the hell would try to*

stop me from going to Arlington and taking a piss on the grave of a dead,
racist white man, in order to appease a dying, racist black man? Maybe the
culprit was a groundskeeper at Arlington who took especial pride in his
work.

"I don't know," I said.

Tamika walked over to the patchouli stick burning in the
sandalwood holder. She removed it from the holder and carried it
around like an Olympic torch, trying to mask the smell of the pot
smoke.

"Cops want to close my shop, because of the pipes. If I got rid of
those, I could get rid of a lot of hassles. I'd also get rid of a lot of my
business."

"Yeah, I'm pretty sure frat boys wouldn't walk down here to buy
The Conspiracy to destroy Black Boys. That's not on an Economics
syllabus."

She giggled, waving the incense stick in the air. "The most
important question isn't who's doing this to you, or why."

"What's the most important question?"

She walked the incense stick back over to the holder, satisfied that
she'd successfully masked the smell of the weed. "The main question
is how to get your power back."

"Okay, let's say I ask you that question. How would you answer
it?"

"If I didn't really care for you, I'd tell you to buy one of these." She
walked across the room, to a carousel where little crystals hung from
hemp pendants dangling on wooden hooks.

"What are those?"

"Cayce crystals." She spun the carousel and walked away from it,
back behind the counter. She folded back the flaps of the cardboard
box and continued pulling out the rest of the merchandise Jah Son
had brought in the Mystery Mobile. "They're for healing, aiding in
successful child birth, and telekinesis."

"Do they work?"

She shook her head. "They're for novelty purposes only. I think
Cayce was like Madame Blavatsky or Uri Geller. He was a fraud.
Cayce crystals are about as real as spirit photography." I didn't even

know what that was, but it sounded fake.

"So what works, then?"

"First, if and when that succubus posing as your old girlfriend shows up-"

"Tutor," I said, interrupting her. I don't know why, but I felt the need to stress the platonic nature of our relationship.

"Tutor," Tamika said, and walked over to the wooden shelf where the stereo system sat. She picked up a small tube of Visine and squirted drops in her eyes. I didn't think her eyes were bloodshot, but it was her business. "If your tutor tries to suck your cock again, don't let her."

"Sperm didn't come out. It was that weird ectoplasmic stuff that I found on the floor at the VA."

"Now you know what she's after."

"You mean 'it'?"

"Or he," she said, and I got queasy again.

"Okay. Is that it? Just turn down a blowjob and I can have my power back?"

She chortled, and the laughter brought out that sexy little mannerism about her that I liked. She licked her already-glossy lips and made them wetter. "No, you also take this." She reached inside her Dashiki and handed me a necklace that truncated in a small burlap pouch, which smelled of herbs and spices.

I took it and put it over my neck. It was warm from where it had nestled against her skin. She told me what it was before I could ask. "It's a Tituba sack. Do you know who Tituba was?"

I nodded. "We read *The Crucible* in high-school."

"Nobody knows Tituba's ethnicity for certain. Some of the Puritans thought she was an Indian."

"Like West Indies Indian?"

"Tituba said she made a witch cake for her mistress in Barbados in her deposition to the witch finders. It's possible that she was West Indian, but no. I think they thought she was Native American."

"What do you think?"

"Tituba's a Yoruba name. I think she was a sister."

"Like you?"

"For all I know I might be a reincarnation of her."

"Sounds like you've been taking Ambien."

"You don't believe in reincarnation?"

"About as much as I believe in transubstantiation."

"That's right," she said. "You were raised Catholic." She walked the Visine back over to the shelf.

"I went to Catholic school," I said. "My mom was Protestant and my dad was Jewish."

"What does that make you?"

I shrugged. "Nothing."

"Nobody's nothing."

That elicited another shrug. "I'm about as close to nothing as you can be while still breathing."

She pointed one of her long fingernails at the sack around my throat. "Sleep with that around your neck tonight. Don't take any wooden nickels from any succubae, then try to tune into that special frequency you've got going for yourself again."

"Will do." I wanted to stay in her shop all day talking about Catholicism, witchcraft, and about everything else. I was tired from my last shift, though. My arms also still hurt from massaging Thigpen's legs. If I could work in an appointment with my shiatsu foot goddess before making the flight to D.C., it would definitely help with the pain.

I walked toward the door, opened it, and the bell chimed. "Make sure you report back to me," she said. "You're an interesting case. I mean, you're an interesting person."

"You, too." I smiled, yawned, and walked out into the misty morning. I stopped at the *Free Times* kiosk, opened the face of the rubber newsstand, and took out the top fish wrap. I held the local newspaper under my right arm and inserted my key in the door of the apartment building. I trudged up the wooden stairs. Tiffany was attuned to the sound of my footsteps, and started barking.

I ran the rest of the way, despite my exhaustion. I didn't want to risk waking my neighbors with her barking. Not everyone kept my hours. I opened my door and scooped Tiff up in the arm not carrying the paper. She sniffed me. Then she pressed her cold, black snout against my chest, and smelled the Tituba pouch curiously.

I walked into my bedroom, took my shirt and pants off, and lay in bed reading the *Free Times* for a moment. The main story was an article about police brutality, headlined *Clifton Cops out of Control*. The irony was that the victim of brutality was a childhood bully who terrorized me, named Jason Ramundo.

His family was what my buddy and ex-bandmate Max once called "gaslight rich." His parents owned a pizzeria, a few properties, and an upscale tailoring shop. Jason had been in and out of trouble with the law since a young age. He always had the best hydro weed when we were younger, but he liked to shoot me with his bb guns. According to the story, his girlfriend went to a local bar with another guy, and Jason got word somehow and went up there to confront them both with a pistol. Only he wasn't a kid selling weed anymore, but rather an adult selling and doing blow. That meant the gun he had this time didn't shoot BBs.

The cops showed up, and a confused melee took place in a crowded roomful of drunks. Both police officers hit Jason with their stun guns, and he'd died of cardiac arrest. Toxicology reports showed he had cocaine and marijuana in his system at the time of death. Every witness who spoke said he had a gun in his hand, but this was a free newspaper. That meant they were going to call it police brutality rather than cause and effect.

I threw the paper to the floor, and accommodated Tiff as she hopped up onto my lap. I was shirtless. There was now no barrier between the dog and the new smells, and she licked the little Tituba bag's burlap. I hoped the pouch was doggy-safe, and also that it would give me my mojo back.

I closed my eyes, cracked my knuckles once, and breathed deeply with the dog lying on my chest. I felt bad for Jason who died at the bar, Jah Son the Trustafarian, and Brook the bassist. Last but not least, I also felt sorry for myself.

CHAPTER ELEVEN: GAMESMANSHIP AND THE ASTRAL EDGE OVER THE HOUSE

The Tituba sack must have had some secondary aphrodisiac powers, because I had morning wood for the first time in a long while. I pulled the comforter off myself and hobbled with my erection to the bathroom and took a leak. Claude Thigpen spoke in my ear, as if his voice came through a cochlear implant.

"Today's a big day for you."

"Oh?" I flushed the toilet and washed my hands, dried them on the bath towel hanging from the shower curtain. "You going to get me the money to go to D.C.?" It was a Friday afternoon, and I had off until Monday.

"Yes, I am."

I walked back into the bedroom, into the kitchen. I gave Tiff a can of Caesar wet dog food. My vet told me I was overfeeding her, but she didn't look fat. I opened the fridge, took out a carton of orange juice, and drank until it was empty. "How are we going to get the money, exactly?"

I dropped the empty carton in the trashcan and grabbed Tiffany's leash, slipping on my terrycloth slippers over my bare feet. "We're going to Belterra," Thigpen said.

Belterra was a casino in the suburbs, near the house where my father lived with his girlfriend, a fellow psychiatrist. It was about five minutes away from the place I shared with my brother when we lived together. It also wasn't far from the offices of my chiropractors. "I've never had much luck there."

I'd only been once or twice. There were no tables, no roulette wheels, just slot machines. I didn't see the appeal, despite having taken some 101 level courses on psychology and learning about

Skinner boxes and operant conditioning.

"You ain't gonna need luck with me in your corner. Speaking of luck, want to tell me what you got around your neck, and where you got it?"

"You know where I got it." I tugged the burlap. The sack gave off a musk that reminded me of catnip and jasmine. Tiff had not torn through it last night, thankfully.

"That some old hoodooing thing?"

"Something like that." I glanced down at my erection, tried to think of algebraic equations in an effort to get the thing to wilt. I wasn't going to go outside with my pajama bottoms on and risk my cock sprouting through the weak cotton fabric of the fly. "It looks like it's giving me my groove back."

I hooked Tiff with her leash, and did an old trick with my erection. I pulled my cock upward and cinched it with the elastic of my PJ bottoms, and covered those with the fabric of my untucked t-shirt.

Back when I was stationed at Fort Bliss, Texas, I'd attempted to drown my PTSD with heavy drinking and nights spent in strip clubs. I deliberately wore sweatpants to the clubs in order to make friction orgasms easier. At my lowest ebb, I went to a hole-in-the-wall in Juarez right across the Mexican border and got a lap dance in a "private booth" that consisted of chicken wire. My cock came free of my sweatpants (I wasn't wearing any boxers), and the stripper grinded her thong against my naked cock. I came and jets of semen shot onto the sawdust floor of the shack. Like I said, it was my low point.

I walked down the stairs with the dog in tow, yawning and scratching my chest. We headed outside. "You know," I said, to Thigpen, "I don't know much about what comes after this life, but do you really want your last act on Earth to be this petty vengeance? I've heard that your state of mind when you die determines where you end up, on the next grind of the Wheel of Life or whatever it is."

Some Indian students from the university passed me on the sidewalk, heading into Tamika's shop. I gripped the charm in my right hand, and pressed the crosswalk button. Thigpen said, "My grandpa told me about this ex-slave who fought with the Fifty-Fourth in the

Civil War."

The "walk" light came on and I ran across the street with Tiff. My dick was limp now, and I subtly shifted my pajama bottoms so that my flaccid cock dropped into my trousers. No one was the wiser. Thigpen said, "This slave died in battle, but his soul haunted the battlefields and all the blue coats until they agreed to bury his body in West Africa."

"Why don't you worry about where you're going to be buried then, rather than pissing on some white man's grave?"

I walked Tiff over toward the naiad fountain, and she did her business. "You let me worry about my soul. You just take care of this last bit of business for me, and then I'll be out of your hair for good. You have my word, and my word is my bond."

"If you say so." I walked back across the street with the dog, and up the stairs. I didn't feel like kenneling Tiff for two days, so I poured her a giant mound of dry dogfood, and a large bowl of water. I blanketed the rooms in puppy pads, got together a rucksack filled with supplies to last me two days, and set my bugout bag by the front door.

I took a combat-speed shower, and spoke to Thigpen as the hot water splashed off the tile and fogged the grimy shower curtain. "Just don't ask me to go near Section Sixty."

"What's there?"

I turned the water off, and stepped out of the shower. "That's where the vets killed in Iraq and Afghanistan are buried. That's where my buddy Dunfy's buried. Sergeant Dunfy," I added.

He was a specialist when he died, but they promoted him when he got killed. That might seem stupid and pointless, but the death benefits paid out to families are based on the rank of the soldier in question. Thus, the promotion at time of death actually mattered.

"I ain't interested in young white cats," Thigpen spoke as if he was a big game hunter. "I want me a white man from the Jim Crow days. I don't want a white boy like you. I want a white man."

I unplugged my phone from the charger in the wall, coiled it in a ball, and placed the charger in my pocket. I dialed a cab for myself and gave the dispatcher my address. Then I grabbed my bag, leaned down to Tiffany, and kissed her on her gray and wiry head. "Bye, bye baby."

I hoisted my bag on my shoulders and left the apartment. I was excited to be heading to the casino and leaving town, for all of my initial reluctance to complete this mission. I walked downstairs, where Claudine was waiting for me.

She wore a peasant blouse frilled and ruffled like a nightgown. Her eyes, hair, and freckles were the same chestnut color. "Can we go upstairs to your apartment?"

"You're not Claudine."

"That's right," Thigpen whispered in my ear. A man balancing a floral arrangement walked by me, and I said, "Excuse me, sir."

He stopped, moved the flowers from his face. "Yes?"

I pointed at Claudine. "Do you see a woman there?"

He looked at the space where I pointed. "No. Did you get stood up or something?"

I looked back to the succubus. "No woman would turn down cunnilingus like you did, and few would be as eager to give head as you were. Goodbye."

I looked away from her, toward the cab pulling up to the curb. "Damn skippy," Thigpen said. "Fuck that cracker."

"Which cracker?"

I was confused. I thought the succubus was a sexless figment of my imagination. "Never mind," Thigpen said. "Time for you to *di di*." I thought about throwing my rucksack in the trunk, decided to keep it on my lap in the backseat. I opened the door and got in. I shifted my weight on the cigarette-burned upholstery, through which foam leaked. I leaned forward to the hack, who wore a leather Kangol hat and ruby-tinted specs. He glanced at me in the rearview. "What's your poison?"

"Belterra, *mo ricky-tick*."

He smiled, revealing a mouth filled with teeth yellow from cigar smoke. "My man. You had a uncle in Vietnam or something?"

"Yep."

That was the truth, too. My mother's brother was a medic in the Marine Corps. My father got a deferment and spent the Vietnam War as an Ivy Leaguer in med school. He was part of the Students for a Democratic Society and was a very vocal member of the antiwar movement. Despite all that, though, he respected my uncle with something verging on reverence, and once confided to me that he felt guilty for getting out of the war.

I'd asked my father, "You really thought the War was morally wrong, though, right?"

My father just shook his head. "If you were antiwar and poor or working class, you went to Vietnam. I didn't get out of the war because I was antiwar. I got out of the war because I was an upper-middle class kid."

My mother said my father actually tried to serve in the Medical Corps near the tail-end of the war, but my uncle called her from Saigon and said that, due to his involvement in the antiwar movement, my dad had a file that could choke a snake. The government was worried he wanted to join in order to monkey wrench the war effort.

"You gonna make some money?" The cabbie looked at me as he steered.

"Gonna try." I spoke to Thigpen, but figured the cabbie would assume the words were meant for him. "They're not going to let me bring a rucksack into the casino, so I'll keep the meter running while I'm in there."

The cabbie shot me another one of his trademark, yellow-toothed smiles. "You must be a high roller."

"I just got a good feeling about today." I gripped the Tituba sack as if it were my lucky rabbit's foot.

Uptown gave way to the ghetto, which led to the highway, and on into the suburbs. We drove through Mount Washington, where I had lived with my brother when he accidentally got a girl pregnant and made me an uncle.

Mount Washington had once been middle-class, but Section Eight vouchers brought the ghetto to the suburbs. White Flight left the area half-blighted, and half-tenanted by middle class families hanging on for dear life against the proliferation of spray paint and roving groups of boys on foot and low-rider bicycles. The kids brought traffic to a standstill by walking wherever they wanted and not bothering with crosswalks. The most expensive restaurant in the neighborhood was a Little Caesar's pizzeria, and the walkways and gazebos of the parks were littered with syringes and torn condoms. Cop cars were everywhere.

"This ain't shit," Thigpen said. "Go to the Southside of the Chi-Town if you want to see a real ghetto."

"No thank you."

"What?" The cabbie asked.

"Nothing."

We passed into the whiter suburb of Anderson Township, where there were churches and real estate agencies, expensive Thai and Indian eateries and big box department stores. Most of the cars on the road were piloted by trophy wives riding high in Land Rovers and Mercedes SUVs. The women were wearing hard, surgically-enhanced expressions and sunglasses.

I knew, beyond a shadow of a doubt, that I had fucked my life up. There were times that I would look at a beautiful, young trophy wife and think, *I should have devoted my life to getting money, from something like the age of twelve. I should have thought about nothing but money.* There was another part of me that sensed the lifestyle was somehow a trap, that marriage and wealth and outward success could be a lie that masked something suffocating, ugly, and permanent.

I might spend my life in pursuit of money, become a frustrated ball of repression from having to constantly compete and go through the social graces and rituals that the nouveau riche had to put up with. I'd do it until I was publicly powerful, but privately wearing women's clothes and spending the money I made on financial derivatives and hedge funds to pay some man to fuck my wife, because I'd been driven insane by the American status game.

The cabbie parked in the lot of Belterra, and the car jerked to a stop, bringing me out of my thoughts, thank God. "Okay," I said. "I'll leave the bag here." I spoke to Thigpen. "How long will this take?"

"Not long if you do what I tell you to do."

"I don't know how long this will take," the cabbie said. "You tell me."

"Not long," I said. I got out of the cab and walked toward the giant fortress of a casino. Its body was made of flimsy corrugated tin, and the shelter obscured the racetrack that was here before Cincinnatians voted to allow casinos in city limits to cover the school and museum tax levies.

The track once actually had a scruffy, beer-soaked charm. There had been an open-air grandstand that smelled of cigar smoke and horse stables. There had also been a clubhouse from which one could gaze out on the emerald greens and relax with a drink, while the compulsive gamblers squandered rent money on simulcast chariot and greyhound races broadcast on the TV monitors welded to the ceiling. That was a long time ago, though.

"Shit," I said, and reached in my pocket for one of Tiffany's dog poop bags.

"What?" Thigpen asked. "Don't go to pieces on me now."

"I'm having one of my OCD fits." I gripped the metal door handle at the main entrance of the casino with the dog poop bag over my hand, feeling germ-phobic at the worst possible time. I might get some weird looks while pulling the crank on a one-armed bandit, but I didn't think it was illegal to play the slots with a dog poop bag on one's hand.

Barry Manilow's voice came from the speakers, and I regretted that I sold my Walther to a pawnshop some months earlier. I'd always made a vow to myself that if life ever became unbearable, or the ass-fucking that Uncle Sam gave me proved too onerous a memory, I wouldn't conscript other people into my nightmare. I wouldn't shoot up a mall or a movie theater. I would shoot myself in the head and leave humanity in peace.

It occurred to me now that if I was going to go on a shooting spree, though, I might as well try a casino. I'd never heard of someone rampaging in a house of chance. I'd heard of people shooting up subway cars and churches, but never casinos.

The doormen didn't guess the nature of my thoughts, and both wore ill-fitting red sports jackets and earpieces. "ID?" The older and sadder-looking of the two asked me.

I pulled out my driver's license, handed it to him, and waited. "Thank you." He handed me the card back and I put it in my wallet. "Okay." I took a deep breath, looked out over the sea of slot machines. I scanned the glowing ocean of neon tubing, blinking lights, and the people hovering over the slots. There seemed to be as many oxygen tanks and Rascal mobility scooters here as at the VA. I guessed there were quite a few mamas using their social security disability to cop them a new pair of shoes, or perhaps some gourmet treats for the bichons and Siamese they left at home, their only friends in the world aside from video poker machines.

"Jesus, this is worse than the fucking VA," I said. "Congrats, sir. You have found the most depressing place on earth."

I looked around, trying to filter out the noise so I could better hear Thigpen's voice. There was a gaudy beauty to the place that could be enjoyed as long as I didn't think too hard about the blue rinse senior citizens and over-the-road truckers being bled on the gaming floor. I took in the various themes, the Greek gods and pirates with their chests filled with doubloons and parrots on their shoulders. I watched the fruit fall and the strobe of lights as jackpots paid out.

"Go stand over there," Thigpen said. I felt myself being drawn to a stool next to a woman with a bald spot, a fanny pack, and varicose veins exploding in fissures on her bare legs. She played a machine called *Brauhaus*. To her right was a man with a faded Woody Woodpecker tattoo on his liver-spotted hand, slapping the glowing "repeat bet" button for all it was worth.

"She's gonna play two more times, then you're going to step up to the plate."

"Okay."

The balding woman looked over her shoulder at me, then turned back to *Brauhaus*. German pretzels, Bier steins, and *Mädchen* wearing dirndls fell, but none of them fell in a winning pattern.

"Goddamn." The woman tried again, had no luck, and stood up from the machine. She held a troll doll with magenta hair and a matching gem lodged in its navel in her left hand, and a pack of Virginia Slims in her other hand. She smiled. The flesh of her face, wrinkled as gizzard meat, crinkled even more. "Smoke 'em if you got 'em."

I smiled back at her, and sat down on the warm stool. "Put a hundred bucks in the machine," Thigpen said.

"I've only got two-hundred in cash on me." I opened my wallet.

"Then put two-hundred in."

I shook my head, but did as I was told. I fed twenties into the machine's slot, until all ten of them had been devoured by *Brauhaus*. It was prettily designed, I thought. A German girl with ample cleavage, bunched like grapes from the strain of her corset, held out a foaming pitcher of dunkel brew to the player. There was a fachwerk village and cobblestone streets in the background behind her. I didn't miss the Army or Iraq, but I missed the hell out of Germany.

"Hit 'Max Bet'."

"You better know what the fuck you're doing." If I fucked this one up, I'd have to go to the ATM machine and get some cash for the cabbie. The meter was still running. I slapped the "Max Bet" button and waited.

A croaking sound came from my right, and the guy with the Woodie Woodpecker tattoo said, "I like to see a fella go all in on his first bet." The German curios and tchotchkes whirred and spun, and I asked the guy next to me, "What's the most one of these machines ever paid out?"

He nodded toward the back of the gaming hall. "Oh, a lady back there won a hundred grand earlier."

"Really?"

"Yeah, but it's a sickness." He pointed toward a banner draped above the vendor windows where casino employees in red vests and bowties paid out to the few winners. The banner was a black and white ad, featuring a man gripping his head in his hands. "Have a gambling problem? Get help now. Game responsibly." There was an 800-number listed below that. The dude next to me jerked his head back toward the rear of the casino, where the woman got her hundred grand payout earlier. "She'll feed the monkey until that hundred grand's gone. You watch."

The screen in front of me blinked and pulsed, and five Aryan blonde goddesses smiled at me with their hair in pigtails. "Congratulations! You've hit the Jackpot!" I watched the dollar amount scroll from two-hundred upwards until it was four digits, and my jaw dropped. The four digits became five.

I had won ten-thousand dollars. Thigpen's voice whispered in my ear. "Don't say I never did nothing for you."

"Holy shit." The array of buttons on the console before me glowed, offering everything from "Max Bet" to "Cash Out."

"Cash out," the man next to me whispered. "You don't know how lucky you are. Get out, before it bleeds you dry and sets you up for the big hurt."

"You better listen to that cracker," Thigpen said. I pressed the "Cash Out" button with my trembling, poo bag-covered hand. I expected a rush of coins or cash money. Instead, the dispenser shot out a receipt. I reached in the tray for the waxy sheet of paper. The man next to me nodded at the bag on my hand. "You got a Howard Hughes thing going there. Whatever brings you luck, I guess."

I stood up with my ticket and walked toward the two doormen in headsets and ill-fitting blazers. "Where do I take this?" I held it out to the younger of the two.

"Depends on the dollar amount. If it's below a certain amount, the machines over there." He glanced at the ticket, and his eyes widened. He stifled his reaction, regarded me now as if I were his pit boss, rather than some loser off the street. "Over there, sir." He pointed toward the windows below the Gambling Crisis Hotline ad.

"Thank you." I walked across the thin industrial carpet, which was patterned like a migrating army of Monarch butterflies. There were few big winners, which meant there was no wait for the line. The girl at the window behind the grates had a jeweled stud in her pale nose, a gothic pallor to her skin, and a slight gap in her teeth. I was happy that I had a ton of money in my hand to mask the insecurity and anxiety I always felt in the presence of attractive females.

"Hello, sir."

"Hello, ma'am."

She smiled at that. I handed her the ticket. "Wow!" She beamed. I think she was genuinely happy for me. "Congratulations."

I shivered. "I'm not used to winning."

"There's a lot of winners." She spoke in a half-whisper, as if her candor could get her fired. "They just don't know when to cash out." She handed me a form to fill out.

"I didn't know I had to do this." I signed my name, filled in the various fields.

"Yeah, it's for the IRS." I handed her the form back, and she counted my money out. I watched Ben Franklin upon Ben Franklin form a creamy stack. Butterflies flitted in my chest as the cash pile grew. I knew ten-thousand dollars didn't make a man rich, but it made me feel like a Rockefeller. I licked my lips like a savage animal and didn't try to hide my greed.

I spoke to Thigpen. "Can we do this more often?"

"It's a one-time deal," he said.

The cashier giggled. "I'm here whenever you are."

She handed me my ten-thousand dollars, and I slid a hundred off the top. She spoke in the same half-whisper she'd used before. "We're not allowed to accept tips."

"That's cool, because that's not a tip. It's a hundred I forgot."

She mouthed the words "Thank you," and the silver of her tongue ring glinted in the lights of the casino that reflected off the mirrored ceiling. I stuffed my money in my wallet, and walked past the two doormen. I headed toward the escalators, and passed a new Mercedes SL on display. The luxury car rotated on a pie-shaped pedestal, roped off behind velvet.

I took the stairs, too excited to wait for the escalator to get me where I was going. "Slow your roll," Thigpen said. "We'll get to D.C. with time to spare."

I slowed down, walked out into a bracing wind. I drank in the air through my nostrils. "How you like me now?" Thigpen asked. "It ain't gonna cost you ten grand to get to D.C. and back. Keep the change. You're welcome, motherfucker."

"Thank you." I opened the backdoor of the cab.

The cabbie looked up at me, furtively ground out his stogie in the ashtray. He looked as guilty as a kid caught masturbating. I quoted the woman who tried her luck at *Brauhaus* before me. "Smoke 'em if you got 'em."

He retrieved his stogie and lit it with a Seabee Zippo. "If you don't mind." He started the car. "Where to now?"

"CVG Airport, my friend."

"Sounds like you got some spring in your step. I'm guessing you broke the bank?" He smiled at me in the rearview mirror, cracked his window, and puffed his cigar.

"I did alright." I wasn't about to tell him that I was walking around with ten-thousand dollars cash in my pocket. I would tip a hundred over whatever the meter said, though, when we got to Cincinnati/Northern Kentucky International Airport.

I looked out my window as we drove on the highway. "You know," Thigpen said, "an interviewer once asked Miles Davis if he had one wish, what he would wish for."

"What did he wish for?"

"To get his hands around a white man's throat."

I smiled. I was safe, since I was destined to remain a white boy, no matter how old I got.

CHAPTER TWELVE: SULLY AND THIGPEN DO D.C. IN STYLE

My bankroll was depleted by nearly three-thousand dollars by the time I got settled in D.C. I bought a first-class redeye ticket on United for nearly a grand, sipping Disaronno Amaretto on the rocks and watching the terrain pass below me from the comfort of my window seat.

The seat next to me was empty on the flight. Thigpen went from voice in my ears to passenger, still wearing his hospital gown. The buttons of his robe were unsnapped to provide easy access for either his wife's comb or the shock paddles. I thought of something as we were touching down on the tarmac, just as the sun rose.

"I forgot to pack my meds."

"Can you hack it?"

"I can do it, but it's going to hurt." Clonazepam helped me feel as if I barely existed, which helped with the mental pain. I didn't like the tranquilizers and drugs that turned one into a shuffling zombie, but feeling as if I was only half-there made the days easier to endure. The Fluoxetine helped me see the glass as always half-full, and the Percocet helped me cope with the more literal pain.

The morning was muggy as we deplaned. I regretted drinking the amaretto, whose heavy chocolate liqueur swam inside of my otherwise empty gut. I bought a croissant and a scone from a Starbucks in Reagan National Airport and headed toward baggage claim to get my rucksack.

I touched my jaw, which was still aching from where I broke one of my teeth in half a few days ago. "Can you do something about my pain?"

"The fuck I look like?" Thigpen walked next to the conveyor belt running alongside the concourse shuttles that flowed from terminal to terminal. "I ain't Florence Nightingale."

There were advertisements for various hotels, eateries, and attractions in glowing posters running up and down the walls of the concourse. An ad for a hotel called Moonrise Georgetown caught my eye, and I decided to stay there.

I finished up my scone and croissant, fought the choking urge to vomit, and headed toward the baggage claim carousel. I snagged my rucksack, and then walked to an Enterprise agency. I asked for the most expensive vehicle they had, aside from the stretch limousine.

I paid almost another thousand dollars for a Cadillac Escalade fit for a drug kingpin or a foreign diplomat. The interior was all Corinthian leather and woodgrain. It was climate-controlled, with a sixteen speaker Bose surround sound audio system and power sunroof. I'd never been inside of a car so nice, let alone driven one.

Thigpen stretched out in the backseat, and I listened to an oldies satellite radio station. The Ronettes sang, "Be My Baby," and I sang along with them. I set the GPS course for the Moonrise, Georgetown.

"This is the life," Thigpen said. "It beats the hell out of a hospital bed."

"It beats my apartment." I turned left, as the female voice instructed. I hoped Tiffany was doing alright at home alone. My landlord might get a call if she barked too much, but this had to be done.

"Jesus." I looked at the city around me, thrown into relief by the rising sun. It had been years since I was in D.C- decades, actually- on a field trip with my elementary school. I still believed in all sorts of things at that point in my life, like my family and the future. I may have still even believed in America.

There were multiple quarries' worth of marble arranged in Second Empire and Greek Revival buildings spread out before us. There were churches and basilicas with stained glass windows, museums and government buildings with mansard roofs. I was in the heart of the Great American Karnak, the halls of power. I rode high in my SUV and took it all in as if I was on safari, with still more than seven-thousand dollars in cash in my pocket.

The Washington Monument was visible no matter where I drove. I went through a series of streets where the traffic was bumper to bumper for some time, but there was more than enough at the roadside to distract the eye. There was a parterre embroidered with daisies and azaleas. The white and red flowers were so bright in the sunlight I had to squint even though the windows of the Escalade were tinted. I could also smell the spring bouquet even though I had the windows rolled up.

"You wouldn't know it from looking out the window," Thigpen said. "But D.C.'s got some of the roughest ghettos in America."

The colorful, sunlit portions of the land were interspersed with shaded terraces and double rows of lindens that cast imposing shadows, on the other side of which were more orchards shimmering in full bloom.

"Quit trying to bring me down," I said.

The spirit of Thigpen sat up in the backseat. "Don't forget why you're here."

"I know why I'm here. Don't worry. I'm drinking plenty of fluids."

He laughed hoarsely. I activated the Bluetooth car kit nestled in the dashboard's console that glowed like a vintage jukebox. I silenced the GPS and activated the speaker feature of the SUV's built-in phone. "Moonrise, Georgetown."

"Moonrise, Georgetown Hotel. Is that correct?"

"It is."

The line rang. We passed the Iwo Jima Memorial, the six bronze soldiers struggling to raise that American flag on the sand. I didn't have much patriotism left in the tank.

"Moonrise Hotel," a receptionist said.

"Hi, I'd like a room for tonight, and I'll check out Sunday morning."

We were getting closer to the Washington Monument and Lincoln Memorial, and the polished granite of the Vietnam Veterans' Memorial. Thigpen sat up in his seat and pressed his hand to the window's glass. "Blood—"

The hotel clerk said, "All we have left is the handicapped suite. Would that be alright?"

"Sure, I'll pay cash." I glanced down at the muted GPS. "I'll be there in less than twenty minutes."

"That's fine, but you have to use a credit card for the deposit."

"Not a problem." I turned left.

"And your name, sir?"

"Joseph Sullivan."

I got trapped behind a government motorcade, flanked by two leather-clad cops on motorcycles with a team of black Suburbans moving in a tight formation. "Very good. See you soon, sir."

"End call," I said, and turned the GPS volume back on. I then turned up the oldies satellite radio station. Chuck Berry soloed his ass off, shredding hard enough to snap strings.

"I might take a trip to the Memorial," Thigpen said, and I knew which memorial he meant.

"You want me to drive you there?"

"Nah, I can go there on my own."

"Then why do you need me at Arlington?" I asked.

"I'm projecting, right now. I can see, but I can't touch. All I need to do at the Vet's Memorial is see the names of some Bloods I left in the bush. I need you to do something that requires a..."

"Corporeal presence?" I tried.

He snapped his fingers. "Exactly. You're cooking with butter now."

I pulled into the parking lot of the Moonrise and stopped in front of the valet's podium. The valet stepped back a few paces from the gunmetal behemoth I drove. I hopped down from the bucket seat, got out. I went into the back of the SUV, grabbing my rucksack.

"Self-parking is free," the valet said. "Our service is twenty dollars a day."

I went into my back pocket for my wallet, took out a hundred, and handed it to him. "There you go. Keep the change."

He snapped to attention like a private on the parade field. "Yes, sir!" He got into the car. The engine was still idling but was whisper-quiet.

"Slow your roll," Thigpen said. "Stop wiping your ass with money."

"When will I get another chance? Be real." I stepped through the automatic doors. "I think I'll have a beluga omelet this morning." I lugged my rucksack on my aching shoulders, my whole body pulsing from Percocet withdrawal. The clerk was an ebony bombshell with a box Mohawk and dyed red braids. I yearned to oil up her redbone ass cheeks, spread them, place my face between them, and then allow the round mounds to close around my head with a thunderous clap.

"Hello, sir."

Behind her was a massive photo negative from Georges Melies *Voyage Dans La Lune*, the moon cringing as a rocket ship landed in its left eye. "Hi, I just called. Sullivan, Joseph." I set my rucksack down and massaged my shoulders. I dug my wallet back out. Next I handed her my credit card, ID, and five one-hundred dollar bills.

"Keep spending like it grows on trees," Thigpen said. "See what that gets you."

"I need a hotel room. What do you want me to do? Pay with acorns?"

The amazon looked confused. "No, cash is fine. We just need the credit card for deposit purposes."

She slid me my room key and change. "Room 234."

I slid a twenty-dollar bill back towards her. "Tip," I said.

"At least it ain't a hundred this time," Thigpen said. "If anyone's got it coming, though, she deserves it more than that white boy out there parking cars."

"Thank you," she said, and tapped my keycard with an acrylic nail covered in Greek Comedy and Tragedy masks. "You need that to activate the elevator and to get to the rooftop bar."

I slid the keycard in one of the sleeves of my wallet. "I'll hang onto it," I said. I picked up my rucksack and walked toward the bank of elevators. Golden Age SF paperbacks were stored in glass cases, dusty jackets for A.E. Van Vogt's *Null A* series and Heinlein's *Starship Troopers*. There was a mobile on dangling wires hung above us that featured spacecraft from the old Buck Rogers and Flash Gordon serials, battling with flying saucers that looked like spray-painted hubcaps.

I pressed the "up" button on the elevator, and a maid in a black outfit with a white doily collar got out as I got on. I inserted my keycard in the slot, as instructed by the desk clerk, and pressed "two."

This elevator was a sight better than the one in the VA. The walls were mirrored, the ceiling Vitruvian marble speckled with gold flecks.

There was a golden handrail running around the four sides of the car. The bell dinged, the door opened, and I hopped off onto carpet too soft to register my footfalls even though I was wearing my heavy desert combat boots.

"Shit, I'm tired."

"We got business to take care of first. You can splash your face with water and have a cup of coffee, but we're at Arlington by thirteen-hundred hours or I'm taking your ass on another tour of Vietnam. If you think shit got hairy during Bell Telephone Hour, I can show you something that'll put your ass in the bughouse for good."

"I believe you." He was right, anyway. I never liked to have anything hanging over my head. If I took care of this, I could lay in my handicapped suite and spread out on the bed. I'd drink amaretto on the rocks while the AC blasted in the corner of the room, and I alternated between bites of prime rib and scoops of cold ice cream from my hot fudge sundae. First, I had to piss on the grave.

I slid the keycard in the door and turned the knob. The room was dark, the sun barely cracking through the heavy curtains bunched like an accordion over the window. I closed the door behind me, dropped my ruck, and plopped down on the bed. It was made of that space age memory foam I always saw advertised on TV but never thought I'd ever have the money to buy.

"This is the life. If I had those curtains and this bed, I wouldn't need Percocet." I stretched out, fanned my arms, and yawned. "I need coffee."

I walked over to the little darkened kitchenette, tore open one of the house blend packets, and set it in the Mr. Coffee's filter basket. I filled the pot with tap water and poured that into the top of the machine. Next I closed the top, and then turned the machine on.

The sound and smell of brewing coffee comforted me. I kept the lights off, turned the sink faucet on, and splashed my face. I glanced at my watch. I'd gotten a cab to the casino yesterday afternoon, and it was now about 11:30 a.m. I dried my face with a hotel towel and walked over to the menu card laid on the dresser next to the television.

I went to open the room service menu, and Thigpen said, "We eat when we get back."

He was no longer in his hospital gown, but instead he wore his green Class A Uniform. A blue braid of rope was over one shoulder. "I didn't know you were in the Infantry," I said.

"I suspect there's a lot you don't know, about me and about everything else, young buck." He stood at parade rest, as if ready for inspection and betting that not even Baron Von Steuben could gig him on any part of his uniform, down to the highly-polished golden buttons.

I remembered our drill sergeant at Benning shouting, "Why is the sky blue!"

"Because God loves the Infantry, Drill Sergeant!"

"What makes the green grass grow!"

"Blood, bright red blood!" If that was true, Iraq would be as green as Ireland.

I suddenly flashed back on my drill sergeant making us lay down just outside of his "kill zone" in the barracks with our backs on the ground and our heads barely lifted off the floor. Our necks were sore and aflame after ten minutes of holding this position, massive knots forming in our occipital lobes. The cords rippled on our necks, until I was sure the veins would snap and we would all bleed to death.

The drill sergeant had shown us the video of insurgents decapitating Nicholas Berg earlier that morning, making more than a few of us lose our breakfasts on the floor of the barracks. "Hajji wants to cut your fucking heads off, but I will not let him. By the time you leave Fort Benning, your necks will be too strong for his blade to cut through your flesh."

I stood back to inspect Thigpen. I turned on a lamp so I could better look at him. He was highly-decorated. The area above his breast was a veritable fruit salad of campaign ribbons and awards, and there was an Expert Infantryman Badge and a Ranger's tab on the green coat.

"I figured you would have thrown all your medals away," I said.

"Why's that?" Thigpen tugged his sleeves.

My single cup of coffee was finished brewing and I walked over to the Mr. Coffee, and poured myself some Joe into the complimentary mug. "I don't know." Steam rose from the cup and I blew on the hot surface of the muddy sloshing coffee. "I thought you would be all

'This is the white man's war' and 'Fuck America.'"

I was a white male, and despite all the unearned privileges I discovered I had when I got to college, I myself was still fairly bitter about my military experience. I suspect that if I was black, I would be dead or in jail by now.

Thigpen tugged his lapels. "I went through too much shit earning these medals to just throw them away. I still say fuck the white man and his government. And when my wife ain't around, I say fuck his God, too." He dusted his shoulders off. "Ida's a Christian, and I don't want to hurt my baby."

I took a sip of my coffee. It was still hot but drinkable now.

His eyes bore into me, and he asked, "You ready to go to Arlington?"

"Yup, just keep me away from Section Sixty and I'll hold up my end of the bargain."

"I don't give a crippled crab crutch about Iraq or Afghanistan."

"Good, then." I took my coffee and walked over to the edge of the bed. I guessed that I could set the mug down on one portion of the mattress and jump on another part of the bed. Not a drop of coffee would spill, just like in the commercial. I was too tired to try, though. I reached forward and turned the TV on, got the local weather forecast.

It was going to be a sunny day, a perfect seventy-five degrees, ideal for a stroll through our nation's most hallowed grounds.

CHAPTER THIRTEEN: OCEAN OF STONE

The Escalade drank gas like a parched camel. When I stopped at the gas station, I picked up another cup of coffee. I was wired by the time my GPS led us to Memorial Avenue. I rolled down my window and tried to grab a ticket from the dispenser, but my seat was too high and I had to get out of the car to get the ticket.

"Maybe you should have got something a little less showy." Thigpen was still tweaking his Class As, fogging the golden buttons with his phantom breath before shining them. I got back in the car, the tollbooth arm lifted, and we drove into the garage. "I love Caddies, but I ain't used to this. When I think Cadillac, I think El Dorado."

"Get with the times, old man." I cut the wheel, pulled into a parking space, took a deep breath. I got out of the car and walked toward the endless greensward that was dotted with white marble markers to the horizon. The view was interrupted here by stands of trees and there by special graves for the unknown soldiers, or the especially well-known generals and politicians.

The sun was warm and mellow, filtering down through the tops of the black and Japanese cherry trees. It highlighted the eastern red cedars and spangled the red oaks. *Stay away from Section Sixty*, I thought. I said, "I guess if you die without a name, they make a big deal. If you die with a big name like Kennedy, they make a big deal. If you just die, you get a basic headstone."

A wind picked up, rustled the grass and the leaves of the trees. The gust carried the distant report of a rifle crack and the sounds of dueling bugles from separate funerals, one blowing *Taps* and another tooting *Amazing Grace*. I laughed.

"The fuck is funny?" Thigpen asked.

I sipped my coffee. We walked together past the visitor's center, where there were several info kiosks set up. "I remember when I was at Fort Bliss, *Taps* was automated on the speaker system." I had another quick slug of my coffee. "Whenever it played, you had to stop where you were and salute. So once guys heard that first note, they would rush inside and try to get out of saluting. Even if you were driving, you were supposed to pull over. A lot of dudes never did."

The smile dropped from my face, and I stopped walking to allow a solemn procession to pass. I could tell from the youth of the widow and her two sons in tow that they were heading for Section Sixty. Both Thigpen and I automatically went to parade rest. I found it difficult, but not impossible, with the Styrofoam cup of coffee in my hand.

Horseshoes clopped as the steeds pulled the wheeled caisson along the paved road. The widow pulled her veil aside, and dabbed her tear-stained eyes with a Kleenex. I watched the funeral cortege pass. I admired the color guard's satin billowing standard, the flags fringed with golden brocade.

I whispered to Thigpen, "I used to be the guide-on bearer for our company. Top gave me the job because I was a fast runner. I could do the two-mile in thirteen-flat, so I would run around the entire brigade on *espirit de corps* runs with the flag in my hands held high." Thigpen watched them pass. The catafalque rattled, and the American flag draped over the coffin rustled slightly from the choppy motion of the carriage as it drew along on ancient, wooden wheels.

They passed us, and we resumed our march through the cemetery. I noticed the Jewish tradition of leaving small stones atop the markers was observed for the dead of many faiths here, that headstones featuring crucifixes as well as the Star of David were littered with individually-placed pebbles. Tiny American flags staked in the mulch fluttered where the miniature pennants were moored.

"You want to know something?" someone asked. I turned toward Thigpen, and saw it wasn't him who spoke. It was another black man, a young sailor in a white service uniform that contrasted with his dark skin tone.

I looked at him. There was something vaguely familiar about his features. "What?"

"I've been here for more than sixty years, and you learn something spending that much time in a cemetery. You learn quite a lot."

"You look good for being that old," I said, dumbfounded.

Thigpen scowled at me. "He's dead, you shit bird. He's a ghost."

"More than a million Negroes served in World War II, but not one colored fella earned the Medal of Honor."

Thigpen's anger shifted from me to the dead sailor. "'Colored?' 'Negro?' You old Uncle Tom!"

The dead sailor squared his stance. "Who you calling 'Uncle Tom,' boy?"

"Who you calling 'boy,' Uncle Tom?" They swung on each other at the same time, their fists passing through their ghastly shells.

"I wish I was alive right now," the sailor said. "I'd beat some manners into your uppity hide."

"That's right, keep cooning for Massa, and maybe he'll leave you some fatback when he gets done in the mess hall."

The sailor shook his head. "A boy like you is a lost cause. I can't talk sense into any of the younger Negroes." He pointed toward the graves behind him. "You think you had it bad in…What war was you in, Korea?"

Thigpen ran a finger along his sky-blue Infantry braid. "Vietnam, you sorry-ass 'Bama."

"Vietnam, okay." The sailor nodded, cupped his ear like a mariner listening to the roar of the sea in a conch washed ashore. "Listen to that, boy."

The necropolis, silent aside from the bugles and horses until now, picked up a dull roar that sounded like an army of cicadas hissing. At first I thought it was just the water sprinklers chugging along, but the hiss grew into a moan. The ecstatic screams of men possessed by the Holy Ghost were mixed with shrieks of lung-tearing terror drawn by the slice of an overseer's whip, splitting black flesh and then salting the wounds of the weeping field hands.

"You hear that?" The sailor asked.

Thigpen grew meek, docile. His lower lip quivered, as if the sailor was his father and he was his son who'd just gotten beaten with the razor strop. "You want to know what that is?"

Thigpen didn't speak, but I figured he didn't want to know. The ghost sailor told him. "Those are contraband from Section Twenty-Seven, liberated slaves. Epitaphs only tell a small part of the story. I've been listening to that for decades. You through puffing your chest out at me, Negro?"

Thigpen looked down at the tips of his shined dress shoes. The dead sailor silenced the moaning of the ghost slaves with his hand, like a conductor of a massive, agonized symphony. He looked at me. "What you got around your neck?"

I pulled the sack out, gripping the thong. He asked, "Tamika give you that?"

"How do you know her?"

My question annoyed him, and he looked almost as put out with me as he was with Thigpen. "Let's see. How do I know Tamika? One tends to know their daughter." He glanced back over at Thigpen, who was still looking at his shoes. "Unless they're the type of Negro to knock a girl up and run from their responsibilities."

"You're her father?"

"Yep." My surprise didn't mean much to him, and I wondered if he had anticipated our arrival. "Walk with me," he said.

Thigpen and I walked with the ghost of the sailor. "As I was saying, not one Negro received the Medal of Honor in World War II, the nation's highest military honor for bravery."

We passed two Mexican laborers hovering over a tombstone. One of them used a level, while the other one eyeballed the grave and tried to see how far from plumb its angle was. Another Mexican in the distance ran a pressure-washer over a headstone, laving its soft marble with his hose.

"Bill Clinton retroactively gave the award to seven colored fellas. The hell of it was that only one of them, a Negro by the name of Vernon Baker, was alive to get his award."

"Do you think you deserved the Medal of Honor?" I asked.

Tamika's father stopped on the road. "I was nothing but a steward. They wouldn't let me be anything else."

"Yeah, I think Tamika told me something like that."

Thigpen regained some of his composure, and smoldered at my mention of Tamika. The seaman pointed at Thigpen. "He's right. I had to do the Stepin Fetchit, soft-shoe routine. I wore me a white jacket and shined shoes. I was a personal valet, at the light-colonel's beck and call. I did laundry, pressed clothes. You name it, I did it."

Thigpen winced and wore a sour grimace. "I'm glad my black ass was in the bush, and I'm glad that when I was a rear-echelon motherfucker, that at least I was in an all-Blood clique."

I gripped the Tituba sack, rustled the herbs through the burlap material of the pouch. I looked at the old sailor. "Was there a message you wanted me to give Tamika?"

That earned me a peal of laughter. "I talk with her every night. She knows how to commune. No, we don't need no intermediaries to get our Red Cross messages through."

He disappeared, faded in a blur, and Thigpen said, "This way." I walked with him. We headed toward a detachment of Old Guard soldiers from the Third Infantry Division. They carried M-14s with bayonets fixed. I'd never used a bayonet outside of basic training, drilling to stab and twist between the third and fourth rib. I wondered if a single casualty from either the War in Iraq or in Afghanistan came via bayonet; I highly doubted it.

We stopped beneath a tree, about fifty feet from the detachment of ceremonial troops. "This is what we're here for." Thigpen shook hands with the ghost of another black seaman, this one in a blue dungaree uniform. The ghost was shirtless, with a crosshatched pattern of straight-razor scars traversing his face. He had an anchor tattooed on his chest, rising from his pectoral muscles. One of his two front teeth was capped in gold.

"What you got for me?" Thigpen asked.

The sailor stuffed his hands into his pockets. "Look a here."

I was inside the body of a man with the physique of Jack Johnson. This was quite a change from being a fairly frail white guy who'd had two surgeries on his left shoulder. I felt like I could bench-press baby grand pianos, but my muscles didn't give me any confidence. In this situation, they were nothing but a liability. I'd been put on magazine duty because I was the most powerful Negro on-board, and also because I mouthed off to the petty officer a few days back.

I was six stories beneath sea-level. I could feel the pressure of the ocean around me, the roiling of the currents and the rumble of strange sea monsters. The hatch above me was closed and locked, but I shouted at the white man on the other side. "Look a here, Mr. Baines. There's no windows and nothing but bombs down here." The water was up to my waist now. I was shivering, and my teeth were chattering. I didn't want to show fear because then it would feel like I was putting on a minstrel show, and I didn't want Baines to get too much *Amos n' Andy* joy out of my suffering.

The magazine trembled from the force of a torpedo that barely missed our destroyer. I braced myself against the metal scaffolding. The booms were getting closer and closer, like a giant octopus slapping the sides of our ship with its tentacles.

Petty Officer Baines spoke to me, over the roar of the incoming torpedoes and through the dull lead and metal separating me from freedom. "That compartment is flooding and I'm mighty sorry about that, but I'm not about to open this hatch. You can make it out to be a colored-white thing if you wish, but I'm not willing to jeopardize the lives of three-thousand men just to save your sorry, tar-baby hide."

"Mr. Baines, that's a cotton-picking lie, and you know it!" The water was up to my chin now. I had to raise my head to speak, my nose almost flush against the cold metal of the hatch. "If I was white, you'd open that hatch and give me a fighting chance."

The white man laughed from the other side of the riveted metal hatch. "Say hello to Davy Jones when you get to his locker. I'll make sure to give your regards to Broadway when I get back home."

"You …" Any cussword I could come up with was cut off by the water filling the room. I swam until I ran out of breath. My lungs filled with water. The laughter of the white man followed me to my grave. It rang in my ears for years, decades of limbo after death as I haunted Arlington up until this moment where the Negro and the white man found me beneath this tree.

The Negro in Class As looked at me and said, "What was Mr. Baines' first name?"

"Michael," I said, still in the body of the ghost. How the hell could I forget the name of a man who drowned me and left me in purgatory for damn near half a century? His ass was buried with full honors. I gave the Negro the section and grave number, so that he and the white fella didn't have to mess with that newfangled machine by the visitor's center. The Negro looked at the white kid with him, who was jitterbugging from leg to leg like he had to piss.

I left the body of the man who could pass for pugilist Jack Johnson's twin, and I walked with Thigpen toward the grave in question. I had my initial misgivings about this mission. It sounded disrespectful from the start, but the coffee was running through me now and my bladder was full. I didn't see the harm in relieving myself here, provided none of my piss splashed onto an adjacent grave.

We waited for another cortege to pass us, this one for a bigwig. The horse was caparisoned, and a saber and cavalry boots were fitted backwards in the stirrups of the riderless mount facing Thigpen and me. The procession marched on, toward the distant sound of another rendition of *Taps*.

I walked to the grave of Michael Baines. I listened to *Taps* blaring, glanced around, and quietly unzipped the front of my pants. The aphrodisiac powers of the Tituba sack still had me half-erect, and I took my penis and aimed it toward the headstone.

I pissed. The ghost of the old, drowned black sailor and the spirit of the dying black Vietnam vet looked on and smiled. Thigpen said, "You've got a big dick for a white boy." I looked at him, smiled and said, "That's what every black girl I've fucked has told me."

That wiped the smile from his face, but the old sailor still grinned from ear to ear. I wasn't sure if it was because someone made of flesh and bone finally gave him a measure of closure, or if it was because he couldn't believe how much society changed in the last sixty years or so.

I finished pissing, and shook my cock to get the last few drops out. Thigpen said, "You jiggle your Johnson more than twice and it's a sin."

"Stop looking at my dick, please." I buttoned up, looked around, and left the tombstone drenched in piss.

"Let's go," I said. I walked quickly across the road, weaving between headstones. "I don't want to pay more for parking than I have to, and I damn sure don't want to run into the ghosts of any of the dudes I left in Iraq."

Section Sixty was far away, but I didn't want to risk seeing the spirit of Dunfy. I would see him when I died, whether that was tomorrow or thirty years from today.

CHAPTER FOURTEEN: BURDEN LAID DOWN

There was a printed note taped to the front door of my apartment when I got back to Cincinnati. I removed the note and stepped inside my apartment. I got a strong whiff of Tiff's used puppy pads, which smelled like a soiled diaper that needed changing. She sulked in a ball near the stove, apparently having resigned herself to the idea that I might never come back. She watched me with her sad eyes, as I crossed the room and headed to the pantry. I took out a garbage bag and leaned down, balling up each of the soiled pads. I knotted the garbage bag, set it by the door, and went to the sink to wash my hands.

"Sorry I was gone, girl." Tiff stood up, walked over to me, and sniffed my legs to make sure it was really me. I dried my hands on my pants, and stepped into the hallway outside my apartment to grab my rucksack. I pulled it inside, and then rushed over to the shelf in my bedroom where I kept my meds. I uncapped each bottle with shaking hands, and ate my fill of everything but Ambien. Chills worked their way through my body, and I shivered.

"Alright, Tiff, let's go for a walk." She was excited now, looping her way through my legs. I picked the note up off the counter, took my dog's leash down from the peg, and cinched it to her collar. I read as I walked her outside.

"Mr. Sullivan, your dog barked all weekend and we reported you to the manager. If this happens again, a petition will be taken up to have you removed from the building. We are pet-friendly, but we have our limits. Space is hard to come by in the Gaslight District. If you don't want to respect the rules of our building, we will be happy to find someone who will. Sincerely, your neighbors."

I counted signatures as I walked down the stairs with Tiff. Every tenant had signed. I guess I had it coming, and that I should be grateful that I'd been given a warning. I picked Tiffany up and kissed her on her warm, grey head. I bounced her in my arms as we walked outside.

It was warm, perfect weather. A light breeze carried the smell of sidewalk chalk and tarred blacktop on the wind, mixed with the scent of Indian curry and Chinese takeout comingling in the air. Couples walked by pushing strollers, and older kids kicked their way down the street on skateboards. The neighborhood was alive and buzzing, and the Percocet burbling in my stomach promised to make me feel like my blood was made of blessed sunshine for the next twenty minutes or so.

I glanced over at the front of the Third Eye Boutique, wanting to tell Tamika about my encounter with her father's ghost. Through the window I could see a Buddhist chant group was in session, with Tamika in the center. They stood with arms linked and eyes closed, as incense smoke wafted through their midst. I walked Tiffany down the street, yawning from exhaustion. The last couple of days had kicked my ass. The good news was that I neither sensed Thigpen's presence in my mind, nor saw his ghostly form walking alongside me.

I walked until I came to Amol India. There was a homeless man dressed in unseasonably warm clothes sitting outside, wearing multiple layers of heavy coats and wool sweaters. He was a permanent feature of Clifton, with red-rimmed hollow eyes and a guitar case that made me think he may have once been a folkie with promise, but ended up an acid casualty somewhere along the way.

"Hey, man," I said, "can you watch my dog for a moment?" He nodded, and took Tiff's leash. She sniffed the crushed velvet inside of his guitar case, where there were several coins and a couple of crumpled one-dollar bills.

"Thank you."

I went into Amol, took a Styrofoam takeout box, and loaded it down with Naan and Tandoori chicken. I walked it to the front of the restaurant and handed it to the waiter in his red Pagri turban. He weighed the box, then said, "Thirteen seventy-five, my friend."

I handed him a twenty. "Keep the change."

The Indian man smiled. "I'm sorry, sir, I cannot. This is too much." I pointed at the jar for some children's charity. He accepted that with a nod. I walked out of the restaurant, and back to Tiffany and the homeless man.

"Thanks." I dug a hundred out of my wallet and dropped it into the guitar case. The man was too tired to glance up at the bill I threw in the case, and probably assumed I gave him a single. I suspect that eventually he would figure out how much I'd given him.

I took Tiffany's leash and walked her back toward the apartment. My Monday morning shift started at Midnight. That still left me plenty of time to eat, relax, and launder the clothes I'd brought with me to D.C. I was beat, though, and I didn't give myself good odds of lasting more than another hour or so after I ate, unless I brewed an extra-strong pot of coffee. That might work too well, and keep me awake all night.

I decided I was too tired to try to do laundry, that my clothes would sit in the washer all night if I tried. If I left my stuff in the machine overnight, I would only end up pissing off the tenants even more. I was already on thin ice with them, thanks to Tiffany's marathon session of barking that probably lasted the better part of the whole weekend.

I walked back upstairs with the dog, went into my apartment, and rushed toward the bed. My terrier was close behind. She burrowed under the covers. I pulled my pants off, removed my wallet from my back pocket, and stuffed five-thousand dollars beneath my mattress. Then I got into bed and pulled my pillow over my head. I slept, and dreamed of neither Iraq nor Vietnam for the first time in what felt like quite a while.

* * *

Hasford had the news for me when I arrived that night for my Monday shift. He stood outside the nurse's station window, at his regular sentry. He spoke softly. "Thigpen passed in his sleep, on Saturday."

I didn't say anything. I looked up and down the corridor, as if expecting to see his spirit haunting the hallways. A new janitor was on his hands and knees, scrubbing at the ectoplasm coating the floor like a glaze.

"What was it?"

"A perfect storm of factors." Hasford scratched his Winchester tattoo. "He had really bad Type 2 Diabetes."

"I know." I'd seen his chart.

"It's a common illness for African-American men, but it can also be a result of exposure to Agent Orange."

"He spent a lot of time in the bush," I said. "So he definitely got more than his fair share of exposure to defoliant."

Hasford's eyes narrowed. His voice, already reduced to a half-whisper since the subject was death, grew even fainter as the topic turned to the supernatural. "I think you helped him in his last days, and my guess is he contacted you first. But do me a favor." He drew himself up to his full height. "Don't abuse your gift. Stay out of my head."

I felt like shrinking from the hulking sniper who'd probably killed more people than I fist-fought, but I held my ground. "I'll stay out of your head if you stay out of mine."

He smiled at my show of heart, pointed at the scar on his neck. "I already told you. My wound's too low to give me that second sight."

I glanced up and down the fluorescent-lit corridor again, an uneasy knot growing in my stomach as a question formed in my mind. "You think any other vets will try to contact me? I can deal with vomit, colostomy bags, and catheters. I don't get paid enough to deal with their nightmares."

Hasford gave the question some thought, and he pursed his lips. "I don't know. I guess you'll just have to wait to find out. In the meantime, suit up and then come back here and stand tall before the man." I assumed he was talking about himself.

"Yes sir." I walked into the changing room, prepped, and then returned to the front of the nurse's station. Hasford was gone. He returned a moment later, pushing a cart with some supplies lain out on the top.

There was a wooden tongue blade wrapped in gauze, a tube of moisturizing gel, and some Chapstick. There was also a box of suppositories, resting on a sheet of cardboard. He pointed toward the room where Thigpen stayed until a couple of days ago, where Norman Jones still resided.

"Chemo's shrinking the watermelon in his head, but it's dehydrating the hell out of him. He's in and out of his coma. The patient's presenting with a strong fever and he's on mechanical ventilation."

"I'm guessing the fever's not caused by an infection."

"You guessed right. It's just a sign that he's in the last days. Doctor Shah's not too sadistic, so he said stress comfort and don't worry about doping him up. The fever's not going to respond to antibiotics."

"What do you want me to do?"

"Do what you can to make him comfortable. If he's awake, get his pain rating."

"You want me to ask him to hold his fingers up? He's not going to be able to talk."

Hasford pulled the sheet of cardboard from under the box of suppositories resting on the cart, accomplishing his trick as smoothly as a magician removing a white cloth from a table covered with dishes and silverware. He held up one of the old-school Wong-Baker charts with the faces ranging from smiles, indicating a total lack of pain, to an openly-weeping red-faced character.

I didn't know Norman Jones, certainly not like I knew Claude Thigpen, but I guessed he would feel patronized and a little pissed even in his weakened state, if I showed him the chart meant for children and the mentally-impaired. I didn't argue, though. Instead I took the chart and turned with my cart. I wheeled my way down the hall, past the janitor who used all of his elbow grease to remove the plasm from the floor.

The wheels of my cart passed over the ectoplasm as if it was Vaseline, so lubricated that they ceased to squeak and made no sound as I made my way into the hospital room. I noticed that the goop on the floor was even heavier now than before. I decided it either meant that this janitor wasn't as good as the last one, or that the level of paranormal activity on the eighth floor of the VA was increasing rather than decreasing.

Jones was propped up in his bed, wisps of hair light as spun sugar sprouting from the top of his skull.

Thigpen's empty bed somehow filled me with sadness, and I tried not to look at it as I wheeled my way over to Mr. Jones. "How are you this evening, Mr. Jones?"

I didn't know whether he was in or out of his coma, but it didn't matter. Hearing is not only the last sense to go as one approaches death, but the sense of sound becomes even more acute as eternity nears. At least that's what we're told in nursing school. Thus it makes sense to talk to the dying, even when they are in a coma. It's also best never say anything within their earshot that the dying might not want to hear, no matter how deep their coma appears to be.

He was apparently awake earlier, whether or not he was conscious now. He gripped his call light in his right hand like a remote control. My father was getting older, and something about this man's frailty reminded me of the old man, my father who terrorized me and beat me when I was child. I now loved my dad like a child himself, when I saw him in his recliner as *HBO*'s late-night programming droned on and he slept with his mouth open and aimed toward the ceiling.

"I hear you're getting better," I said. "You've got a fever, though. I'm going to do what I can to make you feel more comfortable." I picked up his left arm, the bone so soft that it was indistinguishable from the flesh. The whole limb felt like sponge cake. I was afraid that if I gripped it too tightly, his arm would shatter like a dry maple leaf in autumn. I felt his pulse with two fingers of one hand and watched the ticking hands of my Swiss watch on the wrist of my other hand.

His heart was at one-hundred and twenty beats per minute, and I guessed it had been there for a while. I would report it on his chart (where I wouldn't be surprised to see something about the rapid rate already noted in the narrative). I didn't think it was something that could be treated, much like the fever. It was just another sign that death was only a few days to a week away, at the most. Pretty soon this bedroom would be empty, and then two new bodies would be here.

I had let myself get too attached to Thigpen. I had grown to love his bitterness and depend on his hatred for me and his incessant litany of racial slurs. I'd also made a mistake by noting the similarities between Norman Jones and my father. Now I was going to have to feel something when he died, too. I wondered if I would feel pain every time a patient died, and the thought disturbed me. Then again, the idea that death eventually wouldn't disturb me was just as bad. I had to find some balance; I had to seek the ability to recognize death and feel its presence and power, without letting it drain the life from me while I was still alive. I would have to talk to Hasford about it during a smoke break. Maybe I would end up borrowing that book from him.

I squeezed the hydrating solution from the tube onto the gauze on the tongue blade, preparing to moisten the patient's mouth with the swab. The high pulse, just like the fever, was a sign of dehydration. It accompanied changes in the hypothalamus- the body's thermostat- as it went into overdrive and death became imminent.

The man was awake now, and shook his head. The wires attached to the cannula in his nostrils moved as he emphatically said, "No" with his gesture. I guessed that not only wasn't he in the mood for the tongue blade or the Chapstick, but that he also wasn't interested in pointing out one of the stupid faces on the Wong-Baker scale.

"How about some cool cloths?"

Once someone was this close to death, everything required more energy than they had. Speaking would be impossible for him now, but even following the thread of a conversation was tough on a mind and body this addled. I didn't want to live to be as old as him, unless my nephew really wanted his Uncle Joe around for that long.

His foggy eyes focused, hardened, and achieved some light. The man he once was came back for the moment. He nodded, firmly. "I'll put some cool cloths on your face, neck, and groin. I think some anti-fever suppositories should make this less painful for you."

The call button fell from his hand. He reached for something on the right side of his bed, near the railing padded with bath towels. I saw he had a dry-erase communication board, and a black marker. He held the board in a tremulous grip, and scrawled like he was automatically writing in a séance.

He turned the board toward me. The words were squiggly, but legible enough. "Nothing in my ass. I die first."

I nodded. "It's your body, and you have a right to refuse treatment. You've been through enough."

His deteriorated muscles slackened, and his teeth unclenched. He eyed me with a soft gaze. There was gratitude in the mute expression. I guessed he was relieved that I wouldn't be humiliating him, subjecting him to a suppository goosing over his objections. I figured that he'd been prodded, radiated, poked, and intubated quite enough at this point.

I'd researched the subject of death back when I'd been suicidal. I'd discovered the defunct Hemlock Society, which was replaced by the Australian group, Peaceful Pill. I'd even bought the *Peaceful Pill Handbook*. I knew their suggested method of suicide, phenobarbital, was more than doable for me. It was supposedly painless and available over-the-counter in Mexico. If I could find a woman to give me a lap dance until I orgasmed in a chicken wire cage with a sawdust floor in Ciudad Juarez, I figured it would be nothing to walk into a Mexican pharmacy and cop some phenobarbital from off the shelf.

Norman Jones hadn't asked me to kill him, but if he wrote a request for suicide on his little dry-erase board, I would have found it difficult to refuse him, no matter what the consequences might be for me.

"Alright, aside from the cold towels, is there anything else you want me to do to make you comfortable?"

Norman Jones nodded again. "What?" He wiped the board clear with the skin of his arm, which was translucent except for a rash that resembled untreated psoriasis. He wrote with a hand that shook so badly I instinctively rushed to his side, held his hand in my own, and gripped his trembling palm in my strong fist.

My eyes widened in surprise as he finished writing, and I read, "You can help me like you helped Thigpen."

CHAPTER FIFTEEN: HIDEKO MATZUZAKA

The first time I floated outside of my dying body at the VA, I drifted along Ludlow Avenue and stopped inside China Kitchen. I watched the woks simmer and drank in the smells. My spirit could not cry, but I believe I did weep when I returned to my body at the hospital. One of the Chinese dishwashers looked a little bit too much like Wang, whose name we pronounced "Wong."

Wong could have survived the war with no problem, if he hadn't helped us build a radio receiver. He was put in the same hut with the GIs, as a punishment. The white pigs were lower even than the black pigs, the natives on the island who were smart enough to run away whenever they saw the Japs coming.

Just as I will feel a common sympathy for every Chinese man I meet for the rest of my life, I will also feel fear and hatred for every Japanese man I see. When I attend college on the GI Bill after war, a young Japanese student will sit next to me in one of my classes. I will then get up and sit somewhere else. I do not mind being called racist. I am.

This is one of the few things that Thigpen and I have in common, aside from the fact that we're both dying. We both hate. If his experiences with white people were half as bad as my experiences with the Japanese in the Pacific, then I don't blame him for his hatred. I wouldn't frankly hold it against him if, one day when he's changing his colostomy bag, he walks over to my bed and pours his shit in my mouth and ties a knot in my oxygen line.

It is the rainy season, and I don't know if the natives of this island have anything like American Indian rain dances, but their sky gods are angry. Raindrops fall with the weight of lead, through the bamboo and atap. The huts the Japanese have are well-built; we built them when we were still strong enough, and rations still abundant enough.

The floors of their shacks are not covered in mud and dirty water, although it is hard to tell what is mud in our shacks. We all have dysentery, and we white pigs (with one yellow pig added to our number) kneel on bamboo that makes our knees bleed. Blood leaks from our asses and when our watery and bloody shit hits the rainwater, it forms an oily scum that sits on top of the raindrops. The water floats around and touches each of us. It soaks us, stains us. We are dyed with blood and shit.

I am dying with a fever in a hospital, but the fever of a dying man is nothing compared to the fever of one trying to live. We all have beriberi and cannot stop shaking. When the Japs speak to me, sometimes I cannot hear them. Sometimes I am too weak to speak, and that brings more beatings from the hilt of the *Kempeitai's* special samurai sword.

Corporal Meeks once whispered, "They're trying to out-Nazi the Nazis." That gets laughter. It is quiet laughter because any sound brings beatings. In a heavy rain, we can sometimes get away with Morse code, but I'm now too tired to tap the wall behind me and get the attention of whoever hasn't died in the hut behind ours.

Meeks quietly sings a variation on a Noel Coward tune. "Don't let's be beastly to the Japs."

I try to smile. A couple of the other American POWS actually do smile. Wong doesn't laugh. He is fluent in many languages (making him an asset to the Japs) but he is only conversant in English and doesn't understand the joke

The patter of the rain increases, makes the nipa palm roof shake. One good thing about the weak roof built from mangrove palm is that sometimes the weather gets bad enough that the winds and rain will carry sap. That sap is enough for us to tilt our heads up and get some nutrition.

"Shit," Meeks whispers, and inspects his shaking hands. "I'm yellower than you, Wong." Wong smiles. "Malaria will do that to you."

I feel like I have to shit. I squeeze, but nothing comes out, not even blood. This feeling will last on and off for the rest of my life, long after the dysentery is gone. The doctors will explain that it's a condition called "rectal tenesmus." I will feel like I'm in the middle of a bowel movement, regardless of what's actually going on with my keister. I'll wear adult diapers for a good part of my life, and my saint of a wife will still treat me like a man. By the time I'm shitting in a bag in the hospital, she will have been long dead.

"No!" I shout, and the men around me hiss for me to be quiet. I can't help it. A snake is coming toward me, full of venom and ready to strike. "Snake," I whisper.

"No," Wong says, faintly. "Is vine."

Meeks giggles. He's going to die within the next forty-eight hours, but he will die with his sense of humor intact. He dies trying to escape, and for that reason he will not get a burial in the cemetery with a wooden cross like the POWs who do what they're told. He will be buried on an airfield that gets bombed by the Americans, and his family will never recover his remains and the exact location of his burial will remain a mystery to all but God. That is assuming one believes in God, which I don't.

I blink rapidly, notice that Wong is right. *Is vine*, a bit of creeper used to cinch the bamboo poles together. The front door, which is nothing but soft thatch, shoots open. My hallucinatory shouting has brought three troops and one *Kempeitai*.

I'm too tired to look up at the Jap soldiers, so instead I stare down at the puttees on their legs. They remind me of the wraps on a mummy, and I think about the time I went to the movie house with my ma to see the Karloff picture.

The field officer with the gold star sewn into the front of his Havelock cap shouts something in Japanese. I have not picked up much of the language, and I'm too delirious to understand. The officer leans down to Wong and shouts for him to translate. I notice there is blood on the officer's khaki tunic, stains from where he disemboweled Sergeant Corman for daring to kill and eat a native pig he found while on a jungle-clearing mission.

The officer cut Corman's stomach open weeks ago, removed a length of his intestines, and displayed them like pork tripe in a wooden bowl that sits on a table outside the huts. I first see Corman's guts, blue from rotting and fly-swarmed, when I am taken to the table and asked to sign a non-escape contract. I'm well-versed in the Geneva Convention, and know that POWs are allowed to attempt to escape. The max punishment for an attempt is supposed to be one month of hard labor, but a man who deguts another man and laughs about it doesn't give a fig for international law. I signed.

After I signed, the officer pointed at the sliced strip of intestines and said, "White pig." He laughed. "Black pig too fast. White pigs no run." I didn't exactly receive his routine as if he was Bob Hope. Decades later in the hospital, when Thigpen drones on about chitterlings, he doesn't understand why I want to vomit and plead with his spirit to quit bothering me with his yearnings for soul food.

Wong brings me back to the present. "He says, 'Who screams? Who shouts?'"

I answer the question by using what remaining strength I have to kick the officer in his shin with my right foot. I notice, for the first time, a tropical ulcer on the tendon of my foot that looks worse than a bullet wound. The flies who feast while men starve are so used to me being immobile that they have become stuck to the foot as if the congealed blood was flypaper. It is possible, I think, that some of them have gorged themselves to death.

I am convinced now that I have sealed my fate, that I am going to die. I am happy, pleased as punch. The Jap Nazi *Kempeitai* lifts me up, and the beriberi has me light as a scarecrow. Years later I will see footage of concentration camp victims, and marvel at how similar their starved bodies look to ours.

I, that is Joey Sullivan, can't take my eyes away from the wound on the foot of the man whose body I now inhabit. The bloody sore reminds me of the Leishmaniasis bite I saw on the calf of a soldier in the Green Zone, who got bit by a sand flea. He at least got treatment, though.

In the next moment I, Norman Jones, am dragged into the hut that has no name. Its existence is too fearful for us to acknowledge it with words. I am stretched out on a table, and a wet cloth is draped over my face. I am starved for clean water, so I suck the cloth. As more water is poured, I feel fear. It's something I thought was impossible for me to feel at this point. This is like the time at Coney Island when I was sure I was drowning and my uncle saved me, only there is no uncle to save me this time. I breathe in water through my nose and mouth, and my stomach swells until it feels like I have a potbelly or I might give birth to some water creature.

I hear the creak of a chair, and another creak as someone jumps off it and the Jap Nazi lands with his boots on my distended belly. A gallon's worth of warm vomitus shoots out of my mouth, spreads through the cloth, and splashes back down onto my water-covered face.

My entire body is wet now. I feel hands moving all over me, even though I cannot see through the soaked, darkened cloth. Wet sand is rubbed into my arms and legs, worked and massaged into the fly-swarmed ulcer on the back of my heel. The Nazi wants revenge. He hones in on the painful sore on the heel, presses his finger in it until the wound erupts like a massive, soft pimple. The wound is vulnerable and opening until I can feel his finger touching bone inside my foot. I bite the cloth like an epileptic seizing and I withhold the scream he needs to hear.

The Japs tortured us because we had the radio, but they torture us now with extra ferocity because they know what we heard on the BBC broadcasts. The war in the Pacific isn't going their way, so they hurt us as if the sadism of a few men in a hut might reverse the fortunes of a nation of millions. They have been taught that they are the descendants of Samurai, an indestructible people with an Emperor God. They believed it, and now they're reacting like a people who discovered their God is not real.

The sand is rubbed deep into my skin, like breading worked into raw chicken. Then the sandals come out, and they begin to slap the wet sand until it gets under my pores and hardens like a plaster. I feel like I'm being covered in quick-dry cement that's going to seal me inside. I will suffocate in agony, while to the outside world I'll just look like a statue placed in the middle of a park.

My skin is upbraided, turned raw, until there is no more skin and my body is just a patchwork of rashes. I am now something too disfigured for even the flies and mosquitoes to want. Still I don't scream, because I don't want to make the *Kempeitai* man smile the way he did when he showed me a bowl filled with my friend's intestines.

"You hungry, white pig?"

I try to say "Fuck you," through the cloth, suck more water down my throat and cough. The cloth is removed from my face and I stare into the fiery eyes of the man with the star on his khaki summer cap. He holds a burlap sack of uncooked rice. The hands of two Japs reach inside my mouth, and I taste the dirt on their unwashed fingers as they pry my jaws apart.

"Eat!"

Uncooked rice fills my mouth. I cough, scattering a wedding's worth of rice into the face of my tormentor. Even as I try to spit it, I can't help swallowing some. The uncooked rice travels down my throat, feeling like shards of glass. I can feel each individual grain, like a maggot with piranha jaws chomping its way through my intestines. When the dry rice hits the water already in my body, it grows. It causes the kind of aches that the eating of poisonous fruit causes.

I scream, and the *Kempeitai* laughs. I bite my lower lip until blood comes, angrier with myself than with him. I have finally given him the sounds of a white pig in pain that he wants to hear.

I don't die that day, or the next. I live, while Wong and Meeks and most of the others die. Marines take this base, and take no prisoners. Their plan was to let the remaining POWs kill or torture their brutalizers, but we are too tired and weak. I make it through the war, through the hospital treatments, and I come home to my wife and child.

The birth of my second child is my first son. It is the happiest moment of my life, until I hear about the atomic bombs dropped on Hiroshima and Nagasaki. That becomes the happiest day of my life, as I think about the family members of the Japs torturers who died in the Pacific melting in agony. There is no amount of hatred I feel that can make me ashamed of my hatred. There is no level of revenge that can be quenched.

I am no different from Thigpen, or perhaps I am even worse. He talked about wanting to get his hands around the throat of a white man. I want to sink my teeth into the cheek of a Japanese baby...

...Tiffany was on my chest, the noises of my thrashing and moaning in the middle of my nightmares bringing her to my aid. She covered me with her tiny terrier form. I stood up, walked across the cold, wooden floor of my apartment, over to the shelf where my meds were arranged.

I glanced at my alarm clock. It was two-thirty in the afternoon. I could hear the sounds of life on Ludlow Avenue beneath me: children laughing and singing. A busker strummed his acoustic guitar. I opened the bottle of Percocet, put three in my mouth. I walked across the bedroom, into the kitchen. I turned on the tap and leaned my head beneath it. I drank water and swallowed the pills.

"I can't do this again," I said. Iraq was bad, the visions of Vietnam were horrific, but the horrors of the Japanese POW camp were unendurable. "I'm done." I walked back over to my bed, and crawled beneath the covers. Something told me that I wouldn't make it in to work for my next shift, that I might also not make it through the night. A form beneath the blankets that was too large to belong to Tiffany startled me into standing again.

A young man pushed the covers off his body. His hair was carrot-orange, and his face was hard and angular. His was the face of someone who endured many childhood beatings at the hand of his father; it was a face that had also known hunger, nights going to sleep with an empty stomach and sharing a bed with at least one other brother, probably in a bedroom with no heating.

I knew immediately that this was young Norman Jones. I couldn't compare him to the older version of himself languishing in the hospital bed- unlike with Thigpen-because there was barely anything there left of him on the eighth floor. The only thing this young man and that old man had in common was the hospital gown.

Young Norman Jones stood up and walked over to me. "I need your help."

I shook my head. "I'm done." I grabbed my wallet from the nightstand, and walked into the kitchen. I grabbed Tiffany's bag of miniature porterhouse steak treats, and took one out. I leaned down, and she came traipsing into the kitchen. I placed the mini-steak in her mouth, and then walked toward the door. I put on my terrycloth house slippers and walked down the stairs.

Norman Jones passed through my apartment door as if it was air. He followed me into the street. "This is unfair," he said. "You helped Thigpen."

"I know. It took almost everything out of me." I walked in my pajamas down the street. I passed the Om Café, and a wistful pang hit me like a short hook delivered to the kidney.

I remembered my last meeting there with Claudine. We usually went there to work on *meine Aufsätze*, my essays in German, on her laptop. I had a little data stick shaped like a bullfrog that I would attach to her computer's USB port. This day in the café was her last in America, before she would return to her *Verlobter* in Bielefeld.

She had sipped her frappe and said, "I will miss you and your little *Frosch*."

"*Ich auch.*"

She had leaned back on the ottoman by the bookshelf in the coffee shop, and bumped her head against the exposed brick wall. "Ouch!" Maybe that was why I felt so comfortable with her. She could be as clumsy and awkward as I was, but she was still beautiful.

"Why do you never drink coffee, Joseph?"

I finally told her the truth. It was something I rarely told anyone, but I figured she would be out of the country in less than twenty-four hours and I would never see her again. "I have bad OCD. It happened when I came back from Iraq."

"OCD?"

I didn't know the German word for the condition, so I just listed my symptoms. "If I get a drink from the freezer at the convenience store, I can never take the first one on the shelf. I have to go for the second one because I'm always afraid the first one was tampered with. I can't drink anything that I don't open myself."

I was just scratching the surface, but she shrugged. She looked blasé, in no way put off by what I said. "It is not a problem. *Es ist mir egal.* Everyone has their little things." She'd pointed at her laptop. "If I use someone's keyboard besides mine, I wipe it with a handkerchief."

We'd spent the rest of our last afternoon together at Om looking through a coffee table book on German cinema, flipping from *The Cabinet of Doctor Caligari* to Herzog's *Herz aus Glas*.

"I'm sorry," Norman Jones said, following after me.

He walked until he was alongside me, and I said, "Sorry for what?"

"For taking her form."

I stopped walking. It hit me, so I swung on him. My hand passed through his phantom form and my knuckles slammed into the *Free Times* kiosk, rattling the newsstand.

"Hey, buddy," a homeless man said, staring at me in disbelief. "Those newspapers are there as a free service to the community."

"Sorry." I sucked my knuckles for a moment, stared at the young Norman Jones, and said, "You took on the form of my tutor to suck my dick?"

A hippy mother in an ankle-length frilled skirt walking with her daughter cupped her child's ears as she passed us, seeing only me and not understanding why the lewd lunatic was talking to himself.

"I was jealous of all the help you were giving Thigpen. I needed your help, too. He was hogging you, so..." Jones shrugged. "I took the form of someone close to you to steal your energy. I figured if I couldn't get your help, then he shouldn't either."

"Yeah," I said, "but it only worked that once." I started walking again, grimacing. "Still, you sucked a man's dick."

"Did you see what I went through in the Pacific? What I did in your apartment was *nothing*!"

"I'll admit your experience was maybe worse than Thigpen's."

I walked until I came to the Esquire Theatre. I stopped at the box office and spoke to the employee in his black smock and matching visor. "One ticket for whatever's playing." I slid him a ten-dollar bill from my wallet and he printed me up a ticket. I took it without seeing the title of the film.

"You didn't see anything," Jones said, and followed me into the cool lobby of the movie theater. The place smelled like popcorn.

"How could it be worse than what I already saw?" I didn't just see what he went through, either. I felt it all- the starvation, the anal fissures from the dysentery, the weakness from beriberi. I felt the sand being beaten into my skin with the sandals and the dry rice being shoved down my throat.

"It got worse when they started eating the white pigs." His words took my appetite from me. I got to the concession stand and ordered a frappe in honor of Claudine, since it was her favorite drink. I asked for some Kahlua in order to give the three Percocet in my stomach some company.

Jones said, "You shouldn't mix alcohol and pain pills."

"Oh, no. I might die, and then I wouldn't get to enjoy the time I get to spend with you."

"I'll leave you alone soon enough."

I took my chased frappe and walked to the ticket taker, standing by the velvet rope. She tore my ticket and I walked toward the cool theater where the film played. It was a romantic comedy, starring Renee Zellweger.

It was dark, but I counted no other heads or shadowy forms sitting in the seats. I spoke to Norman Jones shortly after taking my seat. "If I do what you tell me to do, where's the guarantee that another vet won't pop up asking me to knock out some last detail on their bucket list?" I took a sip of my drink, getting too much foam and not enough alcohol or caffeine. "Then another, and another. I signed up to change bedpans, not to heal damaged souls."

"I can't guarantee you that the other vets might not come to you seeking your services."

At least, I thought, *he isn't bullshitting me or making promises he can't keep*. I thought of something else. I remembered a course I'd taken at UC Clermont, the two-year campus, before transferring downtown to Main Campus. I'd minored in history, and had a class with a professor who knew everything about the second World War.

I whispered, even though the theater was empty. Renée Zellweger's nagging voice carried through THX surround speakers. "Cannibalism never happened in the Pacific. Those were just rumors ginned up by the Allied propaganda machine to make the boys fight harder."

Jones glanced once at the screen, winced. "Bogart and Bacall, it ain't." He looked back at me. He wasn't too intent on arguing. It made me think that maybe cannibalism had happened, that white pigs had been eaten.

"My memories don't lie. If you'd like to see more of what I saw in the Pacific in your dreams tonight, I can arrange that for you."

I shook my head. I believed him. "Why would they eat soldiers? They didn't have enough rations?" I glanced around the darkened theater one more time to ensure we were alone. Ours was the kind of conversation that might spoil a good date movie for any couples in attendance.

"They didn't eat us because they were hungry." I looked in his eyes, the irises the color of stone in the light reflected from the projector. I'd also taken an anthropology elective in addition to picking up a minor in history, and I'd learned in that class about the different kinds of cannibalism. There was endo/exo-cannibalism, either eating people from one's own group or from an enemy group. There was ritual and gustatory cannibalism, either where it was part of a religious ceremony or just part of a diet. There were other forms too, but I couldn't remember them off the top of my head. That made sense, as I'd limped out of the course with a low "C" average.

Jones sank deeper in his chair, watched the screen, and said, "We figured they were starving when they started eating the white pig meat. When the soldiers liberated the camp, they found large stores of rice. There were whole granaries and stockpiles of rations." He looked over at me. "They were eating us for some other reason, for a reason I still want to know." Norman Jones paused, and then said, "That's where you come in."

"No." I stood, gulped my Kahlua frappe, and staggered. The combination of Percocet and liqueur made me wobble.

I walked out into the hallway, leaving the dark coolness of the movie theater behind me. A poster featuring giant, red lips stood in the lobby. It was an ad for midnight showings of *The Rocky Horror Picture Show*. I'd never gone to one myself, but I'd seen the people dressed in fishnets and leather lining up at night outside of the movie theater. They were eager to quote Tim Curry's lines and sing Susan Sarandon's musical numbers.

"His name's Hideko Matzuzaka," Norman Jones said. I passed other cardboard movie cutouts, relics from Hollywood's Golden and Silent eras. There was Clark Gable sweeping Vivian Leigh off her feet, and Charlie Chaplin as the Tramp. I passed Audrey Hepburn with a cigarette holder in her hand and jewels around her neck.

"He left before the Americans came. He was one of the few to escape war crimes prosecution."

I pushed the back exit of the movie theater open, walked into an alley where two employees on break leaned against a brick façade and smoked cigarettes. They watched me as I double-time marched away from the spirit pursuing me. I turned left, back in the direction of my apartment.

I'd thought that the old Art Deco theatre would provide a hideout, some kind of sanctuary, but no such luck. Jones wouldn't stop, his voice chasing me up the street. "He snuck into America, worked in a fish canning company in Frisco. He spent some time in an internment camp out West."

I didn't know where this conversation was going, didn't want to know. I glanced once more at the glass front of Om, thought of Claudine again, the real one, not the jealous, ectoplasm-sucking succubus I'd encountered on the floor of my apartment. I'd also told her how much I loved my German feminist professor that same day in the café when I came clean about my compulsions.

"*Ja*, I think she knows how much you like her." Claudine had giggled.

"*Ja*," I said, "*Sie ist meine Konigin.*"

She'd giggled again, plugged her ears, not wanting to know exactly what I meant by saying that my professor was my queen. I smiled for a moment, but the smile dropped from my face a second later. I knew Norman Jones and his voice and his spirit and his demands were not going to go away. Neither were the nightmares, not until I did what was asked of me.

"He's living in Sarasota, Florida, now." I glanced through the storefront window of *Third Eye Boutique*, on the ground floor of my apartment building. Tamika stood in front of the glass case where the bubblers and one-hitters were stored.

I turned away from the store and opened the door to my apartment building. Norman Jones walked up the steps behind me. "I need you to find him." The bile rose in the spirit. It was the same anger I'd felt when I inhabited his body, and I'd savored the news that nuclear annihilation had been brought to Hiroshima and Nagasaki.

"I need you to go to the retirement home where Hideko Matzuzaka lives, and I need you to kill him."

I turned the key in my door, and looked back toward the spirit of Norman Jones. "That's asking too much." I closed and locked the door behind me, and scooped Tiffany up in my arms. I rocked the little terrier and stroked her ears. "Thigpen wanted me to piss on the grave of a dead man. You're asking me to kill someone."

"You've done it before. You did it in Iraq."

I set the dog down, and she scurried across the kitchen floor, her claws scratching the linoleum. "Yeah, well, I'm done with Iraq. I think at this point it would be fair to say that I'm done with everything else, too."

I walked into the bedroom, and Norman Jones rushed after me. He seemed to know what I had in mind, and he spoke in a panic. "You can't kill yourself. I need you to do this for me. I need this to happen before I die. I'm fading fast. I don't have much time before the tumor finishes the job."

I was no longer listening to him. I walked over to the dresser, uncapped the bottle of Percocet, and poured the pills down my throat. I chewed them like a man with bad breath downing a handful of breath mints before he french kissed his girlfriend.

"Think about..." Jones struggled to think of something to keep me tethered to this world, some form of blackmail or bribery. "Think of your mother." I opened the bottle of Ambien and turned it upside down, tapping the little red pills into my mouth. Next came the Clonazepam.

"Think about your brother."

My mouth was bitter from the taste of too many different kinds of pills. It felt as if I'd eaten a whole stick of chalk by the time I swallowed the last of the Clonazepam. I walked into the kitchen, dunked my head under the faucet. I turned on the tap, drank like a man lost in the desert who'd discovered an oasis.

"I should be dead in a couple of hours." I wandered into the bedroom, grabbed my TENS portable electric stimulation unit. I stripped naked, left my clothes in a pile at my feet. I placed the suction cups above each one of my breasts, and turned the electroshock machine up to its highest voltage. It was a battery-operated set, so I wasn't sure if I could electrocute myself, but I was going to give it a try. The strong pulses from the machine shocked my pec muscles into flexing.

The tears were flowing down my eyes now. I picked my terrier up in my arms and held her to my body. Her wiry hair felt warm against my naked skin. "I love you."

I set the dog down, walked into the bathroom, and placed one foot in the tub. I closed the drain and turned on the cold and hot faucets, adjusting both metal heads until the temperature was just right.

"Think of your nephew," Norman Jones said. Daniel was perhaps the one person in the world who could have stayed me from downing all those bottles of pills, but Jones had mentioned him too late.

I heard my nephew shouting "Uncle Joe!" I imagined rushing toward him in the park. I saw myself chasing him around the playset, up the beaten tin slide and through the plastic and PVC tunnel. I ran with him out into the bed of mulch near the swing set, where I finally got hold of him.

"Dirty D!" I shouted, as I lifted him high above my head, and brought him down across my knee. That would teach him who was the heel and who was the face in this wrestling franchise.

His giggling voice followed me into the darkness, and I fell into the filling tub. I pulled the shower curtain down in an attempt to break my fall, yanking each one of the curtain's rings off the rod as I tugged.

The shower curtain gathered around me like a raincoat. Hot and cold water poured from the taps. Tears leaked from my eyes. The distant giggling of my nephew's voice and the barking of my dog followed me through to the other side, to a place where "fresh, new hell" awaited, if I may quote my mother.

CHAPTER SIXTEEN: DYING, LOSING MY MIND, OR JUST SLIPPING THROUGH TIME

A voice called from the dining room. "Joseph, supper is ready!"

I walked down the stairs of the apartment building, which was now a house again, as it once was, so many years ago. The bannister was made of newly-varnished Brazilian rosewood. My mouth hung open as I reached the landing at the bottom of the stairs and stared at the entryway. The walls were marble and the floors terrazzo. I turned right, toward the call of my mother's voice, and entered the dining room. I looked up once at the ceiling. It was frescoed and covered in murals, like the ceiling of the local Catholic church.

Liveried servers stood by in white gloves and seersucker waistcoats. One of them was Thigpen. He winked at me. I walked around to the side of the table where my plate was set, and my silverware arranged. The first course was raw oysters on the half-shell, nestled in a bed of ice.

I whispered to Thigpen as quietly as I could. "What the hell is going on?"

"Don't ask me, sir." His voice was just as quiet and low as mine. "I've never been dead before."

"Joseph," my mother said. It was the same mother I had known my whole life, although she was much younger now. Her face was rouged and powdered. A tight whalebone corset forced her into a posture as rigid as an automaton from *Tales of Hoffman*. "Don't waste the oysters. Ice is luxury which many Cincinnatians cannot afford."

"Yes, Mother." I looked around the table, wondering where my father was. I wasn't sure what time we were in, but I was fairly certain that psychiatry didn't exist. If it did, the old man would be called an alienist at this point.

My mother spoke, as if sensing my thoughts. "Your father is at a meeting of The Society of Abolitionists at the Munich Bier Garten, with some other gentlemen." She looked up at Thigpen. "You are welcome to take a bucketful of ice back to Bucktown with you when you leave."

Thigpen gave a slightly obeisant bow. "Yes'm." I detected a note of irony in his voice, and thought perhaps this play at subservience was an entertaining change of pace for him.

I stared up at the ceiling again, in awe. It was painted in blue and gold. It was decorated with cherubs, golden filigree, and garlands depicted in relief.

"Don't act like you've never seen your own home before, and *do* eat your oysters."

I picked up one of the craggy half-shells and slurped a little rubbery sea creature into my mouth.

"*Bitte*," my mother said. "*Höflicher*."

"*Es tut mir leid*," I said. When I ate the next oyster, I used the fork with the tiny tines provided by Thigpen. His presence over my left shoulder made me feel self-conscious, and I wondered how people could tolerate the constant presence of servants who at best resented them.

"*Viel besser*." My mother smiled. I looked around the room, trying to pin down the exact date. If people were still speaking German, then there was a good chance this was the mid- to-late nineteenth century.

I knew from an elective course that there had been a mass emigration of political and religious dissenters who came to the shores of the U.S. after a failed revolution. They brought ideas ranging from socialism to temperance on the boats with them. I also knew that by the outbreak of the First World War, German-American Identity was taboo. Church masses were no longer conducted *auf Deutsch*, and streets named after Kaisers and Barons were renamed in honor of American heroes.

"I can't," I said, and stood. I pushed my chair back from the table so that it scraped the floor.

"Finish your oysters!"

I walked around the table, ignored my mother, and pointed at Thigpen. "Can I see you outside for a minute please?"

He nodded. "Naturally, sir." He walked around the table, and followed me out into the cobblestone street. Fish mongers and cigar makers plied their trades, in between stalls set up to sell vegetables. The boulevard smelled as fetid as the elephant exhibit at the Cincinnati Zoo, an odor of acrid dunnage. A horse drawn omnibus filled with passengers revealed the source of the smell a moment later.

I looked back up toward the house, which was even more imposing when viewed from the outside. The base featured a row of white Doric columns and the windows were trimmed in bronze.

"What the fuck's going on?"

Thigpen dropped the servile act. "Like I said, I've never been dead before. We're both stuck here." He cocked his head. "We know the diabetes and the Agent Orange put a hurting on me, but what the fuck are you doing here? You seemed to be in good health last time I saw you."

My mother appeared on the front steps, holding a parasol covered in hand-painted roses. She wanted to chastise me for neglecting my oysters, but apparently she didn't want to ruin her complexion. "Joseph, you get back here this instant!"

"Let's go." I tugged on Thigpen's waistcoat and ran up the street. The homes of the Barons of Mount Storm gave way to rooming houses, dry good dealers, and the manufacturers of ready to wear clothing.

I spoke over the sound of horseshoes clattering on cobblestone once Thigpen caught up with me. I tried not to cough from the scent of raw effluvia carrying on a wind borne from the Ohio. "What do you care how I died? I figured you'd think the only good cracker was a dead one."

"Most times maybe, but you did me a solid back at Arlington."

"Yeah, well." I shrugged. "You did me a solid at the casino. I still have some of that money left." I glanced back toward what was once my apartment, where I had five grand stashed beneath a mattress. "At least, I used to have some of that money left."

We continued walking, and things started to look and smell worse. We passed shacks and crib houses, lodgings for rivermen and rag pickers. There was the smell of unwashed bodies crowded too closely together and sharing space, rats fatted from wharf cargo and soaked from swimming in the river.

"What you asked of me was nothing compared to what Jones wanted me to do, and your Vietnam dreams were nothing compared to his World War II ones."

He glared at me. I guessed I'd hit a sore point, the idea that the Vietnam War wasn't a "real war" compared to the Big One. Thigpen said, "Vietnam was no cakewalk."

I decided to leave the subject alone. I didn't have many friends in this afterlife, and I couldn't afford to piss him off. The hearty smell of charred meat came from a local chophouse, complimented by the scent of ale pouring from tapped bungs. My stomach rumbled.

"Yeah, Jones wanted to you eighty-six someone, didn't he?" Thigpen asked.

We walked by a shooting gallery, where revelers dressed in their Sunday best fired rifle pellets at pyramids of stacked glass milk jugs. "How do you know what Jones wanted me to do?"

I noticed I was already speaking in the past tense. I figured it was now impossible for me to accomplish whatever task Jones had set out for me, since I was dead. "I talked to him a lot in hospice. I mean, our spirits used to commune. We'd leave our bodies and go our separate ways in Clifton." Thigpen cackled. "Some days he'd go to the China Kitchen, watch this old cook do his thing, and then he'd start crying." Thigpen shook his head. "I never could figure it out."

Apparently Claude Thigpen hadn't bothered to intrude into Norman's head as often as he pried into mine.

A man in a bowler and greatcoat walked toward us. He swung an ivory cane and sang a song in German about the beloved Rhineland he'd been forced to leave behind.

"*Es tut mir leid,*" I said.

The man tweaked his moustache, and a sanguine expression lit his face and eyes. "*Sind sie Deutsch?*"

"*Ja,*" I said, and he twirled his cane with the aplomb of a vaudevillian.

"*Brauchen sie helfe?*"

"*Ja, wissen sie wo ich eine Zeitung kaufen könnten?*" I wasn't sure about my word order, since the subjunctive case always gave me hell. I should have paid more attention in class.

The Rhinelander snapped his fingers with the hand not holding the cane and produced a folded newspaper from within his greatcoat. *"Benutzen sie meine Zeitung."*

Thigpen spoke up. *"Wie viele schulden wir dir?"*

The man's eyes widened as he turned toward Thigpen. He regarded the black man speaking German the same way he might look upon a cigar store Indian accomplishing the same feat. He recovered a moment later. I wasn't sure whether his initial shock was due to being addressed as an equal by a Negro in the nineteenth century, or if had more to do with the Negro speaking German.

"Nichts," the man said, tapped the cobblestone with his cane. He resumed his travels, after doffing his bowler once.

"Danke." I took the crinkled newspaper in my hands, and spoke to Thigpen as I studied the headline. "I didn't know you spoke German."

He crowded close to me to get a look at the newspaper. "You ain't the only one who was stationed in Germany. I left a few mixed babies in Cambodia, but I did the same in Deutschland. Richard Pryor said they loved them some brothers over there. Hitler must be rolling in his grave."

"Hitler isn't even an infant in Austria yet, I don't think."

"Maybe we should kill his mama's ass before he's born."

I didn't mention the Butterfly Effect, because I had more urgent matters with which to deal. I also suspected that we hadn't exactly time-travelled. I guessed that we were either in a parallel or totally nonexistent world. Nothing we did here would probably affect the world we'd come from and to which we could never return.

The headline of *The Enquire* said: "April 20, 1848: Inquirer Publishes Its First Sunday Edition." It went on. "The editors wish to assure readers of this fine publication that we here are as opposed to work on the Sabbath as the next man, but the readership should derive no small solace from the knowledge that the work that went into this issue was conducted on a Saturday. All was done prior to the Lord's Day. Thus reading this paper, while an enjoyable and informative endeavor, constitutes no greater labor than a Sunday idyll spent in any one of Cincinnati's myriad parks."

I folded the newspaper, stuck it under my arm. "Well, that puts my mind at ease."

"I don't know how we got here," Thigpen said, "but I'm damn sure glad I'm a freeman." Imposing brick structures with only one or two windows in their grim faces loomed above us on the left. There was the sound of clanking glass coming from the bottling works. The waxy smell of suet wafted from the sausage factory in the distance, reminding me of the scent of votive candles.

We passed a fire-gutted tenement that was in the final stages of collapse. The front of the limestone building was shattered, revealing the various floors, water closets, and bedrooms in cross-section. A Chinese hand-laundry appeared on our left. An ancient Chinese matron with passive features worked a sudsy undergarment over a washboard placed above a zinc tub into which scummy runoff spilled. She looked up at us once before returning to her task.

Sunlight broke across Cincinnati's seven hills. It filtered through the stained glass windows of a church before us, turning the depiction of the Return of the Prodigal Son into something like a magical lantern slideshow. The church was a Richardsonian Romanesque masterpiece, with a metalclad dome and steps leading up toward heavy oaken doors with wrought iron handles. It occurred to me that if the newspaper we got from the Hun was of recent vintage, then that meant we were a little less than one-hundred years before the time of the second World War. We were more than one-hundred years before the Vietnam War, and more than one-hundred and fifty years away from the conflicts in Iraq and Afghanistan. Christ, the Civil War hadn't even happened yet.

"Young man," a priest said. He walked down the stone steps of the church, toward us.

I pointed a thumb at my chest. "Me?"

The priest nodded. He was wearing his Sunday vestments, white collar and virginal white gown. He carried a *King James Bible* bound in Moroccan leather underneath his left arm.

"Yes," he said, closing the distance between us. Thigpen kept one pigeon-toed foot toward the street, as if he thought the white man of God might put him in shackles and sell him up the river. Kentucky was a slave state, and was less than twenty minutes away by ferry or steamboat.

The priest held the Bible in his hands, and hefted its leather-bound pages in his sturdy grip. "It is time for your confession."

I looked back at Thigpen for some support, but it wasn't forthcoming. He snapped his white-gloved fingers. "Don't look at me, man. You're on your own." He pointed toward the sea of faded tenements, crib houses, and shacks stretching down the hill. "It's back to Bucktown for this Negro."

"Wait," I said. He sauntered off, ignoring me. I looked back toward the priest. The man held his hand out, smiling.

"Okay." I was resigned to my fate, whatever that might be. The priest scaled the stone steps to his gothic church, opened the brass handle on one of the heavy oaken doors, and waited for me to pass through before him.

I dipped my fingers in the Holy Water font and made the Sign of the Cross over myself. The priest walked to the heavily-ornamented wooden booth. It was varnished to a high shine, like the wooden body of a pianoforte. He opened his half of the confessional booth. I took my place on the other side, closing the door and adjusting myself on the padded seat. His face was visible in profile through the grates of the confessional screen. A spermaceti candle glowed and made strange shadows of our faces.

"It has been ..." I halted. It had been quite a long time since my last confession. Truth be told, I'd gone to Catholic school and even had a friend sneak me a bit of communion wafer to see what the transubstantiated body of our Lord and Savior tasted like, but I'd never gotten confirmed in the second grade. The problem wasn't that I was a bad Catholic; the problem was that I wasn't Catholic at all.

"It has been... a lifetime, since my last confession."

"Go on, my son."

I inhaled, prepared to speak my sins. "Do you know where you are?" The voice was no longer that of the priest, and I was no longer in the confessional. I was in a hospital bed, laying on a gurney. A psychiatrist was seated at my side.

I wondered for a moment if it was possible for me to have switched bodies with Norman Jones. I thought that maybe he played a cruel joke on me, entered my young body and left me in his wizened form to rot on the eighth floor of the VA hospital. I would soon die from the tumor in my head.

My right hand had a wristband on it, but the arm was still that of a young man. I looked up at the shrink, an Indian man with croissant-shaped bags under his eyes. He was the same doctor who processed me the last time I was inpatient.

"How am I still alive?" I asked.

"You're lucky you have a loud dog. She barked for quite some time, and your landlord came and found you in the tub. You're also lucky your apartment is so close to the hospital."

I didn't feel lucky. I did, however, feel the familiar residue of the charcoal emetic given to pump my stomach. My throat was also sore from where I'd previously been intubated for some time.

"Nice try." Norman Jones spoke up, standing over the doctor's shoulder. I ignored his form. I was convinced that he and the spirit of Thigpen were brought on by some sort of subcutaneous bleeding or secondary trauma caused by my TBI.

"How's my dog. Where is she?"

The doctor spoke in a reassuring tone. "A neighbor has her, Mr. Sullivan. Let's worry about getting you a bed for the time being."

"Shit." I shook my head.

"What's wrong?"

I sagged down, dejected. I had been doing so well. I'd gone quite a while without having a severe nervous breakdown. I'd graduated from college and gotten my degree in nursing. Now that was all down the drain. "I'm going to lose my job."

The doctor shifted in his seat, adjusted the Windsor knot of his tie. "You don't necessarily have to disclose your stay here, depending on who your employer is."

I pointed toward the ceiling. "My employer's upstairs. I'm pretty sure they're going to know I'm here." Hasford would definitely know, as prying into other people's files was his forte. My shift started at eight a.m. I glanced down at my wrist, where my watch was, before they confiscated all of my personal belongings.

"Yes," the doctor said, a bit of sorrow in his tired eyes. "They will probably find out. I will not lie to you about that." He stood. "Let's get you a bed upstairs."

"Shit." I didn't know what else to say. I was looking forward to being a productive citizen. Now I was going to have to go back to living on disability, a combination of VA and Social Security benefits, a little stipend the government gave me in order to stash me out of sight. I would spend my days walking my dog in the park, passing the mothers pushing their strollers, busy creating life while I wasted what remained of mine.

"Something's wrong," Norman Jones said.

"Yeah, you don't exist."

He sniffed the air. "I smell fish."

I inhaled, but my senses were too deadened by the aftertaste of the charcoal. "I'll have to take your word for it."

The curtain before the room parted, and a nurse's assistant stood there with a nightgown in her hand. "Hey," Norman Jones said. "We match." I ignored his wan attempt at humor and took the clothes.

"Okay, Mr. Sullivan. If you'll just change into these, we'll wheel you up to Seven West and get you in-processed."

"Yes, ma'am."

The nurse's assistant left, pulled the curtain, and I stripped. "It's Hideko," Norman Jones said, resolve building in his voice. His spirit passed through the curtain. I heard his voice as I finished changing. I slipped on the nonskid booties. "He knows I'm sending you after him, and he's trying to stop us."

"There is no us," I said. I spoke loud enough for the night duty staff at the ER to probably think I was schizophrenic, which I probably was. "There's no way I can get out of here and make it to Sarasota to visit your precious war criminal." I stood up, ready to leave the ER and head upstairs to the psych ward. "Seven West is a closed ward," I said. I no longer had my common access card. It was on a lanyard slung on a bedpost back at my apartment. It was only a matter of time until the VA found out I'd been committed and missed work. They would then deactivate my card.

I pulled the curtain open. "I'm ready."

The nurse's assistant pushed an old-fashioned wheelchair with a leather seatback toward me. "I know you can walk. It's just a formality."

I didn't take offense, and didn't feel like fighting her. "I understand."

"I can get you off Seven West," Norman Jones said, following us down the corridor. I braced my elbows on the cold metal arms of the wheelchair.

"You're just a spirit. You can't open doors."

The nurse's assistant leaned down to me as she pressed the "up" button on the elevator. She said, "If you're having auditory or visual hallucinations, that's something you need to tell the doctor."

Norman Jones ignored the nurse's assistant and said, "Yeah, but spirits can bend rules. Ghosts can get inside machines. It just takes its toll, and makes us tired. Remember what Thigpen did for you at Belterra?"

"Yeah," I said, no longer concerned about how delusional I looked to the woman pushing my wheelchair. "He made me ten grand. What the hell have you done for me except drive me to try to take my own life and lose me my job?"

"You do this favor for me, and I'll leave you alone."

The elevator dinged, and the doors opened. The woman wheeled me inside, and Jones followed us in. He studied the nurse's form with a lingering gaze, not having to worry about her seeing him leer. "I miss women with meat on their bones, the Marilyn Monroe types, the kinds that used to get painted on bombers."

I didn't relay his offensive comments to the nurse's assistant. She pressed the "7" button. A thought struck me and filled me with sadness. We were only going to be one floor away from the place that had given me purpose in life. It had caused me no end of heartache, but a job was at least a distraction from one's thoughts. It was a much needed distraction in my case.

"I'll get you out of here," Norman Jones said. "Just keep an eye out for Matzuzaka and don't take any wooden nickels. Be on guard for his tricks."

"Don't worry," I said, and shifted in the wheelchair as the elevator rollicked upward. "If my tutor shows up again and tries to suck my dick one more time, I'll pass."

"Okay, Mr. Sullivan," the nurse's assistant said, her voice stern. "I'd appreciate it if you don't use that kind of lewd language. I understand you're going through a stressful time. If you're having auditory or visual hallucinations, that's something you need to tell your provider."

Jones giggled. "I got you in Dutch with the little filly."

The elevator dinged again and the doors opened. The woman pushed me out into the hall, and we rolled along with Jones floating behind us. I decided my first call would be to my father. He would be disappointed. He was getting too old to deal with his grown son's psychological problems. I guess I'd let him down, become an underachiever. He was an Ivy League grad who became a doctor; my mother had her PhD and taught English at a two-year college in South Carolina.

I remembered being in Iraq and telling my team chief what my parents did for a living. "Your mom's a doctor and your dad's a doctor. What the hell are you doing as an enlisted man in the Army?" It was a good question, for which I had no sufficient answer. I didn't want to blame everything on the divorce, but it had disrupted my life. I bounced from parent to parent, city to city, and school to school. I was so disoriented finally that I just dropped out and spent my days smoking weed. I ended up working menial jobs in factories or as a pizza man, and then one day I decided to join the Army. End of story.

The nurse's assistant ran her CAC over the door's electronic access point, and we entered the ward. It looked much like hospice care, except the patients were walking up and down the hall, "ambulatory" as we say in the trade.

"Mr. Sullivan's having auditory and visual hallucinations, speaking to someone who isn't there."

The registered nurse at the desk typed something on the keyboard before him, and the nurse's assistant spoke to me. Her voice was chilly now, on account of my previous coarse language in the elevator. "You can stand up now, Mr. Sullivan."

I got out of the wheelchair and stood, scratching my arms and looking around at my new home. Two patients in nightgowns played Wii Bowling on a massive flat screen TV in the dayroom. They looked to be in a trazadone stupor, which might account for all the gutter balls.

"Okay, Mr. Sullivan," the RN said, coming from around his seated perch behind the glass. "Let's get you processed, and then we'll get you some linen and a bed."

"I used to be a nurse." My voice was weak, trailing off.

"Oh?" His tone was friendly. He was bald, with a bullet-shaped head, patchy facial hair, and a potbelly that looked like a baby in the third trimester. "Well, let's get you some help. Then you can get back to helping others."

That reassured me. Just because I couldn't work at the VA anymore didn't mean that I couldn't find employment elsewhere. I could leave Cincinnati, but I couldn't leave the state. All of my benefits and healthcare were tied to Ohio. I could try Columbus, Dayton, or Cleveland. If I was really feeling masochistic, I could move to Toledo, Akron, or even Chillicothe.

I followed the RN toward a private room where I'd been in-processed before. We would sit down together and I would list my symptoms and issues, tell him whether or not I felt like I was a threat to myself or others. Norman Jones walked with us down the hall, and then shouted, "It's him!"

He pointed toward the end of the corridor, whose floor I noticed was slicked in a long trail of ectoplasm, as if a formation of slugs had migrated from one end of the ward to the other. An older Japanese man marched toward us, and I stopped.

Hideko Matzuzaka and Norman Jones both froze in place. I studied the spirit of the Japanese man wiling away his days in a Sarasota rest home. He wore a toothbrush mustache, a nod to the ruler of the other main Axis power. His tortoise-shell glasses heightened the intelligence lighting a pair of eyes betraying no hint of senility. I looked in his eyes, and saw nothing but sneering contempt for the *Gaijin*. His emperor might be dead and his godhood disproven, but his divinity lived on in the burning eyes of the old soldier.

"Right this way, Mr. Sullivan." The friendly RN held his hands out toward the small room appointed with a computer and two swivel chairs. I stood in place, watching the standoff as it developed between the two invisible men.

"Tojo sucks cock," Jones said.

"No." Hideko lifted his bamboo cane, which was tipped with an Arisaka bullet casing. "Roosevelt sucks cock."

"I know he does," Jones said. "I'm a Republican, you fucking slant-eyed nip." He closed the distance between them. As he got closer, the old Japanese man swung his cane. The bamboo, lacquered cane passed through Norman's transparent form. "See the difference between you and us?" Jones said. "We don't worship our leaders."

The old Japanese soldier continued the futile clubbing of his old American prisoner. The RN looked at me, wondering what I saw that he didn't.

"Mr. Sullivan?"

I ignored him and continued to watch the drama unfold. "Oh, there are some other differences between us and you." Jones might not have really been there, but that didn't keep his face from flushing with anger as he released decades of pent-up rage. "We don't eat people!" Jones threw a haymaker, and his fist passed through Hideko's body just as the Japanese man's bullet-tipped cane had floated through Jones.

The spirit of Mr. Matzuzaka stood back a couple of paces, no longer interested in fighting. He struck the stance of someone about to ascend a soapbox. "You killed all the Indians and the buffalo. I read history books. Americans enslave the black man. You make the black man fight and die for you, but don't let him use drinking fountains."

"Yeah," Jones said, not backing down. "But we don't eat black pigs. See the difference, or do you still need some help?"

"You're a racist!"

"You're a cannibal! How do you live with yourself?"

Mr. Jones apparently hadn't been to college in the last couple of decades, since at this point in our political discourse being a racist might have been worse than being a cannibal.

"Mr. Sullivan," the nurse said, growing a bit impatient. "The sooner we take care of this, the sooner we can get you a bed."

A patient passed through the forms of the two old adversaries. He sipped orange soda from a Styrofoam cup and drooled slightly as he did the barbiturate shuffle. Hideko Matzuzaka turned his attention from Norman Jones, and looked at me. I studied his outfit, a blue silken kimono embroidered with dragons and cinched in the front with a tie. I was both a pajama aficionado and someone who had few qualms about leaving the house in his PJs, and I found myself somewhat jealous of the old Japanese man's attire.

He pointed his bullet-tipped cane at me, and said, "You will not bother me at the rest home in Florida." Hideko waved his cane like a wand, and muttered something in Japanese. "*Kokoro no oni.*"

My heart somersaulted in my chest, a pulsing defibrillation. I looked over at Norman Jones, afraid that I was about to go into cardiac arrest. "What did he say? What did he do?"

"I don't know," Jones said. "I never learned to speak nip. Wong did, but the bastards killed Wong." His anger rose again. He remembered the starvation of his friends, and the murder of the Chinese man who ultimately lost his life helping the POWs assemble a radio receiver.

"You killed Wong, you coward!" Jones gritted his teeth until I could hear the sanding of enamel. I shuddered at the sound, which struck me like fingers against a chalkboard. He tried to strangle Matzuzaka, and his hands clutched empty air. "Ever hear of the Geneva Conventions?"

"Mr. Sullivan," the RN said, a bit more firmly this time.

"*Goryo!*" I shouted, and what felt like fissured streaks of lightning crackled inside my body. I fell down on the floor, convulsing.

"He's seizing!" The RN shouted. I could hear only the laughter of the old Japanese man. He addressed me like a dog. "Oni, attack!"

"Don't listen to him!" Norman Jones shouted, but his voice was faint compared to that of the Japanese man.

"*Ushitora!*" Matzuzaka shouted. I had no earthly clue what that meant, but I found myself transformed in my insanity. I glanced down at my body, naked except for a tiger-skin loincloth. My physique was rippled with muscle, my torso like the sculpted and chiseled form of a discus-hurling Adonis. I had spent the last few years in intense physical pain, enduring surgeries and wasting away both physically and psychologically. I didn't know what exact spell the Japanese man had cast over me and I still didn't understand his words, but I was grateful to be possessed by whatever spirit had me in its hold.

I ignored the shouts of Norman Jones to fight the power that gripped me. I embraced it. I found two oxen horns when I ran my hands over my scalp. They were gnarled like shofars, and I felt no horror. There was only the feeling of growing power and pride in my new form. "Oni!" I shouted.

Tsuchigumo earth spiders crawled across the ectoplasm-slicked floor, lifting me up like an army of scarabs hoisting their pharaoh toward his burial vault. I stood and the loyal phalanx of spiders scurried away from me.

"My God." Norman Jones' eyes widened as he took me in. Whether or not the transformation that took hold was real to anyone else, it was now real enough to us three men trapped in this netherworld.

My vision clouded with red that dripped like thick syrup, a sauce for the coming banquet of blood. I looked over at Norman Jones, despising him for his weakness. I hated him for his inability to understand the power that came from consuming human flesh. The rite was sometimes necessary, no matter how much grain and rice a man had. Millet was for the peasants, meat was for the warriors. In the absence of pigs and fowl, our enemies were our meat.

My total embrace of the Oni nature exposed Japanese characters that I could understand better than the German with which I'd struggled for the last few years. I could read it better than I could even read English. *Shuten Doji* picture scrolls written on the parchment made of the skin sliced from the backs of enemies revealed paintings and murals showing human legs severed and waiting on cutting boards. The limbs were hacked from bodies by cleavers and ready to be eaten.

"You're okay?" The RN sighed with relief, latex gloves on his hands and an anti-suffocation pillow held in his grip.

If by "okay" he meant I was no longer in danger of seizing, then I was okay. If by "okay," he meant that I didn't have a desire to taste human flesh and blood, then I was not okay.

I gritted my teeth and walked toward him. "I will take you to *Geshin Jigoku*." Spit slipped between the cracks in my teeth, as I savored the idea of eating his flesh.

"What?" He backed up a couple of paces, glanced around. He was probably looking for the nearest emergency phone, or another nurse he might be able to call to put me in restraints and administer a syringe of something to calm me down.

"It means the hell of pulverized flesh," I said, and took a step forward. My words did not reassure the RN. Hideko laughed and his cackling drowned out whatever advice Norman Jones had to offer. I walked toward the RN until his back was against the glass wall. The two patients were still too engrossed in their game of Wii Bowling to see the mortal danger the poor bald man was in.

"Mr. Sullivan…"

I didn't know who the "Mr. Sullivan" was of whom he spoke, but I did know one thing. "I will have your blood for my rice wine."

"I …"

I lunged toward him. The RN passed out there on the floor, clammy and cold. I reached around his neck for the lanyard that controlled access onto and off the floor. I was apparently listed only as a danger to myself and not others when I was processed into the system. The misclassification was a mistake that would let me leave the ward now.

The laughter of Norman Jones drowned out any sound that Hideko Matzuzaka made. I walked to the door granting access onto the closed ward, and I ran the card over the entry point. The bolt on the door clicked open. "Good job," Jones said, to Hideko. "You lost the Big Won, and now you just helped my partner escape."

I closed the door behind me and ran toward the bank of elevators. "I'm not your partner."

"You're going to Florida."

I pressed the "down" button on the elevator and waited. "The hell I am." I thought about waiting for the elevator to come, but then decided that being seen walking around in hospital garb with my wristband still on was probably not the best look. I was grateful that it was nighttime, and I would use the cover of darkness to make it back to my apartment. I wasn't sure what I would do after that.

The elevator came. I ignored it and opened the door to the staircase. I ran down the cement steps, using the cinderblock walls to steady myself as I went. I wasn't sure what drugs I'd been given while unconscious, but my earlier attempt at overdose still had me groggy and faint.

Norman Jones followed after me. "You can't stay here, in Cincinnati. You've just escaped from a closed ward and assaulted hospital staff."

"I didn't assault hospital staff. He passed out."

"That might not be the way he remembers it."

I pushed the door to the ground floor open, and walked calmly through the lobby with Norman Jones on my tail. The old Japanese soldier had apparently dematerialized. He'd probably floated back toward the Sarasota nursing home, where he would plot his next move and prepare for the arrival of the *gaijin* and the spirit of his old nemesis from the War in the Pacific.

"Alright," I said, walking out through the automatic doors of the emergency entrance. I passed the Plexiglas shell where third shift hospital staff and patients smoked. They clouded the inner walls of the little hut until they turned a milky opalescent with their cigarette smoke. I didn't spot Hasford in there smoking, for which I was grateful.

I walked up the sidewalk. I felt the cold concrete through the thin material of my hospital booties as I marched up the hill. The spell that Matzuzaka cast over me was now past, I was sure. I looked down at my body and saw no tiger-skin loincloth, and I placed my hands reflexively on my temples and felt no ox horns sprouting.

There was a part of me that was disappointed, that enjoyed the rush of power that came with being a Japanese cannibal spirit. The potency was frankly a nice change of pace from the impotent and war shattered, pill popping mess that I actually was.

I walked up to the crosswalk, pulled the sleeve of my hospital shirt over my hand. I pressed the button triggering the signal.

Jones looked at me askance, his eyes narrowing. "What's your problem?"

"I'm scared of germs and I didn't bring any dog poop bags to cover my hand."

He looked at me as if my words made him want to vomit. Maybe even he too thought my transformation into a bloodthirsty demigod might be an improvement, notwithstanding his own horrific experiences with Japanese cannibals. This was assuming that what he told me was true. I wasn't about to argue with him, though. If I did, he might make good on his previous threat and conjure images of *Kempeitai* feasting on white pig meat in my dreams. If I saw that, there was a good chance that I might try to commit suicide again. My dog wouldn't be there to save me this time.

"Tiffany!" I shouted aloud, and my voice echoed in the dark. I wondered which one of my neighbors had my dog, and if it would be possible for me to get her back before heading to Florida. She was my baby and my best friend, and I couldn't live without her. The light changed, the little white figure appeared on the crosswalk sign, and the buzzer chirped.

There was a police car at the stoplight at the intersection. I walked slowly, with my eyes forward. "Easy," Jones whispered in a soothing tone. "Take it easy."

"I'm taking it easy." I spoke through gritted teeth. I walked up the block, past the apartment buildings. They had somehow been restored from their former grandeur as baronial mansions after I overdosed in my bathtub. I was happy to be back in the 21st century, but I wasn't sure that my mind was sound enough to give me any kind of guarantees that I might remain here.

A young girl in jogging shorts and a sorority T-shirt walked toward us. Her breasts jiggled and her thighs bounced as she walked. She saw me, and stopped in her tracks. She turned and crossed the street, braving traffic to avoid crossing my path. I didn't take offense. When I was a student at UC, I used to get constant updates at my university email address, forwarded messages from the local crime blotter. Many of the incidents were robberies and carjacking crimes, but there were more than a handful of sexual assaults and rapes reported.

I was a big guy with a military haircut in a hospital gown, talking to myself and walking toward her in the dark. If I were her, I would have crossed the street too.

I walked on, shivered as a bracing wind from the Ohio reached the hills and moved through the thin material of my hospital gown. Smoke poured from the open doorway of the hookah bar up the street, and sickly mercury vapor lamps illuminated the parking lot of the tanning salon/laundromat where someone was shot a few days ago. Steam rose from the grates at the curbside, and mixed with the aroma of curry spices billowing from the many Indian restaurants in Clifton. The padding of my feet grew sore. I hotfooted it as I stepped on shards from a broken beer bottle, removing the little speckled bits of brown glass from the bottom of my footy. I was grateful that I'd felt the glass with my toes before applying the full weight of my foot to the sidewalk.

I was still walking on one foot and picking glass from the hospital socks when I came to my apartment building. An Econoline was parked at the curb. The leather spare tire cover on the back of the van featured the African continent in tricolors. Tamika stood there. She held Tiffany on a leash, and both she and the dog turned toward me at my approach.

"Oh my God!" Tamika shrieked, and Tiffany strained on her leash.

I leaned down to my dog. "*Mein Schätzchen.*" I picked Tiff up, and Tamika released her hold on my dog's leash.

"Is that her name, *Schätzchen*?"

I kissed Tiff on the head, cradled her in my arms like a newborn. "No, her name's Tiffany."

"Tiffany?" Tamika scowled. "I like *Schätzchen* better."

"Me, too, but it's too late. She came pre-named and I didn't want to confuse her." Tiffany was one of those names like "Crystal." It was white trash; Tiffany sounded like the kind of girl who stripped at night between multiple pregnancies and spent her days watching soap operas in her trailer, calling the shows her "stories."

"What are you doing out of the hospital?" Tamika looked me up and down. "The ambulances and cop cars came, and I locked up the shop and closed early to see what was going on."

The door to my apartment building opened. I walked toward it, holding the door open with my foot as my neighbor stepped out. He pulled the hood of his sweatshirt over his head and sidestepped me. I spoke to Tamika, while keeping my foot in the door and cradling Tiff in my hands. "I'm not going to lie to you. I broke out of the hospital."

"Why? You know that's against the law?"

"I have to see a friend of mine who's dying, in Florida."

Her look softened. I wasn't exactly telling the truth, but I wasn't exactly lying. Hideko Matzuzaka was now an acquaintance of mine, at the very least. He was old and probably approaching death, if he managed to astral project his way from Sarasota to Cincinnati. "I don't have much time to talk." I prepared to run up the stairs.

I halted when she asked me a question. "Who's that?" She pointed at Norman Jones.

He looked at her, his eyes popping in disbelief. "She can see me?"

"Of course I can see you."

"I spoke to your father," I said, "in Arlington. He seems to be doing well."

She smiled, beaming. "I know. He told me." Norman Jones and I exchanged a look, slightly afraid now of this uncanny woman. I ran up the stairs, to my apartment. The door was broken down, probably from where EMTs had battered it in order to get to my body in the bathtub. There was a strip of yellow "Caution" tape wrapped over the doorframe. I pushed through it and ran inside, headed into the bedroom.

I leaned down to the mattress, lifted it, and grabbed the five-thousand dollars I had stashed there. I walked around the bedroom, the wooden floor creaking beneath me. All of my pill bottles were gone. My leather billfold was on the ground, tented in the shape of a pyramid and spilling credit cards from its sleeves. I retrieved the wallet, stuffed the cards inside, and also slid the cash into the billfold. I quickly rifled through my drawers, put a checkered flannel shirt on over my hospital shirt. I slid a pair of grey drawstring sweatpants on over my pajama bottoms.

Tamika was waiting for me downstairs, standing there. "Thanks for taking care of my dog while I was in the hospital," I said.

She looked up the street, toward the VA building looming on the horizon like a medieval fortress. "Maybe you should go back, check yourself in." She stepped toward me, a look of worry on her face.

"I need to get to Florida." I opened my wallet, took out ten one-hundred dollar bills. "I'll give you a thousand dollars to drive me to the airport."

"Don't insult me." She opened the passenger door of her Econoline. Then she walked into the street, getting in the van on the driver's side. Norman Jones floated through the van's frame and into the backseat.

"Just reimburse me for gas," Tamika said. "If it turns out I'm harboring a felon or aiding and abetting an escape, just be ready to make my bail."

"Deal." I got in, sank into the passenger seat with Tiffany still on my lap. "I'm going to give you some extra money to look after my dog while I'm gone."

Tamika started the van. Marimba music came from the CD player, complimented by African chanting. She reached into her ample cleavage, which was ridged with gooseflesh. Tamika extracted an oaken dugout. She tapped the device and a spring-loaded one-hitter that looked like a cigarette appeared.

"My herb's in the glovebox." She pointed at the compartment. "Get it out and pack it."

"Yes'm."

She pulled out and drove down Ludlow Avenue, in the direction of the suspension bridge into Kentucky. We were going past the VA. I ducked even lower in my seat, cradling Tiffany on my lap as I struggled to open the glove box. A pile of Buddhist chant CDs and scattered insurance paperwork surrounded a cellophane baggie filled with a British Columbian strain of weed.

"Holy shit," I said. It smelled like a skunk even through the baggie. "This stuff is too good to waste in a one-hitter. You should only use a bong or a vaporizer with weed this good."

She turned down the marimba music on the stereo and handed me the aluminum pipe that looked like a cigarette. I opened the bag of weed, and Tiff snouted it with rising interest. "No." I waved the dog away, crumbled a choice nugget of the herb, and packed it into the mouth of the pipe.

"That's the sticky icky, Northern Lights, indoor indo."

"Where'd you get it?" I asked. "If you don't mind my asking."

I handed the packed pipe back to her, and she lit it with one of those windproof torch lighters that roared as if she was welding rather than smoking. She blew a stream of smoke over her head, changed lanes, and said, "I get it from Kasha, my ex-husband."

"It smells good."

She held it out to me. "You want a hit?" I shook my head. I'd never liked weed. That didn't keep me from smoking it all day, every day, throughout the course of high-school. It only made me paranoid and caused a knot of sadness to grow in my stomach until it felt like an ulcer.

"Great," Norman said, from the backseat. "A hophead."

Tamika looked at the spirit in the rearview mirror. "If you've got a problem with me smoking, you're welcome to walk, sir."

"Bah!" He puckered his lips, thought of a comeback, and kept it to himself. Tamika shook her head. I wondered what she was thinking about, until she said, "I should have never messed with that fool. He swept me off my feet at a dancehall. His name should have been a red flag that something was up." She shook her head, and her dreads wiggled slightly. They smelled good, like vanilla extract. "I should have read 'Kasha' as 'Caution.'"

"Is he a Rasta?"

She spoke in a mock Kingston patois. "He's a dutty rude boy bumbaclot, but me had a daughter with the worthless batty, and 'im grow da best ganja, so we got a bond that can't no man break."

Red and blue lights flashed through the windshield. Sirens wailed, causing Tamika to lower the one-hitter and pull over to the side of the road. I sank even lower in my seat with Tiff cradled on my lap.

The vehicles passed us, and Tamika pulled back onto the street again and started driving. We were past the VA hospital, but I would breathe a lot easier once we crossed the suspension bridge into Kentucky. I sat up in my seat and asked, "What's your daughter's name?"

"Isis." She pulled on the one-hitter, got the last toke, and said, "It's cashed." She handed me the faux cigarette, whose aluminum body was glowing hot from the touch of the torch.

"You want more?" I asked.

She shook her head. "No, I just needed a little after-work toke to take the edge off. You can help yourself, though." She rolled down her window. Cold air filled the van, causing Tiffany's bristly hair to stand up like porcupine quills.

I petted the dog, stroked her beard, and said, "I can't smoke. I'm a pussy. I get too high and freak out."

We pulled onto the bridge. Tamika sped up, getting in the left lane to pass a slow-moving truck. "Don't equate pussies with weakness, please."

"Sorry, I didn't mean to be a misogynist."

"A pussy is the most powerful thing in the world. It gives life." She clenched her fist. I was convinced she was about to do the black power salute, but she pounded her chest and coughed. Her throat rattled as she cleared resin from it. "You know the whole world came from a black woman."

"Yeah, I know the Out-of-Africa theory."

"Theory, my ass. It's a scientific fact."

We crossed into Kentucky, the rollicking hills upholstered in bluegrass. A giant formation of clouds made me think of the atomic mushrooms detonating over Hiroshima and Nagasaki. I had no intention of killing Hideko Matzuzaka. I did want to confront him, or at least speak with him.

"You get a genetic test," Tamika said, "and you'll see you have some African ancestry, no matter how white you are." She stopped speaking, looked at the road and then over at me. I thought she could tell I was distracted. "What are you thinking about?"

I pointed toward the backseat. "He says the Japanese soldiers cannibalized their POWs."

"They did," Norman Jones said. He placed his hands on the shag upholstery of the front seat headrests. "I don't know why you refuse to believe me."

I looked at Tamika. "Do you think it's true?"

She steered, gazed toward the horizon, appearing to give the issue some thought. An airplane streaked through the dark night sky, taking flight from the runways half a mile or so from where we now were. "Marcus Garvey used to talk about how the white man lied about the extent of cannibalism in Africa. Cannibalism happened here and there in isolated pockets, pretty much everywhere." She pointed toward the dark, Kentuckian hills around us. "Even settlers heading West resorted to eating each other when things got bad, like the Donner party."

An air-traffic control tower appeared in the distance, its lights blinking red in the night. Tamika pulled the van into the curbside drop off lane of the airport, slowing down as we approached a speedbump. I looked over at her. "You don't want to come inside?"

"I'd like to, but I've got to get home and restore peace in the valley." She coughed again. I finished buttoning my flannel shirt over my hospital top. I cinched the drawstring on my grey sweatpants tighter. "Today was Isis's birthday, and Kasha and my boyfriend were raking the backyard to get rid of the leaves, so Isis and her friends could play."

"Did they get into it?"

"Too much testosterone." She giggled. "The herb mellows Kasha out. When he starts drinking his Red Stripe, Lord ah mercy. All bets are off."

I dug into my wallet, handed her five-hundreds. "Please," I said, "take care of my baby." I pressed my lips to Tiff's warm, gray head. "I'm like one of those crazy cat ladies, only I'm a man and my cat is a dog." She counted the five bills while I spoke. "If you don't feel comfortable taking so much money from me, then take her to the doggy day spa and splurge on her there. Spare no expense. Cucumber facemasks, mud baths, the works. Nothing's too good for my one and only." I gripped Tiff's two front paws, lightly touched the padding of her feet. I made her dance for a moment.

Tamika laughed. "You're crazy."

"You're just figuring this out?"

"All right." She folded the five bills and stuffed them into the oaken dugout where she kept the one-hitter. "Be careful."

"I will be. You be careful, too. Don't get pulled over by the cops with that herb on you. If they pull you over for speeding, they'll be able to smell that bud from inside the police cruiser." I gripped the door handle, when I thought of something. "Hey, when I was dying, I started going back in time."

"What?" Her eyes were red from the strong Canadian homegrown.

"After I overdosed, I started going back in time. It was the nineteenth century. Any idea what the hell that was about?"

She took Tiffany off my lap and set my terrier-mix on her own lap. "It's called a time-slip. It's a paranormal phenomenon that happens to a lot of people who tamper with spirits. I've got a book about it I'll loan you when you get back."

I opened the door. "It shouldn't take more than a few days."

"Good luck."

I reached for the Tituba sack, but it was no longer around my neck. They must have confiscated it at the hospital when they admitted me. I felt rather lucky, notwithstanding the absence of the charm. I gave Tamika and Tiffany a wink before hopping down from the Econoline and rushing toward the automatic doors of the airport.

Norman Jones floated after me, like a wraith slithering over the foggy moors. "Wait for me."

I walked past baggage claim and the giant bank of monitors arranged in the center of the terminal that announced arrivals and departures. I was a free man with forty-five hundred dollars in my pocket. Anything was possible.

The glass ceiling of the main atrium was topped by a replica of the prototype plane the Wright Brothers had flown at Kitty Hawk. Ohio was the home of flight, and whoever designed the airport evidently took pride in that. There was a Starbucks on one of the upper levels. I could have used the coffee, but I had no idea if there was some kind of all-points bulletin put out for my arrest since I escaped from the hospital. I thought it would be a good idea to get a coach plane ticket as soon as possible, and get the hell out of Cincinnati.

There was one stop I had to make first, though.

I walked through the concourse, passing people who waited at the top of the escalator for their friends and family members arriving from far-flung destinations. I passed leather, coin-op massage chairs, and a machine that vended synthetic flowers. I walked into the non-denominational chapel/meditation room. There was a sign posted in the entryway that said "No sleeping in the chapel/meditation room for your personal safety."

I walked past the wooden pews and seated myself in the one closest to the slightly raised, carpeted pulpit. There was an open *King James Bible* with a golden tassel bookmark inside of its pages, holding a place in one of the latter Gospels of the book.

"How are you going to kill him?" Norman Jones said, floating on air until he hovered beside me in the pews of the tiny chapel. The sounds of the airport intercom blared from the massive atrium beyond the little sanctuary where I now sat. "You don't have a gun. You going to kill him with your bare hands?"

I looked down at the hands of which he spoke, which were locked in prayer. "I'm not going to kill anyone."

"Then why bother going to Sarasota?" The anger in his voice was so strong that I feared him, even though he wasn't really there.

"I'm going to talk to him."

"Talk!? Talk to the man who tortured me? Who killed my friends?!"

I thought of how best to rephrase it. "I'm going to confront him."

"That's a little better," the spirit said, calming a bit.

I kept my hands clasped together, not sure if I was praying or if I kept the palms squeezed tightly just to keep my hands from shaking. "Jesus," I said, and I still didn't know whether I was just cursing or seeking some kind of salvation in that tiny airport chapel in Cincinnati.

CHAPTER SEVENTEEN: SARASOTA
SLIPPING WITH THE SENIOR CITIZENS

It doesn't matter how terrifying an experience is. Once it has happened once, and it has a name, it can never be as frightening as it was the first time. The same goes for a good experience. My brother told me that the first time he used heroin was the best he ever felt in his life, but he said that he could never get that high again. He said if he had tried to chase that first feeling, he would have died of an overdose a long time ago.

I guess that's why I didn't freak out so badly when the second time-slip happened, and the plane I was on heading toward Sarasota turned into a sternwheeler. I had been sitting in coach on the plane and now I was sitting steerage on a boat. I was across from a family of Irish immigrants whose clothes were mildewed from the Florida humidity. They smelled like a stagnant bayou. I stood to go aboveboard, regardless of what the rules said.

The mother of the family said something to me in Gaelic. She rocked her colicky baby to ease its seasickness.

"I'm sorry. I don't understand you." I looked around and saw Norman Jones floating in his hospital robe that gripped him like a shroud. I balanced myself on a crate of citrus oranges. An alligator with its jaws open appeared in front of me. I recoiled and jumped back until I overturned an orange crate and startled a coop of live chickens. The birds danced in their wire cages and a rain of feathers rose into the air, giving off a fetid smell. My heartrate slowed, and I saw the alligators were just taxidermy trophies. I continued walking toward the steps that led to the top deck. Barrels of guano and local preserves lined the path toward the open hatch, where I could smell cool air and see a patch of blue sky.

I walked to the top deck, and moved to the railing at the side of the ship. The first-class passengers were too enamored of the coastline to notice me, despite my smell. Norman Jones spoke to me in a soothing tone, like someone trying to calm a friend down while he was having a bad trip. "Just relax, partner. This slip will end soon enough, and we'll confront Hideko Matzuzaka."

"I'm not killing anyone." I looked out toward the shoreline.

"No, but you're going to confront him. Right?"

I nodded, gripping the railing and looking out at Sarasota. There was a golf course protected by a Spanish limestone seawall. The wall barely allowed passersby to look over, proles pining for a glimpse of the good life forever out of reach. A lawn jockey with a black face and red lips stood cemented on top of the wall. The statue wore a minstrel's smile and clutched a bulls-eye lantern in one hand, a horseshoe in the other.

I whispered to Norman Jones, "It's a good thing Thigpen isn't here."

The man next to me looked over. He wore a straw homburg with a burgundy silk band, with a boa feather protruding from it. His suit was made of poplin. He brightened, and I could tell immediately he was one of those people who loved to regale the rubes with his store of knowledge. I smiled politely as he spoke.

"Do you know how the city got its name, young man?"

He squared himself to me. "No sir, I don't."

The man was already red as a boiled lobster from the sun, but he glowed when he heard me call him "sir." "Sara Sota was the daughter of a conquistador who settled this land."

I nodded my head soberly, as if this were the answer I had come in search of, travelling from Ohio to Florida to unlock the mystery. We passed an island estate where Venetian statuary, armless men and headless women, lined the neatly trimmed rows of ornamentals.

Now I was genuinely curious, and glad to have the helpful old man by my side. "What's that?"

"You know Ringling Brothers?"

"The circus?"

"That's right." He pointed a beefy forefinger toward the estate. "That's where ole John Ringling winters." The man turned toward the front of the sternwheeler. He pointed to the river spread out in front of us, a shimmering plane of water brown as heavy treacle. A boathouse bobbed near the shore, tied to a pylon rising from the water. Beyond that was a yacht whose sail was bright yellow, like a giant, sun-kissed dandelion. "That there is the *Wethea*." A broad smile stretched across the man's leathery skin. "It's pronounced like 'Why, hi there!'"

I smiled as if he was a potential employer and I needed a job. Norman Jones was under no such duress, and he muttered, "Jesus Christ." He moved aft on the ship to get away from the man who was growing on me despite his corniness.

Another estate appeared beyond the circus magnate's, and my companion said, "That's the hunting lodge of a famous Kentucky distiller."

"What do you hunt in Florida?" I asked. "I thought this was where you fish."

"Hell, boy!" He gave me a slap on the back that he probably intended to be cordial, but it was strong enough to make me fear I might pitch overboard. I got the feeling that we had reached shallow waters. If I did indeed fall over, I might just swim to shore and have Norman Jones guide me to the rest home where Matzuzaka had been hiding for all these years. "You don't have to go hunting for the fish here. They practically jump up on your boat."

I remembered a story of an old Nazi war criminal, who was something like ninety-years old. He was discovered by Israelis trying to bring closure to the lives of Holocaust survivors. He'd been hiding somewhere in the Midwest, and was now to stand trial. It wasn't my place to judge, and I had no right to tell people not to seek revenge. Still there was a part of me that found it impossible to understand what could be achieved by killing a ninety-something year-old man, no matter his crime.

My new friend interrupted my thoughts. He pointed toward the veranda of an inn on the coastline, where several guests posed with their catch strung on a line for an old-fashioned plate camera set up on a tripod. The photographer's head was hidden by a black curtain. "What did I tell ya? Fish in a barrel."

Guests to the side of the inn played badminton, their forms

intermittently visible behind waving stalks of tall sugarcane. The boat drifted until it came to the dock, and one of the crewmen dropped anchor while another hopped off and lashed the sternwheeler to the wooden pylon with a thickly-knotted hemp rope.

"Well, it was a pleasure sharing your company." The man extended his hand.

I shook, and winced from the force of his grip. His palm was as tough as the inside of a catcher's mitt in need of linseed oil. "My pleasure."

The front of the boat was lowered like a gangplank, and the captain said, "All those above deck disembark first. Then cargo, followed by steerage." He adjusted the golden scrambled eggs braids on his captain's hat, and stepped aside. I felt bad for the Irish family below deck, but I didn't feel bad about sneaking aboveboard on my own. I would have dressed like a woman if I'd been on the Titanic, and I wouldn't have thought twice about getting my ass aboard one of those ships that made it to safety. I was suicidal, but I wanted it to be at a moment of my choosing, not the sea's or someone else's.

My feet touched the land, and Norman Jones drifted behind me. "I'm dying," he said. "I don't have more than two or three days, but I'm not going to give in until this thing gets settled."

I looked down at my feet, my brogans dusty and a nail coming loose from the sole of my left boot. "I need to find a cobbler."

"Just wait a bit, and we'll be back in the twenty-first century. Then you won't have to put up with those old shoes."

The path below us was a dirt road, stippled with buggy tracks and the odd imprint of a tire from where a Tin Lizzie had rolled along the street. "Where are we going?" I asked.

"Forward." Jones took point, drifting above my head on a salt-spray wind. Two spotted cows with bells hung around their necks lumbered toward an artesian well and drank to their hearts' content, their udders dangling and heavy with milk. I was thirsty, but not thirsty enough to drink milk straight from the tap. Nor was I willing to sample the well water after the cows had their turn with it.

Chickens danced in the street, making little demented praecox tics and twitches as they picked up scattered bits of feed. They were the lucky ones, I thought. They were the ones not cooped up on the sternwheeler and headed for some butcher's block.

The hotel on our left where the winterers posed with their fish or played badminton was called The De Soto. I pointed toward it. "Is he there?"

"You got something against walking?" Norman Jones turned back toward me. "Keep moving. Turn left at the church." He floated in that direction. Then he doubled back to circle me as I walked, impatient with my plodding pace. There was ringing from the belfry of the church, which was built in the Mediterranean Revival style and announced itself as the First Presbyterian.

Fruit bats scattered from the belfry. They took flight toward the tip of the steeple, no doubt scared from their hiding and stirring up more guano for the traders in the precious commodity. The smell of the stuff was all over my body, on account of me being trapped below deck with barrels chockfull of it.

"Follow me." Jones floated into the tunnel formed by a trellis covered in writhing vines and flowers that glowed like sapphire gemstones in the sunlight. I walked beneath the pergola, feeling shielded from the world. It gave me that same sense of warmth that I got when I hid out in the Esquire Theatre, or pulled the covers over my head in bed and cradled my terrier while the Percocet worked its way over me in warm massaging waves.

I could stay here forever, but the old vet's voice urged me on. He led me out of the shadowed sanctuary and past the vine-covered lattices so dense with vegetation that they reminded me of portcullises on the old castles dotting the Rhineland that I used to see when my unit convoyed for field exercises in Germany. Maybe after this was settled I would take my remaining money and make a trip to Deutschland. I'd visit the *Weinachtsmarkt* and forget that my best friend had died in Iraq. I'd try to remember the good times we'd had as the snow fell and I watched the town of Darmstadt glow with Christmas lights. The smell of rich Swiss chocolate would be in the air, mingling with the scent of firs.

"They used to call him Meth Daddy Dunf," I said.

"Who?" Norman Jones asked, growing impatient. I was now as irritated with him as he was with me. I thought about my buddy Dunfy, who stepped on that pressure plate in Iraq and was now minced in a closed casket in Section Sixty of Arlington. If indeed I did have a gift, I wasn't going to just use it to help other people; I would use it to help myself. I'd avoided my friend's ghost the last time I was in Arlington, but eventually I thought I would have to face him.

"Dunfy was my friend," I said. "He ran anhydrous tanks back and forth all over Missouri for his cousins, who made meth amphetamine and sold it. Somebody called him 'Meth Daddy Dunf' when we were in the Army, and the name stuck."

It beat my nickname of "Porno Tits" they gave me because I could never get any pectoral definition or Mathias's moniker of "Token" that he got on account of him being the only black soldier in our squad.

We arrived at the rest home. A number of Toyotas, Subarus, and VWs parked in the lot let me know we'd made it back to the twenty-first century. Time-slips were disorienting, but they could only last for so long.

A giant wooden sign staked in a bed of mulch fronting a pond announced this as "Valencia Retirement Community." Ducks waddled around the perimeter of the lake, where sprinklers shot water skyward.

A couple of elderly, shrunken women hunkered down in front of the building. They sat in lawn chairs to the side of the main awning where a shuttle bus was parked. One of the women looked to be crocheting with arthritic hands, while the other one worked a ballpoint pen over a crossword puzzle.

I'd always fantasized about living in a retirement home. I liked the idea of a world away from the world, a sort of peaceful community. Meals were always served at a certain hour and time was frozen. People wheeled you from place to place, and the tranquility was only occasionally interrupted by idle chitchat about the weather.

The two old women smiled at me. I smiled back, nodding my head slightly. "Ladies."

There was a massive fireplace in the entryway, dressed in ashlar stone. A bunch of fogies sat in chairs. They knitted, read, or stared off into space. White Christmas lights were strung around the perimeter of the room. There was a piano at the far end of the main lobby, where somebody's granddaughter kicked her white stockinged legs and tickled out a near-perfect *Für Elise*. It was odd and not a little humbling to realize that a six-year old had more talent than me.

I walked down the hall, which was carpeted with little fleur-de-lis. There was a dining hall, with white cloths spread over each table. Silverware was laid out and napkins were tented and waiting to wipe the mouths of the old, messy eaters. I walked down the hall, passing a maid pushing her cart and a physical therapist in scrubs who smiled at me as if I was supposed to be there.

"Turn right down this hall," Jones said.

I obeyed, my feet moving over the soft carpet. I was no longer in hobnailed brogans, but wearing my usual desert suede combat boots. There was a bookshelf lined with dusty paperbacks, set between two chairs. A pang of nostalgia, a pining to be old among the aged, hit me in the pit of my stomach. *Let me stay here*, I thought, *reading Steve Martini and John Le Carre spy novels and watching my VHS copy of* Remembering the Real Ronald Reagan. *Let me fidget with my cochlear implant so that I could better hear how much the QVC lady on TV wanted for the Norman Rockwell Commemorative Plate Collection complete set.*

We passed a wall called "The Veterans' Memorial" where Brokaw's "Greatest Generation" smiled in their official Army photos. They were men in olive drab and peaked caps. There were smiling nurses, all of them looking as if they'd been ripped straight from a *Turner Classic Movies* broadcast.

"Joseph," Norman Jones said.

"Huh?" My mind was a monkey, and tended to jump from branch to branch. The old soldier's floating form hovered before a door, adjacent to which there was a tacky ceramic curio of three schnauzer puppies wrestling. The brass nameplate next to the door said, "Mr. Hideko Lee." A paper note was taped to the door, and someone had written in red marker, "Warning, don't let dogs out when cleaning! The girls are runners!"

"I guess we'd better be careful then," I said, turning from the door. I looked at Norman Jones, who was now shaking like a leaf. "I guess he changed his name?" I pointed at the plate.

Norman Jones nodded back in the direction of the Veterans' Memorial Wall we just passed. "If you were living with a bunch of men who served in the Pacific, maybe you would want to pass yourself off as Chinese rather than Japanese. Don't you think?"

I shrugged. Anger and hate were generally a young man's game. What would they do if they discovered Mr. Hideko Lee, formerly of some West Coast fish cannery, was in fact Hideko Matzuzaka, of the dread *Kempeitai*?" Would they surround him with their motorized wheelchairs and proceed to strangle him with the PVC lines of their portable oxygen tanks? Doubtful. At worst, they would avoid feeding the ducks outside at the same time as the old, Japanese war criminal.

I took a deep breath, and looked over at Norman Jones. "It's open," he said, and I turned the doorknob. Blue light from a giant television splashed over an old man sleeping in a smoke-grey kimono. Football bloopers from onscreen glinted off the man's glasses. I watched a wide receiver with butterfingers lose his grip on the pigskin as a slide whistle sound effect played, followed by a laugh track. I closed the door softly behind me. Norman Jones floated over his old foe. Matzuzaka slept in a Craftmatic adjustable chair with two mini schnauzers coiled close to his chest like pups suckling from a bitch.

"There the bastard is. He doesn't have any conscience, sleeping like a baby." The Craftmatic chair covered in oatmeal shag vibrated, some sort of preset massage routine continuing on a loop because Hideko Matzuzaka held the button depressed in his sleeping hand.

A quarterback on screen caught a hiked ball in the masked portion of his helmet and stumbled blindly around the football field while the canned laughter continued. I wondered why the dogs hadn't woken up. Tiffany would have gone berserk if someone had wandered into my apartment unannounced. I guessed that the dogs were used to the constant comings and goings of cleaners and orderlies, and were now as trusting as the ducks outside that waddled right up to the seniors to eat breadcrumbs out of their hands.

I walked into the kitchen. I felt slightly guilty for prying here, but I was also curious. "Find a butcher knife!" Norman Jones shouted, from the living room. "Slit the nip's fucking throat!"

I didn't know exactly what I was looking for, but it wasn't a knife. I walked into the center of the kitchen and glanced toward the dining room. A half-eaten lunch of Gordon's Fish Fillet and Cracklin' Oat Bran sat on a plastic orange dish on the dining room table. There was a rice paper painting of the Great Wall of China hung in the far corner of the dining area. It was a tacky piece of kitsch one might expect to see hung in a Chinese buffet restaurant, the Asian equivalent of *Dogs Playing Poker*. It looked like Mr. Matzuzaka was committed to his assumed identity as the Chinese man, Mr. Lee.

"What the hell is that?" I turned from the dining room and looked at Norman Jones. He stood over the sink. I walked over to the sink and joined him. The side of the sink with the garbage disposal was stoppered and filled with warm water and a thick scum of detergent. A rubber vagina bobbed in the water. To the right of that was a dishrack where a little tube that said "Cyber Pussy Renewal Starch" sat. Next to that was a metallic vibrating egg that operated by remote, like the Craftmatic chair in the living room.

"It's a pocket pussy," I said. I felt an immediate ball of sadness well in my stomach. The man had probably been without companionship for years. He'd most likely had a wife at some point, who'd been dead for decades now. I'd contemplated buying a pocket pussy, and had even asked my brother if having one would mean I was a creep. His girlfriend was a "sex positive" feminist who played bass in a Riot Grrrl punk group. He'd told me even she thought pocket pussies were now considered about as normal as dildos and vibrators, and that having one wouldn't mark me as a weirdo or a loser.

Norman Jones was from the old school, though. Or perhaps his hatred for his enemy wouldn't allow him to see Matzuzaka as human enough to need some kind of companionship, however artificial. "Disgusting," Jones said.

"Don't knock it till you try it."

Barking from the other room startled me, and I froze. "Min?" It was Matzuzaka's voice.

One of the little schnauzers hopped down from the Craftmatic couch and padded into the kitchen. Its markings were black at the body and snowy white at the legs. It looked like the dog was wearing ankle length, furry boots. The other dog came bounding into the kitchen a moment later. They both scowled at me from beneath their feathery eyelashes, which I thought made them look like grumpy old men.

"Hello?" Matzuzaka said. I still didn't move, or say anything.

"Confront him!" Norman Jones shouted.

"How? What should I do?"

Hideko Matzuzaka came into the kitchen, balancing himself on his bamboo cane and answering the question I'd posed to a man he couldn't see. "You can help me give Min her heartworm medicine."

He evidently accepted my presence here, thought I was a nursing home employee. He wore one of those Life Alert pendants around his neck, and he slowly tied the front of his grey kimono as he spoke. "Lin does not fight me, but we must trick Min." He flicked the light switch. The brightness of the room threw his strong, taut features into relief. He scratched his toothbrush mustache once, and probed the linoleum with the bullet tipped end of the cane. He walked past me and through Norman Jones, opening a cabinet above the refrigerator.

The idea that I might have seen his pocket pussy bobbing in a cleaning solution in the sink evidently didn't faze him. "Which one is Min?" I asked.

I got my answer as the dog with the legs white as the coat on a Himalayan cat fled at the sound of the pantry opening. "She knows what is coming." Matzuzaka set the heartworm medicine on the counter, and looked over at me. He tried to muster a solicitous expression, but the pain of years wouldn't allow the muscles or the skin of his face to move. "Will you help me?"

"Sure." I walked over to the counter and popped one of the pouches on the blister pack. I took out the heartworm pill.

"*Danke*, my friend." I wondered why he was thanking me in German. I had an idea, but it disturbed me. He shuffled past me, back into the living room. "Come." He waved his right arm and I followed.

"Great!" Norman Jones shouted. "You're really sticking it to him. You travelled all the way to Florida to help him with his toy poodles."

"Schnauzers," I said.

"Yes," Hideko said. "Mini schnauzers." Lin was perched on one of the oatmeal shag arms of the chair. The Craftmatic had ceased to vibrate, but I guessed it was heated and that the dog enjoyed that.

Matzuzaka grabbed a package of dog treats from the glass coffee table in front of his television. He opened the seal on the bag. I saw they were chicken-flavored pill pockets. His hand trembled as he extracted one, and gave it to me. I kneaded the greasy pocket and placed the heartworm pill inside.

"I don't believe this," Norman Jones said.

"Good," Hideko said. He trembled and I didn't know if it was Parkinson's or PTSD, or some combination of the two. "Min, treat time."

The little dog scurried out from its hiding so fast that it stomped on a remote control as it bounded toward the treat in my hand. The show on the big TV changed from classic football bloopers to a QVC segment on hair products. Two women with hairspray helmets stood over a woman they were about to makeover in their image.

"It's a thickening style cream," one of the women said. "Just like with all our beauty products, it can be yours in three easy payments."

The other woman waved her palm like a hand model over their victim's coiffure. "Notice how it's penetrating. It's not just lying outside of the cuticle." Lin the schnauzer's fluffy gray eyebrows twitched as if she was considering buying the product advertised on TV.

Min gobbled the chicken treat from my palm, completely unaware of the pill hidden inside. Hideko sat back down in his chair. He exhaled heavily, searching for the button which would make his seat vibrate again. He found it, and pressed it. Both he and his little doggy rumbled from the hidden massaging fingers inside the upholstery of the chair.

"Okay," he said.

"Okay?" There was nowhere for me to sit, so I stood, and Norman Jones stood by my side.

Hideko Matzuzaka took off his glasses, and set them on the coffee table before us. He regarded me with eyes that were milky with cataracts, but saw through me nonetheless. "I tried stopping you with my little Oni trick, but it didn't work. You are here on behalf of a white pig. You know who I am, just as well as I know who you are." He leaned all of his weight on the curved handle of his bamboo cane. "What do you want?"

"Norman Jones wants me to kill you."

That didn't startle or disturb him in the least. If anything, a wan smile crept across his face. "Do you want to kill me?"

"No."

"What do you want to do?"

It had been awhile since anyone had asked me that. I'd been so busy carrying out other people's final wishes here on Earth that I'd forgotten to have much of an agenda of my own. What I wanted was my job back. Since I'd had a nervous breakdown and was involuntarily committed, and I'd escaped from a closed ward, I didn't think that was going to happen.

"Did you do it?" I asked.

I think he knew what I was asking him, but he still said, "Do what?" in order to buy himself a little more time.

"Eat white pig meat?"

He stood so fast that the chair rocked hard enough to eject both of the schnauzers onto the carpet floor. "Okay." He looked around the room, searching for the ghost he could not see. Hideko Matzuzaka was no longer interested in me. "I will make you happy, white pig. You have waited this long for your revenge. Here is your reward." He walked away from me, stabbing the carpet with the Arisaka bullet jacket that capped the end of his cane.

"Wait!" I followed him.

"Good." Norman Jones grinned. Whether or not Matzuzaka was a cannibal and a sadistic soldier in the *Kempeitai*, I hated Jones more in the moment than I did his brutalizer. I walked down the hall, after the man whose pace was quite nimble for an octogenarian.

"Slow your roll!"

We were in his bedroom now. He opened the closet, and dug through effects. Ancient memorabilia flew across the room. A little piece of metal came flying from his hands and slapped me in the center of the forehead. I picked it up. It was a trench lighter engraved with Sig lightning runes. I tried to spark it, to no avail. It was probably sixty-years old.

Hideko looked at me and laughed. "I got that on a joint exercise between the *Kempeitai* and the S.S. The Nazi who gave that to me is probably long-since dead. I have other things in this closet." He continued rummaging, and stopped when he seized on a treasure that brought him out into the bedroom. It revived memories that were strong enough to free him from the other ones weighing him down.

He held a little velvet-lined box in his hands. I expected it to contain a wedding band. I thought it was maybe some relic leftover from his marriage whose passion he now had to simulate with that pocket pussy bobbing in the sink filled with detergent.

His trembling fingers flipped the case open. He revealed a military award dangling from a length of silken ribbon. The two schnauzers came into the room, sniffing the little medal. When it was apparent that it wasn't a treat, both of the grey little old men in dog suits turned from the bedroom and ran back to the comfort of the Craftmatic couch.

Hideko ignored me and stroked the ribbon. I asked, "Did you win that in the Second World War?"

He shook his head. "This is the *Jugun Kiso*, from the Sino-Japanese War. It is my father's." He stroked the engraved flower crests on the rusted medallion, the Paulownia and Chrysanthemum flanked by two miniature flags. "The way of Bushido was to respect the weak, and to accept the defeat of the enemy with grace."

Norman Jones was no longer angry, just confused. Hideko Matzuzaka looked up from the award. He stared at me with his filmy, sad eyes. "We were told to brutalize the white soldiers for the benefit of the Chinese workers we had with us."

"I don't understand."

"The Chinese were like the Indians. They had been conquered by white men, or colonized by them. They respected and feared them too much to treat them like prisoners. We had instructions to treat the whites like animals, so the Chinese would understand they were not gods. Do you understand?"

I nodded. He closed the little box, let it fall from his grasp onto the carpeted floor. "Your friend is right, and I will give him what he wants before he dies." He reached back in the closet. I expected him to come out with a gun, perhaps a German Luger a *Sturmbahnfuhrer* had given him that he'd somehow snuck through Customs when fleeing the Pacific and coming to the shores of America. Instead, he held a gold-inlayed Kitana in his hands.

The blade had no sheath, and he stood with the handle outstretched toward the bed before him. The point of the sharp edge touched his stomach. It made a slight dent in the weary flesh of his gaunt belly, which was naked and revealed since the tie on his kimono had come loose. He made as if to lean forward, to impale and then perhaps disembowel himself. I rushed toward him and shoved him until he fell backwards into the closet, landing among clothes and old photographs that smelled of formaldehyde and mothballs.

"No!" Norman Jones shouted. "Let him do it!"

"Please," Hideko said, his eyes widening as he now saw Norman Jones in his own delirium. He stared into his old enemy's eyes and said, "You are right." He looked back at me and struggled to stand. "You don't belong here." I offered my hand to help him up, but he slapped it away. He struggled like a turtle on its back, unable to stand. Both of the schnauzers returned, sensing the trouble their master was in. They barked and snarled at me, their short-clipped tails wagging and the gray hair on their backs bristling. I grabbed the Kitana by its handle.

"I'm tired of pretending to be a Chinese coolie in this…graveyard with old white pigs, playing Scrabble and eating pudding." He finally managed to gain his footing, and reached for the sword I gripped in my hands. "Let me die like a Bushido."

I kept the sword down at my side, as if it were sheathed in a scabbard at my hip. He lunged for me. When he got close, I depressed the little Life Alert button he wore around his neck. It was no larger than a dog tag, and a red light blinked.

"No!" He bucked against me as if he was having an epileptic fit, and Norman Jones shouted so savagely that he drowned out the barking of the dogs. I didn't hear the EMTs come in.

I stood up, dropping the sword as I did so. The two EMTs glanced around the room, holding their supplies in latex-gloved hands and looking confused. One of them asked, "Did Mr. Matzuzaka press his panic button?"

"I pressed it for him." I pointed toward the sword, the award, and all of the paraphernalia he'd scattered across the room. The other EMT picked up both barking dogs and placed them in the bathroom, closing the door and sealing them in to lessen the confusion. "He tried to kill himself," I said.

"Tell them!" Norman Jones said. "If you're not going to kill him, at least tell them!"

I struggled to regain my breath, and spoke between gasps, "I have reason to believe this man is a war criminal who escaped justice in the Second World War. He was involved in the torture, and..." I paused. "Cannibalization of POWs."

"Victor's Justice," Hideko said. He wept some more. When he next spoke, it was in Japanese. None of us could understand, and one of the EMTs leaned down to the patient and the other one spoke to me. "We're not police officers. We work for Valencia Retirement Community."

Another EMT entered the apartment wearing a stethoscope around his neck and pushing a wheeled stretcher. "Mr. Matzuzaka?" The EMT on the floor asked. Hideko continued to weep, switched back to English and said, "Tojo shot himself in the chest, but missed his poor heart. They hanged him. I want to be hanged like my emperor."

"We're going to take you to the hospital now, okay? We don't want you to hurt yourself."

The other EMT scowled at me, as if it was my fault that Hideko was in the state he was in. It was at least partially my fault. I didn't have to listen to Norman Jones. I could have left the poor old man here with his Craftmatic chair and his QVC and his miniature schnauzers, in peace. If there was some sort of afterlife, whether it was a kind of Buddhist karmic wheel or a Valhalla of eternal war, the state of his soul would eventually get sorted out without my damn meddling.

I should have been strong enough to tell Norman Jones to go to hell. If he'd just left me alone, I might still have my job.

"What are you doing here, anyway?" The EMT asked.

"Emperor Hideki!" Hideko shouted, "I apologize for failing you!"

I decided to come clean, to give up. "I attempted suicide a couple of days ago, and was committed to the main VA facility in Cincinnati." Mr. Matzuzaka was lifted onto the stretcher, and the other EMT and I cleared a path to let them go by. Lin and Min continued barking and the men carried the old *Kempeitai* soldier out of his room, and out of the nursing home.

"I escaped from the hospital," I said. "I guess I need to go back. I'm suffering from PTSD. I was in Iraq."

"Why don't you ride along with us?" The EMT said, extending a gloved hand. "We'll commit you at Sarasota Memorial, and then you can get transferred back to Cincinnati."

I nodded. It was time to go home. I was tired. "Sounds like a plan." I took one look back toward the spirit of Norman Jones, but he was gone.

I assumed that he let go, allowed himself to die at that moment. He didn't get to see Matzuzaka die, as he'd initially wished, but he did get to see his mortal enemy reduced to tears. Norman Jones saw Hideko weeping and carted away from his father's medal and samurai sword and his miniature schnauzers. I guessed that was enough to satisfy his spirit and let him cross over into the next world.

As for me, Joey Sullivan, my work was just beginning.

Purchase other Black Rose Writing titles at www.blackrosewriting.com/books
and use promo code PRINT to receive a 20% discount.